The Recital

The Recital

Kyle V. Hiller

Seven in the Afternoon

Published by
Seven in the Afternoon
319 Reed Street
Philadelphia, Pennsylvania 19147

Names: Hiller, Kyle V.
Title: The recital: a novel / Kyle V. Hiller
Description: First Edition | Philadelphia, Pennsylvania
Seven in the Afternoon Artisanal Publishing, 2016
Summary: Edith Madeline Solstice begins seventh grade with little
expectations. She's a straight-A student hoping to win a piano recital,
but she's also got a crush on her friend Nemo Daniel Jones. When
she tries to kiss him, her hands cramp and they get hot—like a fever
in her palms that doesn't go away for days. She soon discovers that
this fever is her awakening as a witch, but it happens in the worst
possible way: she nearly kills Julie Suzanne Cherry, her rival at
school who's captured Nemo's heart.
ISBN: 978-0692679388
Subjects: Coming of Age - Young Adult Fiction. | Witches - Urban
Fantasy
Promotional & Cover Art: Jessica Bastidas
Editor: Kate Angelella

http://www.sevenintheafternoon.com

For Nanny

Hey, but a lot can happen over a year. I mean, you could come back next fall as a completely normal person.

—*Samantha, Sixteen Candles*

1

Everything changed after the first day of seventh grade. At most, I hoped I'd grown an inch or two, maybe start wearing a little bit of makeup, and become the sort of girl my classmates admired for being cool, aloof—sophisticated. Seventh grade was going to be the year I had my first kiss, charming the boy I'd been daydreaming about all summer. If only I'd known that I carried an unimaginable darkness within me, and it was about to make its escape—like a tsunami of black smoke gathering a terrible momentum with every passing second, poised to take out everything, and everyone, in its wake. Seventh grade was when I had a near-death experience. I'd never thought I'd be one to almost kill a girl.

Classes were over, and the hallway was empty. I was alone, standing in front of The Sacred Wall of Heights. I stepped close to the wall, leaned my head and my hands against it, then pressed my lips right below the line initialed *NDJ 6/97*. I clutched at its cold, straight hips, pretending with all my might that it was him. The wall was no longer ivory, but was smooth and mahogany like his skin. I yearned to run my fingers through his hair, but a first kiss shouldn't last this long. This was the third or fourth kiss I was practicing. I'd fallen so deep into my imagination that I could smell his musk.

Then, a rush of heat scurried up my hands. I leapt back, letting out a gasp as an ache arrested my palms and my fingers. My porcelain tone reddened and my heart raced. Shock and alarm slipped from my tongue in a hot whisper that was more of a sound than it was words. I tried to round my fists but it hurt.

I heard my name called from down the hall. *He* was walking towards me. I nearly fell right then, even though I was standing still. I'd gotten so dizzy with emotion that I'd turned into a flurry of feathers. What in the world was this pain? And why was it happening then?

I swallowed the pain and the nerves in a hard gulp, shutting my eyes with a whimper as I did. *I'm okay*, I thought. *I'm fine. This is fine.*

"How was your first day?" he asked.

"It was great. I can't believe we're in seventh grade," I said with stammered breath. I'd never been so thankful that my uniform skirt had pockets. I shoved my hands in them and looked him dead in the eye. *I'm not scared at all, Nemo Daniel Jones.*

"Neither can I," he laughed. He took out a marker from his afro and uncapped it. He was prepared for this moment, wasn't he? He knew he'd find me here. I hoped he didn't see me making out with the most sacred wall in the whole school. I hoped he didn't see me freak out about the fever that had sneak-attacked my hands. I could feel the warmth seeping through my pockets onto my thighs. I wanted to cry. I wanted to run away. "You want me to measure you?"

"No," I said, trembling.

"Why not?" he asked.

I had to look away from him. I spun around and found my initials from June. I swore I was never going to grow again. I went into middle school at four feet and eleven inches. Then, at the end of sixth grade, Nemo measured me. I'd grown an inch! There was my growth spurt. I was forever going to be the short girl. Five feet *nothing*.

This was the Sacred Wall of Heights, the wall where every student measured how tall they were at the beginning and the end of each grade. There were lines dated as far back as 1984. I even saw my older brother's initials from a few years ago. It was a big deal for the students here. It was a ritual.

My heart was pounding against my chest as he came close to me. "Come on," he nudged me. "Let's do it. I'm sure you've grown."

As much as I wanted to dash down the hall, I wanted to stay. I hadn't felt this stuck since I'd gotten trapped in my closet playing hide and seek with my brother and sister one time a couple of years ago. I had wailed and screamed and when they finally got there, they couldn't open the door.

I wanted to wail and scream right then, too. Sweat gleamed on my face and down my arms, the heat and the ache swelling in my pockets. I'd rehearsed this moment for weeks in my mind. I'd practiced this in the shower or at my mirror or on my pillows. I was going to get this right. It was going to be perfect.

I walked up against the wall and he drew a line slowly over my head. I wanted to tug at him and pull him close to me, lock his lips with mine, and start seventh grade off with my first kiss. I was drowning from everything. His face was so close to mine, and I held onto my breath as I stared at him. This moment had felt so long. I wanted it to both last forever and hurry up and end all at the same time.

"Alright," he said, backing away.

I put my hands against the wall, its coolness took some of the pain away. A shiver shot through my body. "Did I grow?"

He said nothing.

"No?" I spat.

"I'm sorry," he muttered.

Nothing. Five foot nothing! The line was next to the same one from June. I took the marker from him. "Your turn."

Okay, here it was. This was how the ritual was supposed to go. I had to measure Nemo since he had measured me. It was good luck, and it meant that we'd be friends no matter what, at least for another school year.

He stood against the wall. "Can you reach?"

I scowled at him. "Yes, I can reach!" I couldn't get a firm grip on the marker. I winced as I snapped the cap. *Ignore the pain, Edith. Here's your chance.*

I leaned onto him, standing on my toes. I was going to take my time. I didn't know whether to measure his hair or not. That'd be an extra few inches. When I went to start the line, my hand cramped and I dropped the marker. He laughed at me as he picked it up.

I clutched my hand. When he asked me if I was okay, all I did was stare at him. At his hair, at his caring eyes. I leaned onto him again. I fixed at his lips, like Claire did to Bender in *The Breakfast Club*. I leaned my face close to his. His hands landed on my hips. The tips of our noses touched. I closed my eyes and could see all the butterflies and the fireworks waiting at the edge to burst away into flight. There was but an inch keeping us away.

Nemo lightly pushed me back as I heard someone call his name from down the hall. I felt like I was jerked from a dream, shaking and mired in a blushed daze. Julie Suzanne Cherry, my least favorite person in the world, came skipping down the hall. I backed away from Nemo. He glared at me with narrow eyes and slightly shook his head. I didn't know what that meant, so I kept looking at him, waiting for him to say something.

Julie slid into the tiny space between Nemo and me, her backside and her long, raven-black hair brushing against me. She took his hands into hers. "How was your first day?"

"I think I'm ready," he said.

"Good! And you'd been going on all summer about how afraid you were of being a seventh grader. Like it's a big deal." She leaned into him, pushing him against the wall. "Do you want me to measure you?"

He glanced at me but quickly returned his attention to Julie. Julie caught wind and looked over her shoulder. She narrowed her eyes and pursed her lips. "You need someone to measure you? You're going to have to wait. Obviously."

A chilled twinge shot through my neck. I'd barely gotten to see Nemo this summer. We didn't spend as much time together as I wished we did, and the reason why was standing right in front of me. Her arms were around Nemo. She'd won the grand prize, and all I got was a consolation prize of embarrassment. My cheeks burned as I remembered leaning in to kiss him.

"I was just leaving," I shrugged. "You two can, you know, whatever." I glanced at Nemo again but my hands were getting hotter, like I was holding them over a stove fire. I scurried off down the hall and into the girls' bathroom. I turned the cold water on and shoved my hands under the water, splashing with little care. The heat cooled after a minute. I turned off the water and sat in silence—the kind of silence that doesn't want to be silent, the kind where echoes are screams brooding like water just about to boil. The whole floor would hear me if I screamed, like I wanted to, but I bit my lip as hard as I could. I stared at the fogging mirror, fighting urges to cry and to throw up. They were probably kissing right now. That witch had stolen Nemo away from me. And here I was, alone and terrified from some weird, excruciating fever in my hands.

I left the bathroom and walked back to the Sacred Wall. I stopped right before I got there, peeking around the bend to see if they were still around. Nope. My chest tightened when I saw two new lines where we had been standing: *NDJ 9/97* and *JSC 9/97*.

Julie had grown two inches this past summer.

I wanted to scribble over every line on the wall. So many students had grown. So many of them were taller than me. It was bad luck that I didn't measure Nemo in return. I hated how much I cared about rituals and superstitions. I would be scribbling over everyone else's aspirations and their hindsight and their good fortune. If I couldn't have any of those—if I was going to be stuck being the same old Edith forever—then why did I have to watch everyone else celebrate their happiness and their stupid traditions?

I had a red marker in my pencil case. I fought through my books and dug into my backpack, grunting as I pulled it out from the bottom. I found the marker. I looked up at the wall, scanning for each time I saw Julie and Nemo's heights. I wanted so much for this to be how I keep them still. They would never grow again, just like me. And no one would've known it was me if I'd ruined the wall.

"Edith?" someone called out to me. Evanthia Katsaros, my favorite teacher, was walking down the hall. I shoved the marker in my case and threw it into my backpack.

"Hi Miss K," I said softly. "I'm sorry, I was just about to head to the auditorium."

"It's okay. I'm late, too. You want to head down together?"

I nodded. I took one last look at the wall. Something had gotten into me, tugging like it wanted me to fall and break into pieces. I didn't fight it, either. I had let it wrestle with me. I stayed there, looking at my initials. I'd never been so upset before.

2

I clung to the edge of the auditorium stage with my toes and spread my arms. I was flying. Silence, warm late summer sunlight, and swarms of dust motes poured from the tall stained glass windows. I had dreamt many dreams in the auditorium. Sometimes, I'd take naps in the balcony instead of going to lunch. I would daydream when I was worried about a test. I didn't study much. I didn't have to. I was naturally a straight A student who'd gone unnoticed, and as much as I wanted to keep it that way, I knew that if I wanted to do *this*, I might have to sacrifice some of my solitude.

I'd flown a long way in my mind, all the way to December. I'd landed at the annual Christmas Eve Festival. The auditorium had filled up with kids and their families dressed up in Santa hats and ugly sweaters. Aromas of gingerbread and spruce and gift wrap billowed as the festival was about to commence. Applause was brooding and the grip of my toes tightened. Their eyes would be on me. Murmurs of who this girl was would thread amongst the kids, especially the eighth graders. But in the center of the crowd was the reason I was doing this.

"Where did you go?" Miss K said, whisking me from my dream. "Were you flying again?"

She sat on the piano bench behind me and tilted her head in a way that reminded me of how my little sister looked at me. Miss K was earnest, sweet, kind and pure. She knew me well. I thought of her more as a friend than as a teacher.

"Can I play a song for you?" I asked.

"That's what I was hoping we were here for," she said. She stood from the bench, opening her palm as she curtseyed.

I sat at the piano and relaxed my fingers down on the cold keys. The odd fever from earlier had crept back into my hands, but I shook them and told myself *it's okay. It'll go away again. It's been a nervous day.*

I felt alive as I played the song for Miss K. I'd swallowed the pain from the fever and from Nemo long enough to reach the end. Then it all came rushing back to me as I lingered on the last chord.

Miss K clapped and cheered. I forced a smile as the pain crescendoed.

"That was wonderful," she said.

"Thank you," I stuttered. I clasped my hands in my lap between my knees. I bit my lip and told myself to keep it together. This wasn't even the hardest part.

"You've come a long way," she added, sitting next to me and wrapping her arm around me in a side embrace. "I'm so proud of you, Edith."

"The song isn't finished yet. Me and my Dad are still working on it," I said. "But I was wondering—"

I trailed off. I couldn't look at Miss K. I stared at my hands and at the keys, then into the empty auditorium. If I wanted my dream to come true, I had to ask. Being around Miss K made me feel like there was nothing to worry about. I would've bet she had enough warmth to bring world peace if she wanted to. But part of me was still scared. What was I doing to myself? What was coming over me? Where did I find the nerve to try and kiss Nemo and play a song in front of someone other than my Dad? Was this why my hands had gotten so hot?

"Wondering what?" Miss K said, nudging me back from space.

"I—I was wondering if I could play at the Christmas Eve Festival." That took the last bit of wind out of me and I got dizzy and sweaty. Then my stomach churned and I spat more words. "A recital. Not too long. Maybe three songs? I don't know. This song, too!"

My shoulders tightened. I wanted to tuck my face into my blouse and hide. But words kept spilling, staggered and coy. "It would be my Christmas present. To my Dad. And—"

I wanted him to see me, his precious little Snowpea, playing the piano on the biggest stage that I could. We'd been writing this song together all summer. I wanted him to see an entire auditorium listen to our song. I wanted the song to echo against the walls and seep into his heart in a way that it wouldn't in our living room. He would think I was beautiful in a flowing white dress with silk gloves and heeled shoes that clicked with every step. Even if for a moment, I'd be the best daughter in the whole world. Everyone would ask me about the songs and I would tell them: I wouldn't have been able to do it without him.

He was the reason that was in the center of the crowd.

"Oh, Edith," she said. Her whole face opened up. Her nostrils, eyes and ears lifted as a smile blossomed like a sunrise over a plane horizon. She nodded and didn't say a word, like I had taken her breath away.

I couldn't wait to go home and tell Dad.

3

When I got home, I was alone. My hands were still hurting. I took a cold shower until the fever went away. Shivering, I got dressed and went to the kitchen for ice cream. I was going to be absolutely sure that I'd froze this fever away. But when I scooped the ice cream into a bowl, I'd started to warm up again. I held the bowl and watched as the ice cream melted. In not even two minutes—I watched the microwave clock—my ice cream became a hefty portion of chocolate milk. I poured the ice cream out. I didn't bother to wash out the bowl. I didn't want to touch anything anymore. What in the world was happening to me?

My Mom was a nurse at the hospital. I wanted to call her and tell her what was happening to me. She would know what was wrong. She always knew how to treat us whenever we got sick. It wasn't often that I caught a cold, let alone a fever. I never liked taking medicine. If I called, she would tell me to take something.

The pain made me wince when I picked up the phone. I wanted

to cry and I wanted to fight it, too. I wanted to be strong. I didn't need medicine. Mom always said when people get sick, it's usually because of stress or not eating right. I did eat three slices of pizza for lunch. And then there was Nemo and Julie. I didn't want to tell her about all that.

I went to my room and leapt onto the bed. I replayed the scene at the Sacred Wall in my head. I squeezed my eyes shut and held a pillow over my face to drown the memory. No luck. It only got more vivid. The solvent scent of permanent marker tinged my nose. The scalding look Nemo gave me that made me feel like I was just another girl. How weak my legs felt when I leaned in to kiss him, and how his slight push nearly made me fall. I piled the pillows and swung and punched. I took one of the pillows and pulled at its sides. I wanted to rip it apart, grunting as I brought strength from as far down as my belly. I tossed it across the room without looking, hitting my desk lamp. It toppled to the floor and shattered.

I left the lamp in pieces and plopped down on the bed. The lonesome afternoon stillness embraced me, like a hug brimming with sympathy. The day was telling me it was going to be okay. And for a moment, I believed it. I listened to the birds singing in the tree outside my window. I heard children playing in the distance once I opened my ears.

Then, I buried my face in my pillow and cried.

"Why her?" I whispered.

"Wake up, wake up," I heard over and over. I awoke and beside me was my little sister tugging at my shoulder. Her name was Jenna, but we all called her Cannoli. She had an obsession with the Italian dessert pastry, and we were certain the sugar this little girl ate made her the sweetest kid in the world. It was nice to wake up to her beaming smile and her wide hazel eyes.

"I'm up," I said. The afternoon had passed by and the evening sunset flushed my room with crimson.

Cannoli wore her backpack. This woke me up for sure.

"How was your first day?" I asked.

"We put our supplies together, and we colored our name tags for our desk! And we had to think of a word that rhymed with our name. And then the teacher took us to recess and we played games with each other!"

"Did you tell the teacher your name is really Cannoli?"

"No! That's not my name. That's my nickname!"

"Yeah, but did you cry when Mom left?"

"I didn't cry. Mommy cried."

"Did you give her a hug when she did?"

"A hug and a kiss. And I told her I loved her. And I told her that I was going to be home soon! And then she stopped crying."

I laughed. "Is Mom downstairs?"

"Mm-hmm. She got cannoli for us!"

"She did? How do I know you're not lying just to get me out of bed?"

"I'm not lying! Cross my heart and hope for pie," she said, drawing a cross over her chest. "Come on!"

Cannoli jumped off the bed and scurried out of my room and down the stairs, shouting "Mommy! Edith was asleep! I woke her up. She's coming!"

She hadn't noticed the broken lamp. Thank goodness. She would have gone and told Mom right away and I wasn't ready for that conversation.

As I climbed out of bed about to pick up the pieces, I noticed the fever was gone from my hands. I could move them without them tightening and aching. I breathed a long sigh. It was like I had woken up from a bad dream. Maybe it was stress and too much pizza after all.

I picked up the broken lamp pieces and threw them into the trash, then took a book from my desk and made my way downstairs. Mom was in the kitchen. As usual, she wore bubble-gum pink scrubs, and her long hair was tied up in a bun. Her back was to me as she slumped over the sink, lathering her hands with soap and water. Cannoli sat at the table as she munched on her cannolo, swinging her feet and humming a song.

"Hi Mom," I said.

When she turned, I knew what she was going to ask. I didn't want to talk about it.

"Hey Snowpea," she said. "How was your first day?"

"It was fine." I leaned against the wall with my hands in my pockets. "It's just school."

"Don't tell me you're bored with school already."

"No. I'm not."

She began to unpack the grocery bags on the counter. "You should join a club. Or try sports. You and Lenore could play softball together."

I wasn't athletic. And I didn't want to play chess or be a tutor for the elementary kids. I wanted to play piano. We had one in the living room. Why would I want to stay after school when what I wanted was at home? I didn't want her to keep pushing suggestions, so I nodded and promised that I would think about joining something.

I had fallen in love with piano over the past year. I had Dad to thank for that. Every Sunday, he would play records with me—from jazz to classical, to soul and funk and rock-n-roll. He would sing all the words or hum along with the instruments, waving his hands like he was a maestro. We would make hot chocolate and then we'd practice the melodies we'd heard on the piano. He could pick up from the middle of any song and play. As baffling as it was, he always insisted that songs were like people: they may seem different, but they are all so similar, and once you've met enough of them, it gets easy to figure them out.

"Is Dad coming home tonight?" I asked.

Mom stopped loading the refrigerator and sighed. "I'm not sure, Snowpea. I haven't heard from him."

The last few weeks, whenever Mom came home, she would go straight for the kitchen and open a bottle of wine. She talked to Aunt Tegan on the phone for hours, complaining about how stressful being a nurse was, and how no one appreciated her enough, especially the doctors who thought they knew everything. She always put a desperate emphasis on *everything*, like it was her last breath. She and Aunt Tegan would talk for hours. Mom and I barely spoke a few minutes. Even though she was home, I missed her.

"Do you need help with dinner?" I asked.

"No, I got it."

I settled on the living room couch with and opened my book. I was reading *Mrs. Frisby and the Rats of NIMH*. Miss K had given it to me as a present at the end of sixth grade and I was reading it for the second time.

But tonight, I got distracted. I snuck upstairs to Mom and Dad's room, carefully opening the creaky door. They always kept their room neat. Their king size bed was made and their lotions and sprays and polishes were lined straight on the dresser. I picked their cordless phone up off its receiver and held it tight. Then, I took it to my room and locked my door.

I dialed and waited for it to ring.

"Harper, Dalbey, DeLaMater, Manhattan office, this is Fiona, how may I help you?"

I paused. I wasn't expecting a secretary to answer. "Is Da—I mean," I stuttered. I asked for him by his real name.

"He's left the office, may I take a message?" Fiona sounded kind and gentle and southern.

"No, that's okay. Thank you."

I smiled. He was on his way home! And when he got here, I would tell him about my recital.

I was excited when I heard the front door knob jangling. But it was only my older brother Yaden. He got home just in time, as it was a little after seven and Mom and I were setting up the table for dinner. It was important to her that we have dinner together as a family as much as possible.

"I'm sorry I'm late," he said.

"It's okay," Mom said. "How was work?"

"Great!" He was wearing a green work polo with his gray school uniform slacks. He had started a job at a video game store called FuncoLand. "I have to do training for a few days but I got to sell a few games."

"That's nice," Mom smiled. "You're a working man, now."

He chuckled. Yaden had stayed in his room all summer playing video games, or going over to his friends' houses to play more video games, so it was kind of funny to think of him with a job. He had gotten a haircut over the weekend and I noticed he must have lost weight over the summer. He was getting chubby last year. But right then, he looked sharp and grown up. His transformation didn't make sense to me.

Yaden was a senior in high school. He'd been working his part-time job to save up for a car because he was going to go away for college. He'd applied to Syracuse, University of Pittsburgh, and Hofstra University. I remembered those because they were all far away. Not to mention Dad was always asking about it over the summer. Mom wanted him to stay home and go to a school here in Philly. I wanted him to stay, too, but I never chimed in. I only listened. I was happy for him, but I always felt down and I'd lose my appetite at dinner. My brother was a dork and he played video games and he teased me all the time, but I loved him and I didn't want to see him go.

"Should I set up a plate for Dad?" I asked Mom.

"No, don't worry about it," she said. "I'll set aside some leftovers." Her smile faded as she set Cannoli's plate on the table.

We all sat down and Mom stared down at her plate, picking at her food. I watched her for what might have been a whole minute and I don't think she blinked once. She gazed as she twirled linguine noodles with her fork.

Cannoli was always the most talkative at dinner. "I had a dream last night and there were rainbows in the snow. And I drew it at school. The teacher liked it."

"Bring it home. I'll put it on the fridge," Mom said. Her voice was low.

"Yeah!" Cannoli quickly swallowed a mouthful of pasta and carried on. "And a girl in class has pigtails. I want to have pigtails, too. Can I have pigtails, Mommy?"

"Sure." She met Cannoli's cheer with a dim nod. Mom hadn't even taken a bite of her food yet. She got up from the table and opened a bottle of wine.

"I can do Cannoli's hair, Mom."

"Okay," she said as she popped the cork from the bottle and poured a glass.

"What time is Dad coming home?" Yaden asked after a crunchy bite of garlic bread.

Mom sat back down and took a gulp of her ruby red wine. She picked up her napkin, dapped her lips and took in a breath. She looked at me, and then at Yaden.

"Your father won't be home tonight," she said, looking at the empty seat across from her.

"Why not?" I whined. I wanted to snatch the words back into my mouth. I sounded rude, questioning her like she was another seventh grader I called Anita instead of Mom. But that was my eagerness all built up, waiting to tell him the great news.

"He's still working," she said.

"Is he staying over Aunt Tegan's?" Yaden asked.

I bit my lip and grasped my silverware tight in my hands. What a maddening day it had been. And the one exciting thing that I was happy about I couldn't share yet.

Mom tilted her head back, shifting back and forth and around like there was a tightness in her neck.

"He's staying over," she said. She took another long sip of her wine. "He's not staying with Tegan."

Sister Maggie was the teacher who everyone feared. No one dared to say a word in her class. The eighth grade boy whose locker was next to mine had told me yesterday that she would shut the windows when it was warm or open them wide in the winter if anyone broke the rigid silence.

Sister Maggie had sharp eyebrows and small lips. She was round with salt and pepper frazzled hair, probably from the stress of teaching The Good Word to kids like us. She was classically militant like a nun from the nineteenth century. The eighth grade boy told me Sister Maggie kept whips, belts, and wooden spoons in the locked classroom closet. She also archived detention slips and framed copies of tests from students with failing grades. I wasn't too worried about all that. I was quiet and failing Religion class was almost impossible.

Nemo had this class with me—he sat in the back of the room. I looked back at him, my line of sight clear in the last two minutes before the period bell rang. Nemo never noticed me staring; he was too busy slouching over his notebook.

I wondered if he could hear my heart thumping. I wanted to whisper his name and wave at him. I wanted to sit next to him and read what he was writing. He was deep in thought, biting his pencil. He erased a line before scribbling again. I wondered if it was one of his poems. He wrote the best poems. They weren't sapped with love. He talked about the wisdom of trees and the power of music. I especially liked the ones about music.

I bet Nemo would be thrilled to hear about my recital. He always got excited about the things I was excited for.

All summer, I dreamt of us writing poetry and songs together. He could sneak over to my house on days when Mom and Dad were both at work and Yaden was away with his friends. We could play on my piano and have snacks and when we were exhausted from brainstorming all day, we could sit on the couch and watch *Animaniacs.* I'd sit as close to him as I could, lean on his shoulder— and during commercial breaks, we'd kiss.

"You didn't call me last night!" Lenore said, plopping in the seat in front of me and shocking me out of my daydream.

"I'm sorry," I said. I glanced over at him one more time before I gave Lenore all my attention.

Lenore Roslyn Close had been my best friend since fourth grade and I told her everything. There was one minute left before class, and there was so much I wanted to say. I wanted to tell her about the recital, but not until I told Dad—he had to be the first one. I would have told her about the fever in my hands, but when I woke up that morning, I was fine. I wanted to tell her I hadn't called because I was sad Dad was staying in New York. I wanted to tell her that I missed walking home with her yesterday. But as I was about to open my mouth, she stopped me.

She gripped my hand tight. "Did you do it?" she whispered, leaning close to me with wide eyes.

"Do what?"

"I saw how you were staring. Did you two…?"

"No."

"Did you chicken out?" Lenore asked.

"No." I didn't want to tell her about Julie. "Well, sort of."

"What do you mean, sort of? Either you chickened out or you didn't. Not that hard. What happened? You get cold feet? Sweaty palms?"

I sunk in my chair.

"Look," she said. "It's a big move. So, if you are chicken, just hold his hand. That's how you let someone know you really like them. Do it after class. Seriously."

The bell rang, and Sister Maggie waddled into class, closing the door behind her. Lenore spun around, her straightened raven-black hair whirling with her. I took one more look at Nemo. He shut his notebook, threw it in his bag, and pulled out another as the class collectively muttered, *Good morning, God bless you, Sister Maggie.*

She wrote on the chalkboard in elegant cursive: *Original Sin.* She underlined it with a screeching stroke. "Does anyone know what this is?" Her voice was raspy and I could smell cigarette smoke on her as she paced past my desk. "Anyone?"

Nemo raised his hand. "Is it the sin Adam and Eve committed in the Garden of Eden?"

"Yes it is, Mr. Jones. And of the sacraments we talked about yesterday, which one do we receive to save us from original sin?"

Lenore's hand shot up. "Baptism?" Lenore and Nemo were the smartest kids in our grade. I did have the best grades out of all three of us in the second semester of sixth grade, though. I was catching up. Sometimes, we studied together last year. We helped each other out, but I had decided that I was going to have the best grades out of all three of us this year.

"That's right, Ms. Close," she said. "You are baptized because Adam and Eve deprived you of holy justice with their rebellion in the Garden of Eden. But despite your baptism removing you from sin, you've grown. You're about to turn thirteen, if you haven't already. And now, like Adam and Eve, you're capable of rebellion. You're no longer a guiltless, sinless child of God.

"Children before the age of thirteen are promised into heaven. God forgives you, for you do not know the weight of your sins. Until you turn thirteen. This is why we practice the sacraments. This is why we study religion. Why we go to church. And why we pray." She slammed the pointing stick against the board. "Original sin."

I felt like I'd been whacked with a wild branch in a surprise wind. My birthday was coming soon. On January fourth, I was going to be a teenager. I wanted to tap Lenore's shoulder. Her birthday was the same day as mine. We called ourselves the cosmic twins, born only four hours apart. Did she feel the same abrupt fret I did?

If I died after I blew out the candles on my birthday cake, did that mean I wouldn't get into heaven? Would I be stuck in purgatory repenting for whatever sins I had accumulated? I shouldn't worry. I was a good kid. But maybe it was what I *wasn't* doing that was the sin. Mom and Dad hadn't taken us to church since the Sunday after Easter. I never prayed on my own. And I was guilty about how I thought of Nemo.

I had to be better at being good. I knew I wasn't good enough, even if I didn't want to believe anything Sister Maggie said.

When the period bell rang, I poked Lenore. "Did you hear what she said?"

"Uhh, about what?"

"About turning thirteen?" I said.

"Yeah. So?"

"You're not worried?"

"I am worried," Lenore said. She turned and nodded towards the front of the classroom. "I'm worried that you're going to let Nemo get away."

Nemo was on his way out of the room. Pesky butterflies woke up in my stomach and bounced around. Of course, I was cursed with the clumsiest love butterflies any stomach has ever had in the history of human kind.

Lenore nudged me. "Go. I'll see you after French. And I want details. Don't chicken out."

I sighed. She made it sound like this was easy.

I dodged students, bumping shoulders and squeezing past idle chatterboxes standing in the middle of the hall. I called Nemo's name, and he stopped and turned to me. He met me with a smile.

"Is Sister Maggie crazy or what?" I started as we walked together. Ms. Cutillo's classroom wasn't far—I didn't have much time to do this.

He laughed. "All the nuns are loopy. You know she's just trying to scare us with that turning thirteen stuff, right?"

"I don't know."

"You mean to tell me you bought that?"

I blushed. Yeah I did, but I said nothing. I lowered my head and he laughed at me. But not the kind of laugh that erupts from the stomach, but a chuckle that slips from the throat with empathy.

"You're too gullible," he said.

I kept my head down, watching his hand swing back and forth as we walked. Around the next bend, we'd be walking right into French. I tugged at the collar of my uniform. Then, I let my hand fall to my side and inched closer to Nemo. I felt his fingers brush against mine. He didn't move away from me. I took his fingers with mine, and I nearly fainted.

"Hey!"

I stumbled, shoved from behind. Julie. She glared at me, her eyes narrow and her lips pursed.

"Julie!" Nemo cried out. Other students stared at us.

She gave him the same mean glare before stepping over to me. "What was *that*?" she said.

"What was what?" I asked.

"I saw what you did. Trying to hold his hand?"

"I wasn't." I glanced at Nemo.

"Julie, chill out," Nemo said, getting between us. She shoved him aside.

"I will *not* chill out. Look, Edith. I'm going to need you to stop talking to my boyfriend. Stop walking with him. Stop looking at him. Alright?" She was in my face.

Boyfriend?

Students watched on, muttering *oohs* and other things under their breath. *Are they going to fight? What's going on? Who's that girl Julie's grilling?*

I said nothing but stared back, pretending to be firm and fearless.

Julie gripped my collar. "You hear me?" she said loudly.

Her grip was tight. I choked on my breaths and lost my balance.

"Julie!" Nemo yelled. He pulled her away from me.

The commotion around us stirred. The kids were getting excited. Someone yelled out *girl fight!*

I quivered from my fingers down to my toes. I didn't want to fight. I didn't think I could throw a punch right. I certainly couldn't muster the audacity to hit another person. I mean, there was one time I slapped Yaden when he was teasing me about the first test I ever failed. I had been crying in my room and he kept calling me stupid, whispering the word over and over again through the little space between the door and the floor. I snatched the door open and when he stood, I swung at him with all of my might. He had yelled out in pain, and I had winced, feeling immediately contrite.

Julie wasn't a sibling, though.

"Come on," Nemo said. He took Julie's hand and they walked past me, pushing through the audience.

Everyone looked at me. I wanted to hide, but if I ran, they'd laugh at me. I stood there, staring back with a scowl. *Just go away. All of you.*

Then, I felt what was like an electric shock in the palms of my hands, and my fingers cramped. I slipped past the students. I had to shove most of them out the way. Some of them pushed back at me. I ran for the bathroom and put my hands under cold water.

The fever was back. And this time, it was even hotter than it was yesterday.

5

Lenore stood at the mound of the baseball field, her hair tied up in a messy ponytail. She wore a scowl for the batter.

She and the rest of the team had gotten together with players from Holy Trinity to play a Friday friendly. I didn't know much about baseball, and what little I did know was because I was Lenore's biggest fan. She was the only one on the field wearing a blouse and plaid skirt uniform. Everyone else was wearing button-ups, slacks and ties. She was the best player in St. Vincent, and it didn't matter that she was a girl.

Strike-out! The batter went down swinging. He slammed his bat against the grass and let out a roar. Lenore walked off the mound calmly. It was the end of the inning.

Baseball was a big deal for our schools. St. Vincent had made it to the state championship this past summer. We lost, which tore Lenore apart. Had they won, they would have qualified for the Little League World Series—and Lenore could have been the first girl pitcher to record a win in the series. That was her dream, and it was her last chance to do it since she was going to be thirteen next season, one year too old to qualify.

The day they lost was the only time I'd ever seen Lenore cry. A girl so stoic on the mound collapsed into an hysteria of wails and tears, her face buried in her glove. No one could move her. The other team celebrated. It was a walk-off homerun off of her own pitch. A fastball that could have won the game if it were a strike.

I was there to see it. Everyone pretends to be in that position. Throwing the final pitch or hitting the ball out of the park to win the game. It's one of the most played scenarios in children's imaginations. But no one ever pretends to be on the losing side. No one ever pretends to have their dreams crushed.

Lenore was heartbroken for days, so I invited her to come over that weekend for a slumber party. That cheered her out of her slump. Ever since then, we've had a slumber party once a month. Our first one as seventh graders was going to be this weekend.

As the teams switched to the next inning, with the score at two-nothing St. Vincent, I looked past the two dozen or so students in the bleachers to find Nemo sitting at the top row. He'd been alone the entire game. He hadn't noticed me, but I'd been looking over my shoulders at him the whole time with my hood over my head.

I wanted to talk to him, but I was still sour from the scuffle with Julie in the hallway a few days ago. The courage only came in tiny surges. I'd wring my toes and my fists, wrestling with my cowardice. I was like a mouse hiding in her hole when she knew there was no one in the kitchen keeping her from the cheese atop the counter.

Screw it. If I sat here, the game would end and Nemo would go home alone and I'd hate myself the whole weekend. Another surge came and it lifted me.

I climbed the bleachers. When I was next to him, I playfully tugged his hair. He spun to face me, and I saw his eyes light up. I smiled and then sat next to him, leaving only an inch or two between us.

"This is a close one," I said. "Think Lenore's going to get the shutout?"

"Wouldn't be surprised," he said. "Holy Trinity lost their best two hitters to high school this summer. Their going to have a hard time hitting anything come next season unless someone steps up."

"How do you know so much?"

"I almost went to Holy Trinity," he said. He let out an abrupt yell when a pitch was called a strike against St. Vincent. He shot his arm up in the air, and I noticed he had my only copy of *The Neverending Story* beside him. I had lent it to him last month. Nemo was an enigma. He could talk about sports or science or literature with matching fluency. And he was cute. How he let an average cheerleader get to his heart baffled me. I wondered if Julie had shared any books with him.

I glanced down at the inch between us. I leaned my leg against his, closing that little space. My heart fluttered. I looked at him and he said nothing, nor did he flinch.

"I missed you," I said in a whisper that slipped from my tongue. I hoped he hadn't heard me.

"Yeah, we didn't hang much this summer." He turned to me.

"What are you going to do to make up for it?"

"We'll just have to hang out more over the school year."

"That doesn't look like it's going to happen," I said.

The cling of a metal bat smacking a baseball snapped my attention back toward the game. Lenore had hit a ball deep into left field. All the St. Vincent students stood up. When the ball landed on the ground just past the Holy Trinity outfielder's glove, we cheered.

Lenore dashed past first, watched the outfielder throw as she hit second, then locked onto third base. She dove, impetuously sullying her white blouse. The ball landed in the third baseman's glove far too late.

We sat back down and I stared at Nemo. "What's so special about Julie?" I asked.

He laughed, combing his afro pick through his hair. "I don't know, Edith. She's nice."

"That's it? She's nice?"

"Well, no. She's —"

" — Asian and has big boobs?"

"No! That's not it."

"Then what, Nemo?"

"Why do you care so much?"

I closed up, caught off guard. *I'm the one asking the questions!* I crossed my arms and pouted as I watched the game. I could feel him looking at me. I felt the fever in my hands rise again.

Another hit on the field. A single to right field. The boy who hit it was thrown out but Lenore scored. Three to nothing.

I clapped for her. "I care because you're my friend," I said. "My friend has a girlfriend now. I want to know why he likes her."

"Girlfriend?" he said, blushing. "I wouldn't call it that." He cleared his throat, shifted in his seat, then put his hand on my shoulder. "I know Julie got a little beside herself on Tuesday. I'm sorry. I want you two to be friends, too. She's nice once you get to know her, I promise."

Nice. Is that really the only word you can come up with, Nemo? "Fine," I snapped. "Don't tell me." I got up and stomped down the bleachers.

"Wait, Edith," he called out to me.

I wanted to stop and let him speak. I wanted him to tell me he didn't like her, that he really wanted me to kiss him on Monday. I wanted him to tell me that he'd made a mistake and that he missed me this summer. But if I stopped and he didn't tell me any of those things, he would break my heart, so I put my hood over my head and kept walking, as the fever pulsed in my hands once again.

6

When I got home, I felt the urge to pray. I'd never prayed on my own before. I closed my door although I was home alone, sat on my bed, and closed my eyes. I wanted to breathe in the silence.

I'd been worried about getting lonely in the afternoons at home alone, but I didn't mind it after all. It was my time, and right now, and I needed someone to talk to who wasn't Mom or Lenore or Yaden.

I made the sign of the cross and folded my hands as tight as I could, like the tighter my hands were folded, the louder my prayer would be. My palms ached and blushed red with warmth.

"I'm sad," I said to God. "I'm scared. But worst of all, I'm angry. I'm angry at Dad for going a whole week without calling to talk to me. I'm angry at Nemo for not understanding me. I'm angry at Julie for embarrassing me in front of everyone.

"I don't like being angry. It's terrible. I should be happy— especially for Dad. He's making lots of money so he can take care of us. He's got to do what he's got to do. I'm trying my best to be happy for him, I promise. But it's hard.

"I should be happy for Nemo, too. He's got his first girlfriend, even if he denies it. I'm jealous it's not me." I sighed as the heat in my hands intensified.

"I'm really scared that there's something wrong with me. I'm not sure what to do." Tears fell and a cold quiver caught in my throat. "I'm sorry that I'm angry. I'm sorry for being selfish and jealous. I'm going to try and be a better person from now on. I hope you forgive me."

I recited an Our Father, wiped the tears from my eyes and blew my nose. I hated crying. It was ugly and I got all snotty and my eyes would swell and I always got a headache afterwards.

I didn't know how to feel after I finished praying. I didn't feel any closer to wholesome than I did before I got to my room. I might have felt worse about myself. Was God listening? What did he think? If he could speak, what would he say to me right now? Would he scold me, or would he promise me it's going to be alright?

I fought the tears as much as I could and went to play piano until Lenore got here. Shostakovich, 24 Preludes, Opus 34 was one of the first cycles Dad played for me. Playing it was like building a thunderstorm with my fingertips, gathering the raindrops and the rumbles and filling them in the clouds, only to let a bit of it fall in the distance.

Time flew whenever I practiced and I needed time to fly. This week sucked, and I just wanted it to be over.

I played until I heard the doorbell ring. I leapt from the bench and swung open the door.

"Hope you're hungry," Lenore said, "we brought pizza."

Lenore's Mom, Miss Karen, stood next to her. Miss Karen had a radiance about her—the kind that made butterflies dance around wildflowers. She had short black hair and always wore long, flowing sundresses. She brought me in for a hug, balancing the two boxes of pizza.

Lenore scurried to the kitchen and unloaded a set of jars onto the counter from her bright pink duffle bag. The jars were filled with colorful glistening powders. Then, she took out tiny bottles with handwritten labels on them: strawberry, lemonade, pineapple, and fruit punch. I picked up the jars and bottles, holding them up to the light and turning them upside down to see the powders and the flavored liquids swish.

"We're going to make rock candy tonight!" she said. "But after pizza, of course."

"Cannoli's going to freak out," I said.

"Well," Miss Karen said, "I'll leave you girls to your fun. I'll be back to pick you up on Sunday afternoon, okay?"

"Sunday night?" Lenore pressed.

"Only if you get your homework done before then."

"Deal."

Miss Karen smiled and kissed Lenore on her forehead. "Edith, take care of her."

"I will," I beamed. "Thank you for the pizza."

Miss Karen hummed as she made her way to the front door. She was graceful, like each step she took mattered. When she opened the door, she stopped and called out to Lenore.

She lowered her voice, suddenly somber, and whispered to

Lenore, leaning close as she held her hand over Lenore's ear. Lenore shook her head and uttered goodbye as Miss Karen walked out.

"What was that?" I asked.

"Nothing," she said. "The real question here is, which movie do we watch with pizza? I've got *The Princess Bride, The Goonies,* and *The Lost Boys.*"

"*Pretty in Pink.*"

Lenore sighed. "Again?"

"Yup!"

After Andie and Blane shared their after-prom kiss, and I had broken my record for most slices of pizza eaten in one sitting, Lenore insisted it was time to make rock candy.

Night had fallen and Cannoli was following us like a puppy. She pleaded that we let her help make candy.

"Only big kids get to make it," Lenore said as Cannoli admired the sheen of the purple powder. "But you get to eat as much as you like when its done."

"Okay, Norey," Cannoli said. She sat at the table and picked at the pepperoni on her half-eaten slice of pizza.

"Speaking of big kids," I said, "who measured you on The Sacred Wall?"

Lenore clipped a clothespin onto a wooden skewer and placed it into an empty jar so that the end of the skewer hung about an inch from the bottom.

"My friend Jesse. He's on the baseball team."

"Do you like him?"

"What? No." She poured water into a saucepan, placed it on the stove and turned on the burner. "I don't like boys."

"What do you mean you don't like boys? Not one?"

"No. Not one."

"You have to have a crush on someone, Lenore," I said.

"I don't."

"I don't believe you."

"Oh, well."

Lenore measured out sugar and put it into the water in the pan. I kept my hands in my pockets. I wanted to help but I was afraid to touch anything. What if I turned one of the jars so hot that Lenore would notice? All I could do was watch and hope she didn't ask me to do anything.

"Did you grow?" I asked.

"Two inches since the beginning of sixth grade. Not bad, I guess."

"Ugh. Not fair."

"You're still the same height?" she asked.

I stood next to her and leveled my hand at the top of my forehead, touching hers, too. I stepped back to look. Indeed, she was taller than me. We used to be the same height.

"I guess so," I said, defeated. I wondered who would end up the taller one. Or maybe we'd be lucky enough to end up the same height, like the twins I knew we were. She was letting her hair grow, and it was getting as long as mine. Maybe that was a premonition.

"It's not a big deal," she said. "Girls grow until they're eighteen. You could end up as tall as your Dad. Then you'd be upset because you're too tall."

"I *want* to be tall."

"Being tall is overrated," Lenore said. "I think I'd like you better short."

"Whatever."

The water started to boil and after adding more sugar, Lenore stirred the mixture. Then, she spun around and pointed at me with the ladle. "So why'd you leave the game early?"

"I didn't," I lied.

"Dude, I saw you leave. I had a freaking shutout and you didn't stay the last inning?"

"Are you mad at me?"

"I was. Not anymore. But only because Cannoli is here and she makes me happy."

"I love you, Norey," Cannoli blurted out.

"Hmm, see?"

Steam rose from the pan behind her.

"I left because of Nemo."

"What happened?" Lenore lined three of the powder jars in front of me. "Open those, please. And pour them in the bowl."

I gulped. I pulled my hoodie sleeve over one hand and held on to the jar. The lid was twisted on tight. But I turned it with all my might. When it popped open, I held the lid against my face. It wasn't warm.

"Nothing. He was just being a jerk."

"Can't see Nemo being a jerk. What did you say to him?" She turned off the burner and let the water cool.

"He can be a jerk. To me."

"What do you like about him, Edith?"

"I don't know," I said. "He's cute. He's smart. We share books.

We've been friends for a long time."

"That's it?"

"What do you mean, that's it? That's a lot." I sighed as I poured the last jar into the bowl. A mixture of purple-yellow daffodil and lime green shimmered like sand under the beach sun. "Can we not talk about this?"

"Fine."

Lenore took the skewer, dipped it in sugar and swirled it in the cooling sugar water. Then she poured the water into the empty jar nearly to the top. She put the skewer back into the glass.

"What flavor do you want?" she asked.

"Can you mix strawberry and lemonade?"

She nodded and poured some of the extracts from the bottles into my jar. Colors billowed and the water crackled and sparkled ruby and sunflower. She prepped a fruit punch jar for herself.

"What next? Don't you have to freeze it?"

"Normally, yeah, but..." Lenore sunk her fingertips into the powder in the bowl. She closed her eyes and stayed still for a few moments. She took a long breath, then with a pinch, drizzled the powder into the sugar water. The water cooled and crystals blushed with hue, clinging to the skewer like an old friend you haven't seen in a while.

"Whoa," Cannoli said from the kitchen table.

"Touch the jar," Lenore said with a sly smile.

"Okay," I said.

Steam rose from the water, vapor fogging on the outside. If it were cold, and my hands were hot, the jar might break—I remembered learning that in Science class on Wednesday. I held my breath, hoping my hands would cool.

I reached out, lightly grasped the jar, then recoiled from the icy glass. "What? Lenore, how did you do that? What's that powder?"

Lenore let out a victorious laugh. "I can't tell you. It's a secret."

It was like magic. "Can I try next time?"

"It won't work if you do it, but you can try."

Midnight struck, and our yawns became relentless. Our hands were sticky and greasy from all the popcorn and rock candy we'd eaten. Cannoli was sound asleep on the couch and we laid on the floor. She tried to hang out with us as long as she could, but she didn't make it past ten. I took her to bed while Lenore cleaned up.

Cannoli, half-asleep, cooed about a tummy ache and asked me to rub it away. I did, and I promised her that she'd feel all better in the morning. I kissed her on her nose and told her that I loved her so much. She murmured 'I love you, too,' and fell asleep the next instant. I watched as her tiny hands clutched her comforter. Her lips parted and she purred a little snore.

The fever had been gone since halfway through *The Princess Bride*. I sat in my room while I waited for Lenore, staring at my hands. The fever was like waiting for something to come out and scare you, over and over, and there was nothing you could do to stop being frightened. I promised to myself the next time the fever came back, I would tell Mom.

When Lenore came in, she leapt into bed and nestled with all my pillows. "My stomach hurts," she said.

"Shouldn't have eaten all that rock candy," I said.

"Shut up." She whined and grimaced into the pillows, and before long, she was hiding under the blanket, groaning about how she never wants to see another slice of pizza ever again.

I laughed. "You're going to want some for breakfast."

"No, I'm never eating pizza again. I'm not kidding."

I got under the blanket and took one of the pillows. After a minute, I asked, "Do you think my Dad's okay?"

Her face became serious. "Yeah, Edith. If something happened, your Mom would have told you by now."

"But she's been hiding in their room all week. She's barely spoken to us."

"It's probably just a long business trip. Did you ask your Mom when he'd be back?"

"No."

"Then ask."

I sighed. My eyes were getting heavy. Sleep was coming fast. I reached to switch off the light, and snuggled back under the blanket. Part of me wanted to tell Lenore about my recital. I still hadn't told anyone and it was killing me inside.

"Can we make friendship bracelets tomorrow?" I asked instead.

"Yeah." Lenore was as excited as she was tired.

We talked a little more, planning out our Saturday. We lulled each other with ideas of Saturday morning cartoons, Wicked Royal Penguin nail polish manicures, and blanket forts.

Halfway to my dreams, my thoughts dozed into senselessness. Chords played in my head, and I could taste hot chocolate. It was like I'd fallen into Sunday night, and Dad was home, and we were practicing piano as if he'd never left. As if this week had never happened.

I couldn't tell what was real and what was the dream anymore—until Lenore snapped me awake. She grabbed my arm tight, her nails digging into my skin.

"What's wrong?" I asked, wincing. My eyes hadn't adjusted to the dark.

Her grip got tighter and she pinched into me when I tried pulling away.

"Stop," I said, snatching my arm until I got out of her grasp. I threw the blanket away from me and sat up, staring at her through the dark until my eyes could see.

I felt a sharp pain in my arm. I was bleeding.

"Lenore, that hurt!"

Lenore sat up without using her arms, stiff like a robot. A smile twisted along her lips as she tilted her head. Her eyes were wide and she wasn't blinking, like she'd shot up awake late for school.

"What're you doing?" I asked. I grasped my arm.

She said nothing. She looked at me, motionless.

"This isn't funny," I said. I started to crawl out of bed. As my feet touched the floor, Lenore reached for my other arm. She pulled me back into bed and I landed on my back, nearly slamming my head into the bed frame.

I wriggled out of her grip. "You're scaring me."

Her smile waned to a frown. She knit her brows. "Help me," she whispered. Her voice was low and hoarse.

"Help you how?"

"Get her out of this body."

"Lenore, what are you talking—"

"I'm not Lenore."

She crept over to me, leaning her face against mine. I was against the frame, its coldness clenching my back. "Are you sleepwalking?"

Lenore's stare was ghostly, like she was looking right through me. Her eyes dilated and the whites of her pupils were darkening.

I must have been dreaming. All the rock candy and pizza and fantasies of being Molly Ringwald were giving me a monstrous nightmare.

I closed my eyes. The wound would be gone if it were really a dream. I shut them tight, holding my breath and pursing my lips. By the time I opened them, it would be well into the night and Lenore would be sleeping peacefully beside me. My breaths were rapid and my heart raced.

I opened my eyes when I felt a tremor rattling the bed.

Lenore convulsed violently, lying on her back.

"Lenore!" I cried out. I put my hands on her face. I reached for her arms, held her shoulders. I wasn't sure what to hold or put pressure on. I didn't understand what was happening. I kept calling her name. Her eyes rolled to the back of her head and saliva trickled from the sides of her mouth.

I screamed for Mom, not leaving the bed. I screamed over and over, louder and louder, until she finally came bursting into my room.

7

The ER waiting room at the hospital was like purgatory. I sat in a chair with my hands under me and I kept my eyes lowered to the ground as much as I could. Sickness and despair were tying me in knots.

A man quivered helplessly and held himself. The hair on his arms prickled and his teeth were chattering. Why hadn't anyone offered him a blanket or a sweater or tea? An older man across from me had a loud, dry cough that repeated the same rhythm every other minute, startling me each time.

A woman sat in the corner crying softly, rubbing her stomach. She caught me looking at her. She was wrought with tears. Frazzled hair clung to her face. I didn't look away, frozen by her silent, lonely anguish. Should I go over to her and tell her it's going to be okay? What if it wasn't going to be okay and saying that only made it worse? Hope was not in the stale air, and I didn't know how to breathe or speak without it.

I nestled all of my body into the chair, squeezing my legs with my arms, and burrowed my face at my knees. I couldn't hide from it all. The late-night news spoke of a little boy lost. His name wasn't familiar, but the reporter said he was a Holy Trinity student and was last seen at school. The next story was about a fire that had brought down a house not that far from mine. And then, there was a report of a car that had toppled off the highway and there were no survivors.

I couldn't take it anymore. Was there no good news today?

The television was mounted high on the wall so I stood on top of an empty chair next to it, and reached for the power button. I was too short — just an inch or two away.

The weatherman announced that thunderstorms would bloom overnight, with rain for the rest of the weekend.

I didn't like thunderstorms. I didn't like hospitals. I didn't like being short, and I didn't like not knowing if Lenore was okay.

I leapt from the chair and aimed for the power button. I pressed it in mid-air but it didn't shut off. I grunted, sour with pursed lips. I jumped again and pressed it harder. Nothing. One more time.

A commercial break. And failure. Everyone was looking at me, too. When I turned around, they shifted in their seats and looked away. Except for the woman. She kept looking at me.

"It's going to be okay," she muttered.

I hopped off the chair, walked by her with my head down, and skipped through the automatic doors to get outside. I was met with a chilled drizzle as I found my way to a garden bench. I put my hands on the cool stone, my hands still warm. My tears mingled with raindrops.

I was happy to be alone for a few minutes. I prayed, asking God to take care of Lenore and everyone in the hospital. I left it up to him then, and I shut my eyes and rocked back and forth, shaking the thoughts out. I watched the flowers around me dance with the rising wind. The cold air snuck into the sleeves of my hoodie. I was still in my pajamas. If I'd had a blanket, I would have fallen asleep right on the bench.

"Snowpea?"

I spun around and saw Mom walking towards me. I wiped my face. "Aren't you cold?" she asked.

"No," I sniffled. "I'm okay."

Mom sat and wrapped her arm around me, pulling me close. She nuzzled her nose in my hair and kissed me. I listened to her long, deep breaths.

"Lenore's going to be okay," she said. "She had a seizure. It was diagnosed as nocturnal epilepsy. She'll have to take anticonvulsants, but she's going to be okay."

She tightened her grip on my arm, but I flinched. She had squeezed where Lenore had pierced me. She leaned back and looked at me. She rolled up my sleeve and examined my arm. The wound was red like cinnamon, with three punctures that looked like bites.

"What happened?" she asked, switching to nurse mode. "Does that hurt?"

"It's nothing."

"Did someone scratch you?"

The thought back to the look in Lenore's eyes right before her seizure took hold. I shuddered and leaned my head onto Mom, careful to keep my blazing-hot hands off her radar. I wanted to get out of here and go back to bed and continue my slumber party with

Lenore.

"It was Lenore," I confessed. "She didn't mean it. She grabbed me right before she had the seizure. It's nothing."

"Are you sure?"

"I promise."

"Okay. Well let's get you inside."

The drizzle turned to steady rain. "Mom? I have something to tell you."

"What's that?"

"I was going to wait for Dad to come home. I wanted to tell him first, but..."

Mom kept silent and her eyes cradled me as I took my time.

I sighed. Why was this so difficult to say?

"I asked Miss K if I could play a recital. At the Christmas Eve Festival. And she said yes." I was only half as excited as I thought I'd be when I finally announced the news. I had built it up, like a drum roll patting in my head.

But sitting with Mom at a garden bench outside the ER while my best friend recovered from something scary and awful—maybe it hadn't been the right time. I was cold and tired and my eyes hurt from crying. My hands were burning up and I couldn't get all the sadness from the rest of the world out of my head.

"It's going to be my Christmas present for Dad," I added lamely.

Mom's eyes filled. "That's wonderful," she said.

"Aren't you excited?" I pressed.

She moved strands of hair from her face before looking away from me. Her tone was wilted and wispy. "I'm really proud of you, Snowpea. And I'm sure your Dad will be, too."

"Well, don't tell him, please? *I* want to tell him. I want to see how excited he gets." I wanted to see him light up like a billboard in Midtown Manhattan. He'll be so bright I'll have to wear sunglasses.

"Edith," Mom said. "I love you. I love you so much. And I'm sorry if I've been—distant. I just…" A tear fell down her cheek. I'd never seen Mom cry before. Her voice quivered as she kept on. "I've probably been distant to Yaden, too. And Jenna." She stopped, taking in a long, fluttering breath through her mouth. "You and Yaden and Jenna are the three greatest things to ever happen to me. I really mean that."

I felt like it had been days since Mom told me she loved me. I thought hard as I waited for her to speak again: *when was the last time she told us I love you?*

She took my hands and I could feel her trembling. Suddenly, I was scared of what she was about to say.

She looked me dead into my eyes. "Edith, your father isn't coming home."

"Why?" I asked. "Do you mean he's not coming home for a while?"

"I don't know."

"What do you mean you don't know? Hasn't he called?"

"I don't know because your father and I haven't been getting along for some time now."

"But he was home! You kissed him goodbye that Friday."

"It's complicated."

"What did he do?"

"We'll talk about everything later. Not here. Okay?"

It wasn't okay. I had a million more questions. Where was he?

Why hadn't he called to talk to us? How long was *some time*? Were they not getting along because of me? I fought back tears. The rain was falling harder.

"Let's go inside," Mom said. "We can go see Lenore."

I watched as the numbers counted down for the elevator. Seven, six, five…then it stopped. It stopped for a long time. If Lenore was on the third floor, couldn't we take the stairs? Doesn't anyone take the stairs here?

Four. It stopped again. Mom was next to me, talking to the nurse who had been at the front desk. Her name was Katie and she had shaken my hand firmly when Mom introduced us, saying that Mom told her all about me. I said nothing back to her. I'd been emptied. All I wanted was to see Lenore.

Three. Two.

I tapped my feet and crossed my arms, squeezing them against my chest. I bit my lip, fighting grunts and sighs and all the other impatient things. This was the longest wait for an elevator ever.

One.

The door opened and a man pushed a cleaning cart out, bidding us a good morning. We got into the elevator, and I pressed three before any of them did. Then, when the doors wouldn't close, I punched the door close button with my finger—over and over.

"You know, Edith, you're a hero," Katie said after the doors finally closed. "You saved a life today. That's a wonderful thing."

I glanced at Mom. She smiled at me, but all I could do was look into her eyes. I didn't feel any trace of a smile or a blush or a grin. I was numb. Even the fever in my hands had gone away.

On the third floor, I was two steps behind, my head down as Mom and Katie talked about work. I didn't want to look up and see inside any of the rooms. I didn't want to see anyone else sick or dying or in pain. I wanted to see Lenore and I wanted us to get out as soon as we could. I closed my eyes as we walked.

When we arrived at Lenore's room, she was sleeping in her bed. An IV tube was clipped to her arm, and an EKG's metronome echoed across the room. There was an empty bed on the other side of the room. Raindrops glimmered against the tungsten light coming from outside the window. Thankfully, the TV in the room was turned off.

Lenore's breaths were steady and quiet. She was dressed in a powder-blue, diamond-print hospital gown. She looked brittle. I wished I had brought her things. I'd brush the coils out of her frizzed hair. I'd put her Dr Pepper lip gloss on her dry, cracked lips. Then, I'd have her recite more words from *The Princess Bride* to flush color back into her cold, pale skin.

"I want to stay here with her," I said. "I can't leave her alone."

"That's brave of you, but you don't have to," Katie said. "We'll keep a close eye on her."

"She's my best friend. She'd stay here if it were me in this bed."

"Are you sure?" Mom asked. "Karen should be here any second."

I nodded.

"Alright," she said. "I'll be by to pick you up once she's been discharged."

I reached for Lenore's hand, swallowing a sob.

"She might not know where she is or what happened when she awakes," Katie added. "Be sure to find a nurse when she gets up. All the nurses on this floor are extra-friendly, so don't be shy to ask for help. Your Mom works on this floor, so that should tell you how nice they are."

Katie said goodbye and left the room. Mom lingered there, leaning against the door frame. Thunder rumbled in the distance, followed by a faint flash of lightning.

"I'd better get going back to your sister and brother," Mom said. "I love you, Snowpea. And I'm sorry about your father."

"It's okay."

"You know, there's nothing wrong with crying. I've been crying, too. It helps. Kind of like the rain."

Slowly, she shut the door. Her faint footsteps faded and I turned off the room lights, then crawled into bed with Lenore. I was careful not to pull a cord or nudge Lenore awake. I cuddled against her, uncomfortable with what little space I had at her side. I kissed her on her cheek, whispered goodnight, and let the pitter-patter of the rain lull me back to sleep.

I awoke late the next morning to Lenore calling my name as she shook me gently. "Wake up! Wake up!" Her voice was groggy, but it was back to normal. She was smiling. And the morning had come, filling the room with a soft grayness and the music of a gentle storm.

"What are you doing here?" she asked. "What happened?"

Whatever happened last night, it still didn't feel real to me. Maybe I could choose not to believe any of it. I could lie to myself and say that Lenore had a stomach ache so bad that she had to rush to the hospital. She overdosed on sugar, and the doctors wanted to be sure they got it all out of her system. Everything else was a stupid nightmare, the kind that's scary when you first wake up from it, but it's funny when you remember it later.

"The slumber party got relocated," I said.

She laughed, but it was cut short by a cough.

"The nurse will tell you what happened," I said. "They told me to get a nurse when you wake up."

I went to climb out of bed, but when I did, Lenore grabbed my arm. I flinched, and for a second, I was afraid to look at her. She was holding me right where she had me last night. I grimaced at the pinch of the wound. Lenore sure was strong.

"Wait," she said.

Slowly, I turned to her. "Yeah?"

"Can you hang out here? Just for a minute? I want you here. I'm fine, I know it. This isn't the first time I've woken up in a hospital bed."

"They said it was a seizure," I said, snuggling back into bed.

"I know," Lenore said.

"You knew?"

"It's not my first. Are *you* okay?"

I wasn't sure but I nodded anyway. "Are you?"

"Yeah," she said. "I'm just a little scared right now."

"I'll stay."

"Thank you," she said. She yawned and was already drifting back to sleep. Did she remember everything from last night? Anything?

"I thought I was going to lose you," I said.

Her eyes opened back up. "You can't lose me."

9

Miss Karen drove us home from the hospital. Lenore was still drowsy and fatigued by the time we left. She sat in the backseat of the car with me. She closed her eyes and held my hand, leaning on my shoulder for the ride. Lenore wasn't coming back to my house. The slumber party was over. I pleaded glumly with Miss Karen.

"She needs rest, Edith."

"She can rest at my place," I insisted.

Miss Karen laughed. "I'm her mother. I'm going to take care of her."

"Can I come over to your house?"

Miss Karen kept silent. So did Lenore, her head nodding down and snapping back up with a sleepy sniffle.

When we got back to my house, I quickly packed Lenore's things and brought them to the car. I thanked Miss Karen for dropping me home. Lenore had spread out in the backseat, using her hands as a pillow. I wanted to beg one more time. I didn't want to leave Lenore alone. I didn't want to be alone.

I could have chased them down after Miss Karen drove off; they only lived a block away. I watched the car until I couldn't see it any more, then went back inside.

I watched *Sixteen Candles* then napped the rest of the afternoon. I woke up to the front door slamming shut.

Yaden had arrived home, carrying a small white box and wearing a dripping green raincoat. Cannoli came running down the stairs when she heard Yaden come in. She followed him into the kitchen. "What's in the box?" she asked, over and over.

Yaden had gotten cannoli, something Dad would do every Saturday. I looked at him when he opened the box. Cannoli gleamed over them, yelping and clapping her hands. "Can I have one?"

He looked back at me. Did he know about Dad not coming home?

"Later," he said before moving his eyes away from me. "After dinner."

That's when I realized I hadn't eaten all day. As if on cue, my stomach growled so loud that Cannoli glanced over at me. I laughed, embarrassed, and held on to my tummy. I was still in the pajamas I wore to the hospital.

"Is Daddy bringing some, too?" Cannoli asked as Yaden shut the box and placed it in the refrigerator.

"Not today," Yaden said.

"Geez, where is he?" she pressed.

Yaden turned and I could tell by how long he looked at me this time that he knew.

"Cannoli," I said, kneeling before her. "Dad is on a trip. A long trip. For work. He's not going to be home for a while. But when he gets time, he's going to call us and tell us all about it, okay?" I wanted to hold her hands, but my fever had been pulsing since I'd left Lenore.

"A trip to where?"

I sighed and glanced at Yaden. He kept silent. I guess lying to our little sister was all up to me.

"He's in New York. He's really busy, but when he comes back, he'll have cannoli for you. Lots of them. But hey, at least we have cannoli from Yaden."

Cannoli's face straightened and she swayed her shoulders. She was silent and her eyes grew big and she bit on her finger. "I miss Daddy."

"I do, too," I said. In an instant, a sob got caught in my throat. I swallowed, glanced at Yaden, then back at Cannoli. I forced a smile with everything I had.

"I'm going to make dinner," Yaden said, clanging through pots and pans.

"Why don't you go play, and I'll come with you in a few minutes?" I said to Cannoli.

"Okay," she conceded. She scooted upstairs, her tiny feet covered with rainbow-colored socks, stomping with each step.

"I'm just going to have leftover pizza," I said. "You don't have to worry about me."

"You should probably have some real food," he said. He lit fire under a pan and then poured olive oil into it.

"I don't feel like waiting. I haven't eaten all day." I watched him with my arms crossed.

"You can't wait half an hour longer?" He filled a large saucepan with water and placed it on the stove.

"No."

I took a slice of pizza from the box in the refrigerator, set it on a plate, and put it in the microwave. Yaden walked past me, silent, back and forth from the freezer to the cupboard, and over again. He set chicken breasts in the pan and they sizzled, like a crescendo, low at first and then building in volume.

Once my pizza was heated, I sat at the table. I took a bite, not waiting for it to cool.

"You're a brat," Yaden said, his back facing me.

"How am I a brat?" I said, chewing a mouthful of pizza.

"You don't appreciate what you have."

"How do you know that?"

He spun around, wagging his slotted spatula. "Because you're eating pizza right now."

"So? I wanted pizza!"

"No. You're just trying to piss me off."

"No, I'm not! I just want pizza." I took another bite and chewed and smacked with my mouth wide open, glaring right at him.

"You eat like a cow," he said.

"You *look* like a cow." I stuffed the last of my pizza into my mouth in one ambitious bite. Then, I stood and left the kitchen. Yaden called out to me but I didn't stop.

I barreled up to my room and slammed the door shut. I hoped he could hear it all the way in the kitchen.

How dare he call me a brat? I didn't do anything to deserve being called that. It wasn't my fault I didn't want to wait before dinner was ready. And maybe I would have eaten what he cooked anyway. I didn't want him to have to worry about me.

"It's going to be fine," I said to myself.

But now that I was well and truly alone, there was nothing to stop me from thinking about what Mom said. Dad wasn't coming home. He had disappeared without saying a word to me. I didn't understand. Was this permanent? Or were Mom and Dad so mad at each other that they needed to stay away for a while? I'd never seen or heard them fight or argue. Was it like how I felt about Nemo? I didn't want to see him, but I still liked him.

I hid under my covers and listened to the rain. The storm had gotten heavy. *What's happening to my family?*

I started to pray, but halfway through a Hail Mary, I was interrupted by a knock on my door. Cannoli peeked in, holding her My Pretty Ballerina doll. "Do you want to play now?"

"Just a minute," I said.

She closed the door. I finished the prayer. When I did, I felt myself growing hot. Not only in my hands, but behind my ears and at the back of my neck. I curled into a ball, pulling at my sheets. I muffled a shriek into my pillow, then unfurled a string of punches on my mattress.

A few minutes later, Cannoli knocked on my door again. I let her in, and we played with her toys until it was time for dinner. I wasn't alone that night. Cannoli stuck by my side the whole time. I braided her hair into pigtails and we read stories to each other until we got sleepy. She slept in my room.

Was this what boys and dads did? Love you for a little while, change their minds, and then leave?

10

At lunch, I slipped through the halls to the school auditorium. No one was ever there, and I wanted to be alone. Light poured in from the windows, favoring the floor as I stayed hidden in the shadows of the balcony. This was my oasis. I nestled in my chair and let the quiet wrap around me. I was rattled from the whole week. And I had a test in Social Studies but all I did on Sunday was stare at the same words on the same page before I decided I'd given up.

Last night, Mom had told me that she and Dad weren't getting along and that he wouldn't be home for a while. She promised me that he still loved me, but I wasn't sure I bought it. It had been a little over two weeks since I'd seen or spoken to him. I had called his office in New York only once, but that was once more than he'd called me.

What did he do to make Mom so upset? What made him so afraid to call?

I tried to read *The Secret of NIMH* but I couldn't focus on the words. I left the book in my lap and looked down at the stage. On

Christmas Eve, I was going to be up there playing for everyone. I was sure Mom and Dad would figure things out by then. I needed to be patient, that's all.

The door to the balcony squeaked open. I whipped my head around, hoping it was the janitor, Mr. Ben—the only person who knew about my secret place. He often shared an apple or chocolates and tell me a joke he'd heard recently. I could've used a snack and a laugh.

I frowned. It was Nemo.

"Can I sit down?" he asked.

No, I thought. "Go ahead." He sat next to me, and I leaned as far right in my seat as I could.

"Are you ready for the Social Studies test?" he asked.

"How did you know I was here? Did you follow me or something?"

"You think I don't know you come here?"

"What do you want?"

"I—" He paused. "I want you and Julie to be friends."

"I *told* you—"

"I don't know what's up with you two," he interrupted, sounding annoyed. His words were firm and he stared at me for a long time. We fell silent, looking at each other. Then he wavered back to his old gentle self. "I don't know, but it's like..."

"Like what?"

"Never mind."

"No!" I said loudly, my voice echoed in the auditorium. "What were you going to say?"

He buried his head into his hands and leaned forward. He was quiet, the kind of quiet where you knew the person didn't have anything left to say.

I stood up and swung my backpack on, struggling to get my arm through the second strap. When I did, he was still silent. I stared down at him, waiting for him to say something. Nothing came, and that's when I decided it was time for me to go.

"I miss you, Edith," he said as I was halfway up the aisle.

I stopped.

He walked up to me, pulling at his fingers as he continued. "I don't want you two to not like each other. I want you two to be friends. That's all."

I said nothing. It was hard to look at him.

"I talked to her about it, too," he said. "She said she would keep her cool."

"Keep her cool? Oh yeah, okay." I turned to walk away again but Nemo grabbed my hand. My fever was high and my hands ached. He held me tight. He said nothing about the unusual warmth. But he held on to me, and when I relaxed, he folded his fingers into mine.

"Please?" he said.

I melted. One thing I'd learned this summer was that telling my hormones no wasn't easy. I had thought nothing of boys before then, and now the one I had eyes for inched close to me, took my other hand, and squeezed. His hands were cool and they eased the fever in mine. He gazed into me, like he was saying something in his head and he knew I could read his mind.

Ugh. "Fine," I said.

"Great," he said, letting go. "Look, I'm really hungry and there's only twenty minutes left of lunch. Are you coming?"

"No, but have some french fries for me," I said. *Yuck, I hate myself.*

"Of course," he smiled.

Dang it, his smile was like a bad cold. It got in the system, refused to leave, and made me forget what it felt like to not be sick. I watched him as he left the balcony. I wasn't going to be able to shake the thought of his hands in mine for the rest of the day. When I sat back in my chair, I quivered. I was cold and hot and light-headed.

How could he not know what was up between Julie and me? Was I imagining things on the first day of school? Did he not lean in and almost let me kiss him? Was he playing games with me? If so, then he was winning.

I arrived before the first bell in Social Studies. The class was empty. Shortly after, Julie arrived. She smiled, then sat at the desk in front of me.

"I hear you want to be friends," she said.

"I—" *Well, no.* "Yeah," I forced with a nod.

"I'm really glad to hear that," she said. "You know, I try to be friends with everyone. I like everyone."

Quit the malarkey, Julie. You're not the perfect little girl that you pretend to be.

"What are you doing after school?" she asked.

"Homework, I guess."

"Homework? You can do that later tonight. Let's go to the creek!"

"Why do you want to go there?" I said, raising an eyebrow. The creek was a few minutes away from St. Vincent. There was a playground there and that was where the cool kids went to hang out. But the creek was always empty. That was my other hidden oasis.

"Nemo says you're really good at skipping rocks. Maybe you can teach me. And we can hang out. Be friends." The bell rang. Students were filling the classroom. Lenore came in and stuttered in her steps when she saw Julie and I talking.

"Uhh…" I locked gazes with Lenore.

"It's settled then!" Julie exclaimed. "Meet me at my locker after school?"

I nodded with a faint *uh-huh*.

"I'm really happy about this. I am."

Was she being for real?

The final bell rang. Julie tapped her knuckles on my desk before she moved over to hers. I glanced at Lenore again, *what-the-heck?* written all over her face. I shrugged, and with that, Mr. Hardy entered, shut the door behind him, and class began. He wasted no time handing out the test, despite the amalgam of groans and pleas from all the students that we'd take it tomorrow instead.

"Nope," he insisted, laughing at all of us. "Today's the day. Today is the day."

At my locker after eighth period, I got nervous. Why was I doing this? I didn't want to be friends with Julie. She was a cheerleader in a completely different circle of friends than me. She hung out with the basketball team and all the other popular kids in school. What would *we* talk about? We didn't have anything in common, except Nemo.

I packed my things, wondering if I should bail on her or reschedule for another time. I lingered once I closed my locker. Should I make my way to Julie? What if I took too long and she ditched me? Then, I wouldn't feel so bad.

No, I had to do this. I made a promise to Nemo. I didn't want to disappoint him.

"Edith," Lenore called out to me. Her smile stretched to the edges of her cheeks. "Do you know what today is?" Lenore sang as she arrived at my locker with a jubilant leap. A week had passed since her seizure, but she'd been as zesty and bubbly as ever.

"Monday?" I said.

"Yeah, but what about it?"

"Umm…" I pondered for a moment, dropping books into my backpack. A light sparked somewhere in my brain. "It's the last day of summer."

"Yup! Fall officially begins right before midnight tonight. And you know what that means, right?"

Lenore's face was brimming with so much glee that I thought she was going to burst like a balloon. Another light sparked in my head.

"Ice cream?"

"Yes!" she leapt. "It's a tradition."

Last year on the last day of summer, we'd gone out for ice cream. After that, Lenore and I made a promise to always get ice cream on the last day of summer. I'd forgotten about that until just then.

I shut my locker and put on my backpack. Lenore put her arm around my shoulders, pulling me close. She started to walk down the hall, but I didn't budge.

"Isn't it too cold for ice cream?" I asked.

"Silly, it's like seventy degrees outside," she said. She pulled me. "Come on, let's go."

"Wait, Lenore," I said. "I, uhh, I have plans."

The sunshine drained from her face. Her shoulders slumped. "You have *plans*? *You* have plans?"

"Yeah. I have plans."

"Since when do..." She slouched against a locker. "Seriously?"

"I'm sorry, I totally forgot about today," I said. "Can we get ice cream later? Manuel's doesn't close until seven."

"What are you doing that can't wait?"

"I'm hanging with a friend."

"Nemo? I thought you didn't like him anymore."

"It's not him."

"Then who?"

"I have other friends," I said. "Can we just go later?"

"I have to be home by four," she said. "This is a tradition, Edith, and—"

"No, it isn't," I snapped. I didn't mean to snap, but the words whipped from my tongue and lashed at Lenore. The scowl she gave me was proof enough that I'd hurt her. She'd never looked at me like that before. "Lenore, I'm sor—"

"No, don't," she said. I reached for her arm but she peeled away, spun around and took off. I watched until she went down the stairs, out of my sight. I waited. I didn't want her to pop back up and see me walking to Julie's locker.

I felt awful. I'd broke Lenore's heart.

On our walk to the creek, Julie asked a bunch of questions. She asked how I thought I did on the Social Studies test. I knew I aced it, but I played it off and said I thought I did okay. She admitted she didn't study for it last night, but she still thought it was fine. She asked me what my favorite TV show was and I told her it was *Buffy the Vampire Slayer*. She got excited and squealed, "me, too!" Her favorite character was Cordelia. Of course it was.

We walked through the playground, passing by other kids in St. Vincent uniforms, but none of them saw us. There were other kids, too. Some were younger hanging with their parents. I saw one girl atop the tallest slide in the park eating a two-scoop ice cream cone.

Past the playground, we crossed a stone bridge over the creek. It was the kind of bridge that trolls would hide under—if trolls were real. On the other side, there was a long, grassy plain and a lonely, tall and rusted Virgin Mary statue. At the creek, rocks of all sizes rested by the crackling, glimmering stream. We were alone, the melody of the playground faint and far away.

"So how do you do it?" Julie asked.

I grabbed a flat rock, and rubbed its grainy coolness against my hands. My fever was ripe like a volcano ready to erupt.

"You have to be level with the water as much as possible," I told her. I got low and motioned the rock between my fingers and flicked it across the creek. It bounced three times.

"I can do that," she said. She tried to copy my stance. She tossed the rock and it sunk as soon as it hit the water. "Damn it!" She tried again. And again.

I was bouncing rocks off the water without much effort. Dad had taught me how to skip rocks. I had struggled when I first tried with him.

Was it possible that Julie really wanted to be friends? If she had as much persistence in earning my friendship as she did with learning to skip rocks, then maybe we had potential.

She kept at it. She stomped her feet and scoffed and growled overtime she didn't make it, but then she'd pick up another rock. Finally, she got one of the rocks to skip. One bounce was enough to get her leaping in the air with her fists rounded in celebration. "I did it!"

"Congratulations," I said.

She looked off into the creek, letting out a victory sigh. I skipped a couple more as she lingered in her glory.

"I didn't notice how short you were until today," she said. Her tone had taken a venomous chord, falling down a pitch from the cordial timbre just moments ago.

"I swore you were taller than me in sixth grade. Did I really grow that much?"

I didn't say anything, but I kept my eyes on hers. She got so close that our noses were touching. "I mean, I knew I got taller when Nemo measured me on The Wall, but..."

I backed away.

"What's up?" she said. "Something I said?"

"No."

"Something on your mind? Someone?"

Yeah, I was thinking about someone, and how she probably hated me. I was stuck with this phony trollop instead of eating ice cream with Lenore like I should have been.

Julie picked up a rock, tossed it in the air, and caught it. "What do you think about Nemo?"

"He's my friend."

"Your friend. Just a friend?"

"Yeah."

"I've seen the way you look at him. In class. You stare at him at lunch. I mean, you should just take a picture. Oh! I have some, if you want one. We always take pictures together with his polaroid camera."

I was ready to go home. I wanted to get ice cream, and scurry to Lenore's house before the ice cream melted or fell from the cone. I'd apologize and I'd swear to never ditch her again.

"He hasn't taken any pictures with you, has he?" she asked. "Hmm, I thought you two were like best friends or something."

"It doesn't matter," I said.

"Oh, Edith," she said. "It matters," She stopped pacing and got back in my face. "Stay away from my boyfriend."

My heart scuttled into my stomach.

Her lips bent with a crooked grin and she laughed in my face. "He likes me more. He thinks I'm prettier than you. You're too plain and boring and ugly."

My breaths were rapid and I was shivering all over. "Fuck you."

Julie stared at me straight, until a chuckle popped into her mouth like an air bubble. She held her stomach, cringing with laughter she couldn't hold for long. "Wait, wait, wait! Edith Solstice, did you just cuss?"

I'd never cursed out loud before. I always felt guilty whenever bad words snuck into my head, but not right then. She kept laughing.

Without thinking, I made a fist, pulled back, and struck Julie with a roundhouse. She stumbled over, nearly falling to the ground. I reared back and shook out my hand, which was already throbbing — if it hurt me, then it must have hurt her twice as much.

She leaned over, her hand on her cheek. She sniffled and wiped her face with her arm.

Then, Julie galloped at me with a harrowing yell. I paddled back, but her quick fist batted my chin. I stumbled, falling over the bed of rocks. I winced, but what really hurt was what I felt inside. I was disappointed that Julie had fooled me into coming here. Why had I let myself believe her?

She towered over me, and I snapped out of my daze. She lunged down with a punch, but I rolled out of the way. Her hand hit the rocks, and I clipped her legs with mine. I staggered to my feet, half-heartedly wiping dirt and mud from my uniform. My face was throbbing and my back twinged.

Julie came towards me, but I dodged the punch, grabbed her arm, and slung her towards the grass.

I was out of my mind. I followed her and swung at her. I missed, and she clutched my wrist and threw me back farther. I fell on my face. When I looked up, I saw birds bathing in the fountain at the feet of the Virgin Mary statue. The flock soared, and I heard Julie's footsteps rustling in the grass.

I got up, but I didn't have a chance to react. With a burst of speed, she lunged at me, grabbed my hair, and pulled me back to the ground. She climbed on top of me and struck me hard across my face —once with her right, then with her left—sending explosions of pain through my jaw, my cheeks. It felt like my brain was rattling against my skull. For a second, I couldn't breathe. She was about to strike again, but I thrusted her off with the strength that came from my hips.

I was sick of being nice and reserved. I was tired of holding back tears and pretending I was okay. I barreled at her with a visceral yell, shoved my hand against her face, and we tumbled. She fell down with a muffled grunt. I kept pressing down on her face, like I could drown her in the grass.

Last night, I had wondered what it would be like to not feel. Mom had lit a vanilla butterscotch candle in the living room. The flame danced on the wick, and I went up to it and doused the flame with two fingers. I held on to the wick while my fever surged. I didn't flinch. I thought, how could something smell so sweet and look so pretty hurt me?

Right then, I'd been numb, even though I suffered a burn mark.

With my hands over Julie's face, I was numb again. I didn't care that I was hurting her. I couldn't feel that I was hurting her. But the numbness didn't last. It rose up like a sting that pangs long after the bee has flown away. My hands felt like they were on fire. They were much hotter than they'd ever been, like I'd been holding them close to boiling water.

Julie screamed with a shrill pitch. "Stop! Please! Edith!" Her floundering underneath me dwindled. Her legs stopped kicking and she let go of my wrists. I could feel her strength fading. Julie was crying hysterically, pressing her hands at the sides of her face. "Edith! Please!"

I heard something—felt something—a hiss. I pulled away.

There was steam, and flesh and blood trickled down my palms like sodded goo. Julie writhed and she pushed her palms on her face like she was suffocating herself. Her muffled squeals were like wordless, desperate pleas. I crawled over to her slowly, like a curious cat. I gently clasped her wrists, and pulled her hands down. She flinched, but then conceded to my grip. The blood and the flesh on my hands were not mine.

Julie's face was red, bloody and sinewy. It looked like the skin on her cheeks was melting. Her eyes were shifting, and her lips were busted and trembled. I could see muscle underneath the torn skin of her forehead.

She looked at me, silent with shallow, rapid breaths.

I'd never been so terrified in all my life. What had I done? *How?* I stared at her, my mouth open. I felt cold all over. I couldn't move. "No. Julie, no. No. No."

Suddenly, I felt someone shove me aside. It was Lenore. She put her hands over Julie's face. "Go get help. Now! I can't heal her all on my own. She needs an ambulance!"

The smell of lavender filled my nostrils, and the hum of a wispy viola whispered from — Lenore's hands? A stream of light like a thick morning fog, poured from her fingertips and seeped into Julie's face. The light that missed her face hit the grass and broke like droplets of water.

"I can't," I sputtered. "I did this. I did this. How did I...?" I was dreaming. I had to be.

"Go get someone at the playground! If you don't she's going to die."

"Lenore, what...?"

What was she doing? What was that light? That sound? I couldn't find the words to ask.

What if I did get an ambulance? Would Julie tell them I had

done this? *I* didn't even know what happened. I burned her face. How the hell did I—

"She's not going to remember," Lenore said. "I promise. Nothing is going to happen to you if you get help. But if she dies here, I can't help you."

"How is she not going to remem—"

"Go!" Lenore yelled.

I climbed to my feet. I looked at my hands. There was still blood. I rubbed my hands in the grass. The dirt was moist and cool. I did it until all the blood was gone. My hands were mahogany from the dirt.

I made my way to the playground. I felt like I was in one of those dreams where I couldn't run. When I got there, I saw the girl who was eating ice cream and her dad playing at the swings. He was pushing her and she was going so high. She kicked her feet and laughed and screamed. She squealed each time she went flying, the rusty chains screeching along as they scraped the bar.

I walked towards them. I felt weak, like I was going to fall. "Help me," I said as I got close to them. My voice was vacant, rasping with a hollow whisper.

The horror and the worry and the dismay and the ache froze me. I was too much of all those things to lift my arm and tug at the dad's jacket.

"Help me!"

11

Everyone from the playground had gathered around Julie. An ambulance was parked near the statue. EMT's tended to her before they put her on the stretcher.

Lenore and I stood at the bridge, looking on. Once Julie was gone, Lenore took me by the wrist. "We're going to my house," she said.

I wanted her to let go. Everything hurt so bad that I was dizzy and nauseated. "I should go to the hospital, too," I whimpered. "Something's wrong with me."

"I know," she said. "A doctor can't help you. But I can."

Bewildered, I let her drag me along. A few times we had to stop because I thought I was going to throw up. Once, other St. Vincent boys passed us by while I was hunched over. I couldn't hold it any longer. They stared and pointed, laughing. Lenore scared them off, threatening to punch their lights out if they didn't move it.

Lenore took a bunch of napkins from her backpack. She didn't let me touch them. Instead, she wiped my mouth and my chin for me. She tucked my hair behind my ears as I blushed with embarrassment. I apologized, on the brink of tears, but she smiled at me.

"You're going to be okay," she said.

When we arrived at her place, she shut the door and looked out all the windows. She closed the shades and the curtains at every window in the living room, dining room, and kitchen.

Flowers blossomed tall in the living room. There was a coffee table atop an oriental rug, surrounded by a long pillowed couch and a pair of single love seats. A sweet aroma carried from the kitchen, past the dining room, and into my nose. There was a table with a series of ornaments and knick knacks: owls, dragons, sea shells, and tiny urns.

"Don't touch anything Edith," she said. "Not a thing. Not the table. Not the sofa. Not me. Not even yourself. Keep your palms open and away from anything."

She called out to her mom a few times, shouting down to the basement from the kitchen, and then up the stairs in the living room. She was moving quickly, looking around.

"Come here," she said, taking my wrist again. We went into the kitchen and she told me to sit down at the table. "Keep your palms open."

I looked at the small, amber-colored wooden table. There were only two chairs. "Can I just lay on the floor?" I said.

"Fine."

I laid on my back. The checkered tile floor was cold, like I'd hoped. I spread out my arms and legs, like I was about to make a snow angel. I watched the ceiling fan spin. I was still nauseous, and confused, and scared.

Lenore began to fill a large silver bowl with water from the sink. While the water ran, she searched the tallest cabinet. She knelt, grunted in frustration, then took a chair from the table. She stood on it and reached for the top shelf of the cabinet. She snagged a mason jar from the shelf that was about half full with what looked like thick red jelly, and a whisk and spoon form a utensil drawer, which made a noisy metal clamor.

Lenore turned off the water, then put the bowl on the counter. She scooped three spoonfuls of jelly into the bowl and whisked vigorously. Steam rose after a while.

I stood from the floor while Lenore took a wooden box from the shelves of spices, sugar, and oils. Inside the box, an assortment of colored, softly glowing petals about the size of my palm. She picked at them, smelling each with keen draws of her nose. Then, she held them up to what little light was sneaking in from the curtained windows, tore a small piece off a yellow petal and ate it, taking slow and deliberate bites. She broke the rest of the petal into the bowl, and an aroma of coconut and lemon opened up into the room.

Lenore mixed in a powder that was white and chalky like flour. She crushed some almonds, then drizzled some cinnamon and honey into the bowl. She was silent as she worked with haste. She didn't shoot me one single glance.

Then, Lenore opened her hand over the bowl and a soft white light bloomed from her palms. It wasn't like the fog she spilled over Julie, but like morning sunshine from a window.

"What are you doing?"

"Come here," she said.

I wanted to touch the light as it shimmered off her face and hair, but I folded my hands behind my back. She did tell me not to touch *anything*. I watched as the mixture coalesced into a thin, shiny ruby-red liquid.

"Put your hands in," Lenore said. She took a step back so I could be closer to the bowl. "Slowly."

I recoiled at the sharp pain once my fingertips touched the mixture. I glanced at Lenore. She gave me a nod as she put her hand on my shoulder. "It's okay," she whispered. For that moment, I felt at ease.

I tried again, fighting the sharpness with gritted teeth. The mixture was cold, like making snowballs without gloves. "Keep them there," she said. "I know it hurts."

"What is this?" I grimaced, the ache shivering through my whole body.

"Scarlet wine. It heals siren fever, which is what you have."

"Siren fever?"

"Yeah, it's…" Lenore trailed off. "This is going to sound insane, Edith, but…"

"But what?"

"You're a witch," she said.

I chuckled. Not because it sounded insane. It was insane. But I chuckled because I felt relief. I wanted an explanation so badly that I'd believe anything.

"Siren fever is what you get when your body realizes it. And it usually happens at this age for girls."

"I'm a witch." I said, to see how absurd it sounded out loud.

The pain all over started to go away as the scarlet wine got warm. "This is working," I said.

"Good," Lenore said. "I had siren fever, too. Six months ago."

She took my hands from the scarlet wine and held them in hers. The mix had gotten sticky like maple syrup. She massaged my hands lightly. "They hurt still?" she asked.

I shook my head. "No."

"Okay. Hold them over the wine." Lenore took a hand towel and dried my hands. Then, she opened her hands and had me place mine on top of hers, our palms touching. She closed her eyes and the white aura seeped from her hands and enveloped mine. It was warm and felt like liquid silk.

When the aura faded, she moved her hands away and took a step back. "How do they feel?"

I flexed them, rounded them, stretched them out in front of me. I couldn't believe it. The fever was gone. The ache was gone. "Is it gone for good?"

She nodded.

I took Lenore into a tight embrace. I could breathe again. I could speak again. The tightness all around my body loosened.

"I'm sorry," I whispered. "I shouldn't have ditched you."

"It's fine."

"No it isn't," I said. "What did I do to Julie? What happened?"

"You cast a spell by accident. But I promise, she's going to be okay."

I rested my head on her shoulder and quietly started to cry. She squeezed me tight. I didn't want to let her go.

I wondered if she had ice cream. It was still summer for a few more hours.

12

Lenore scooped chocolate ice cream into a pair of bowls. Then, she sprinkled powder from a jar over the scoops. She handed me a bowl and a spoon, and I admired the shimmering blue crystals.

"This is homemade ice cream," she said. "But it's not ordinary ice cream. It's enchanted. It stops tears and sadness, but only for a little while."

"What's the powder do?" I asked.

"Oh, that just helps the flavor stick to your memory better. It's our last ice cream of the summer. I want you to remember this."

We'd turn to each other and smiled, but we finished our ice cream without a word. It didn't take long for me to finish mine. When I did, my throat and my chest felt refreshed, like I had been drinking peppermint tea on a crisp winter day. My nostrils cleared with each spoonful, and Lenore said my eyes weren't puffy anymore.

"You might get a little brain freeze later," she said. "Only because it's your first time eating the ice cream. But it'll pass. It's better than having a headache after crying." She put her hands on my shoulder and smiled at me. "No more tears today for you. Okay?"

I nodded.

"I have some things to show you." Lenore took my hand and we went up to her room.

Her bedroom was like any other girl's bedroom. She had tall bookshelves filled with books. On her small desk, she had sheets of paper with unfinished drawings and scattered pencils and eraser shavings. Her bed was made up. She had posters of Björk, Nirvana, Hooverphonic, and…

"Your mom lets you listen to Wu-Tang Clan?" I asked.

She laughed. "Are you kidding? *Wu-Tang Forever* was all I listened to this summer. Don't you pay any attention to me?"

There were other posters of people I didn't know. A guitar leaned against her closet door. Her baseball uniform, bat, and glove were neatly piled on top of a basket by one of the windows. She dug into her dresser and tossed a shirt and sweatpants onto her bed.

"Get changed," Lenore said. "Your uniform is a mess. If anyone asks, you were playing baseball with me and made a crazy slide to home plate."

I laughed. No one would ever believe that.

I changed in the bathroom. By the time I came out, Lenore had also changed and was in the hallway, sifting through a closet. She pulled out a long, heavy chest. She sat down, placed her hand over the lock that looked as ordinary as any other metal lock. The lock rattled until it clicked and snapped open. Lenore opened the chest, and inside were books, purple feathers, powder jars, a few daggers, and copper tone charms. A smaller chest was tucked inside, too, but

Lenore told me she couldn't open that one — only her mom could.

"Is your mom a witch, too?" I asked.

Lenore nodded. I felt a pinch in my stomach. I didn't know if it was from finding out about Miss Karen right then or if the ice cream was starting to work its magic. I shook my head when the word 'magic' came into my mind.

I sat next to her as she pulled out a snow globe made out of a mason jar. She shook it, and white flakes swirled around the snowman and the light post. "I made this myself," she said, "right before we moved from Montreal. It's enchanted now, so I keep it safe in here. I only use it when I need it."

"What do you do with it?" I asked as she handed it to me.

"Shake it and find out."

I did. As I looked at the snowman, his tiny orange nose pointing straight at me, I thought about the first time Dad had me play piano. I could hear the music he played and I remembered the taste of the hot chocolate and how soft the marshmallows were. I could see he was wearing jeans and an Eagles football sweater. And I remembered how he sang to me while he played.

Lenore leaned over to look at me. "You feel it?"

"I don't know." I was in a daze thinking about that Sunday from two years ago. It almost felt like it happened yesterday.

"It heals homesickness. When you shake it, and you hold it, it brings back old memories."

"Woah!" I said. I shook it again. "Do you get homesick?"

"Sometimes. I miss my friends. And I miss speaking French," she said. "Maybe I'll go back someday."

"Are you going to tell your mom about me?"

"She might already know," Lenore said. "They say when you get older, you can tell who else is a witch. It's in your intuition or something."

Lenore took out a mahogany, hardcover-bound book thick with off-white pages. She opened it, and the first page was blank.

"Are you going to tell her about Julie?" I asked.

"No one else needs to know but you and me."

"But what about Julie? She's going to tell."

"She isn't going to remember," Lenore said. "Sit tight."

Lenore got up and dashed back to her room. She came back holding a book similar to the one she pulled out of the chest. She sat close to me and set the book between us at our legs.

"This is my journal. It has all the spells that I've learned. When I learn something new, it appears in here."

On the first page was an illustration of a girl with her head tilted back and strokes of lines that resembled vibrations. "When you learn a spell—well, we don't call them spells. We call them poems, but anyway, when someone teaches you or you read about it or you do something by accident, it appears in your journal. It can appear as words, drawings, squiggly lines, rainbows, whatever. It appears on the page as it appears in your head. In your imagination." She put her hand on the page and the papery clap echoed through the wide, dim hallway. "I screamed so loud that I shook the earth. That's when I realized I was witch. I'd had the siren fever, too."

"Wait," I said. "You shook the earth? Like an earthquake?"

"It happened when we were in Oregon. In March. That one weekend? It was a three-point-nine on the Richter scale."

My mouth hung open. I tried to imagine how loud that scream

must have been.

"Where were you? Were you scared?"

"I was terrified. I didn't mean to scream so loud. I was sad, and I was upset. It was at my cousin Heather's funeral. She was only ten, and I was just mad at the world. I couldn't stop crying and then, all of a sudden, I just wanted to scream. Before I knew it, I felt the ground shaking and then I passed out and woke up in a hospital."

That explains her seizure, I thought. She didn't remember anything from that night. Was it really a seizure or was that how the doctors saw it? Was it because she was a witch?

"I'm sorry about your cousin," I said.

"It's okay," she said. "Sometimes I'll have ice cream and shake the snowman when I miss her. It helps. A lot. And hey, no one got hurt. It was a minor earthquake. I get a lot of headaches now, but I know a poem that heals them right up, which is on this page."

She turned to a page with a collage of clouds, pillows, feathers, and flower petals. "This is what I think of when I want to heal someone. I concentrate, then I see all these things, and I cast it through my hands." She held her hand out. "Your fingertips are where your magic pores are strongest. That's what you saw earlier today when I healed Julie."

She turned to another page, and there was a picture of a girl with an empty thought bubble. "This is the poem I used on Julie after I healed her. It's called a Hiccup of Wit. She's not going to remember what happened."

"Are you sure?" I asked.

"Yeah," she said. She took my hand in hers. "She's going to be okay. I promise. And no one knows what happened but me and you.

Not even Julie. I'm sure."

"Could you use the Hiccup poem on me?" I asked. I hadn't stopped thinking of Julie's marred face.

"No," she said, "it's been too long. It only makes you forget the last fifteen minutes or so."

"Did you follow me?" I asked.

"I knew something was wrong," she said after a long pause. "Something told me to look out for you. So I followed you two to the creek. I'm sorry."

I didn't know what to say.

Lenore closed her journal. She took my hand and then put her other hand over the empty journal. Motes of light drizzled from her hands and onto the book. She said something in French. I felt a tingle in my arm, and it crept to my neck as the light seeped into the pages. Lenore handed me the book. Aromas of wood and maple and leather swelled from the book when I opened it. I embraced it close to me and took in the scent, the textured paper rubbing my nose and my cheeks.

"This is going to be your journal," she said. "The poem you accidentally cast is going to appear on that first page. It has my blessing. Our blessing."

"That's the first time I've heard you speak French," I said.

I opened the book again and saw a rough pencil sketch was forming on the first page. I put my hand over it and could feel it vibrating. I pulled back at first, shocked like I had touched a bug and didn't know it. Then, I traced my fingers along the lines as they slowly bloomed.

"Don't beat yourself up about Julie," Lenore said, nudging me out my awe-struck stupor. "I healed her pretty good. She's going to be fine."

The illustration that was going to be on this page was going to remind me every time of the fight with Julie. The sounds of her shrill scream. The flailing of her legs. The ringing in my head from her punches. The sting of my knuckles. The burning in my palms. And the flesh and the blood that I ripped from her face. Was being a witch always going to be this terrifying?

We heard the front door open downstairs. Shaken up, I shut the journal and tried to hide it. Lenore was calm. She shut the chest and locked it with a poem. She returned it to the closet, leaving the snow-jar out. Miss Karen called out to her, and Lenore responded. "I'm up here! With Edith."

"Edith?" Miss Karen said. She started up the stairs and I got stiff. I don't know why, but I felt like I had done something I wasn't supposed to. It was okay to look through that chest, right? Was it okay that Lenore gave me a journal? Was it okay that I was a witch?

"Hi, Miss Karen," I said. I held the journal at my chest, my arms wrapped tight around it.

Miss Karen's eyes widened. "Lenore?"

They talked in French. Then, Lenore turned to me and said: "Elle est une sorcière."

I think I understood what that meant. I looked up at Miss Karen. She was a tall woman, and she towered over me, smiling.

"Edith, this is wonderful news. You're a witch!" Miss Karen said.

"Thank you." I said it more like a question.

"If you ever need anything, we're here for you," Miss Karen said.

"Maybe one day we'll practice some poetry together. If you're up for it. I know it's a little scary at first, but you'll come to love it."

"Okay." I wasn't sure how I felt about that. I was tightly wound inside all of a sudden. I hoped the ice cream wasn't already wearing off. "Well, I should get home. It's getting late."

At the front door, Lenore hugged me tight. "I love you," she said. "I'll call you later tonight. We'll do our math homework together."

I nodded. I said goodbye to Miss Karen and went on my way. The sky was turning violet with orange streaks lingering halfway to the horizon.

When I got home, Yaden was there making dinner. Cannoli greeted me with a monster of a hug, nearly causing me to fall. She told me about how she got to play 'spelling basketball' in class. She had spelled the most words right, and she made the most shots into the basket. She showed me her gold star and she spent the whole night tossing her prized little plush basketball around.

Talking to her was hard. I couldn't even look at Yaden. I was in my head, replaying everything that happened today. I ate dinner without saying a word. Cannoli talked and sang songs about her food while Yaden read an issue of Nintendo Power. By the time Mom got home, we were almost finished eating. Thank goodness she didn't ask how my day was. I escaped to my room and called Lenore on Mom's cordless phone.

We talked for a long while, mostly her reassuring me about being a witch or poems or that Julie was going to be fine. It wasn't until Mom called out to me and told me it was time for bed that I'd realized how long we'd been on the phone. I said goodnight to

Lenore, returned the phone to Mom, and went back to my room.

"I hope Julie's okay," I prayed. "I didn't mean to hurt her. I didn't. I swear—I'm not supposed to swear. I cursed today, too." A tear trickled down my cheek. "I'm a witch. Are witches bad? I don't think I want to be a witch. It's scary and I don't know. I feel weird. I'm sorry for everything today. I hope I can be forgiven."

I said an Our Father before I got into bed. I opened my journal once I was under the covers, and saw that the drawing was finished on the first page. It was of a girl who looked like me. She had my hair and my uniform. Her arms were extended out, and waves penciled in black whirled from her hands and traced all over the page. I touched the drawing, and it felt like I was rubbing tiny grains of sand.

I closed the book and turned out the light. I fell asleep in Lenore's clothes.

13

I hid in the balcony of the auditorium before homeroom. If Lenore was right about Julie being okay, and she did come to school, then that meant I'd have to look Julie in the eyes and pretend nothing happened. I would have to lie, and then lie some more, until I had a pyramid stacked with lie cards—fragile and ready to crumble at the slightest change of breath.

Either way, I'd have to face Nemo. I wanted to delay that as much as possible. He would ask me what happened, since he knew I was probably the last person with Julie before she wound up in the hospital.

The first bell rang—no more hiding for me. I peered out of the balcony door like a mouse looking for traps. A cool wind blew against my face as I scurried to the stairs. The clamor of students neared; I ran all the way to homeroom with my head down. I did my best not to tune in to the locker speak. Surely, word had gotten around about Julie.

I arrived at homeroom tense and out of breath. The students in the class were oddly quiet. It was never this quiet before the second bell. When Nemo arrived, my heart sunk like a ship in a whirlpool. I stared at him. Everyone stared at him. But he just glanced at me, plopped in his chair, and dropped his backpack at his side with a loud thud. He folded his arms and laid his head down on his desk.

Lenore came in and sat in the chair in front of me. "You cool?" she whispered.

I looked over at Nemo. "Yeah."

"He'll be fine. He's probably a little shaken up. Leave him be for now, okay?"

I said nothing.

"Promise?" Lenore held out her pinky finger for a swear. I snagged her finger, and with a kiss on our hands, it was made official. I would leave Nemo alone.

Miss K walked in as the second bell rang, and wished us good morning. She set her books down and leaned her arms on her desk. "Class," she started, "Principal Greene has informed me that Julie will be spending some time in the hospital. She was in an accident yesterday, and she may not return to school for at least a few days. Please keep her in your thoughts and prayers today."

"Is she going to be okay?" someone asked.

"Yes, she will," Miss K said.

I sighed and slouched in my chair.

"What happened?" someone else asked.

"No one knows yet," Miss K replied. "Let's just hope for her fast recovery and quick return to St. Vincent."

Nemo was spaced out, his eyes straight ahead. He sat motionless.

He was like that for the rest of the day. Even at lunch. I watched him from afar, but I went the whole day without saying a word to him. I kept my promise with Lenore through all eight periods.

At the end of the day, Lenore had to go to a baseball team meeting. She said she'd see me tomorrow. I wanted to walk home with her and talk to her about how bad I felt about hurting Julie. I felt relieved knowing that she was okay, but I had done something awful, and I was hiding it, and that was not okay.

Lenore hugged me before she left, and I watched as she walked down the hall. I lingered there for a while. I looked around at the eyes of the other students. Some of them talked about Julie, but no one had any idea what had happened. One of the students whispered: "I heard she's *not* okay."

"Yeah, she's in the hospital," the other student said. "Somebody said she was in a fight or something."

"With who?"

"I don't know. Maybe someone from Holy Trinity? She's got beef with a lot of those kids."

I had to find Nemo. I went to the other wing of the hall. That's where his locker was. He was always slow to pack his things at the end of the day. I peered at the bend and I saw him. I watched as he went through his books in his locker and exchanged the ones in his backpack.

I didn't know if there was a poem that would turn me invisible. There were cloaks and spells and curses that could do that in the books I'd read, but here I was, *a real life witch*, and I had no idea what my potential was.

I could be invisible by not going up to him. I could disappear from his life. How long would it be before he noticed that we hadn't spoken in a while? How long could I hold my breath when he was near? How long could I pretend that I didn't see him?

He closed his locker and then he saw me. He walked towards me, his eyes wide and his steps long and determined.

"What happened?" he asked, standing close to me.

"What do you mean?" Of course I knew what he meant. Immediately, I was shaking all over.

"To Julie. You were the last one with her."

"I don't know," I said. "She stayed behind."

"Why did you leave?"

"Because she made me mad. Can you back up?" I shoved him. "You were the one who put me up to this. You wanted us to be friends knowing we don't get along."

He breathed through his nose and ran his hand through his hair. "It's your fault — "

"I didn't do anything," I said, trying not to raise my voice. I didn't want the last few kids hanging in the halls to hear. But I was nervous and he got me upset. It wasn't my fault. I didn't mean to do what I did. And I wasn't going to tell anyone what happened. Not yet. "And I didn't see anything."

"Are you sure?"

"Yes," I said. I was still shaking. "Do me a favor. Don't talk to me anymore. If you don't believe me, then we shouldn't be talking."

When he took a step close to me, I backed away and put my hands up. "Goodbye, Nemo."

I walked away without looking back.

14

Over a week had passed and October had finally arrived. Julie hadn't been back to school. Miss K didn't mention her in homeroom this morning, and none of the students asked. Murmurs of what was happening still loitered the halls, but with worry and concern. These kids sounded like they were her fans and she was some kind of celebrity or hero. I knew she was popular, but this was getting serious. I'd seen a few girls slip get well cards into her locker, or they'd clog around Nemo so that he could give presents to Julie after school. Others were offering to do her homework. Before lunch, I saw a girl crying at Julie's locker. She was comforted by another girl who assured her that Julie was going to be alright. They'd put an arrangement of fake flowers all over Julie's locker door. I couldn't watch it for long. I got a cold shiver and walked away, and decided it might be best to hide in the balcony for lunch.

My hands were normal. I hadn't experienced any odd sensations nor had I cast anything by accident. The only thing I'd felt was nervous—about what I'd done to Julie. And I was nervous that I'd hurt someone else again.

Miss K gave us our assignments just before the bell at the end of eighth-period English. We had to read a short story called "Under the Rice Moon." It was a story about a swallow bird who had been caged and was bought to be a pet for a young girl sick with a fever. She set the bird free, asking the bird to fly for her, too. We had been talking about metaphors the last few days, and we had to write an essay about what the metaphors were in the story. Those brave enough to read their essays in front of the class would get extra credit.

I wanted to talk to Miss K once class ended and all the kids were gone. But Nemo had beat me to it. I left the room. It would have been awkward sitting there listening to their conversation.

Nemo hadn't said a word to me since last Tuesday, the day after the fight. He'd been silent to mostly everyone, and he hadn't been raising his hand in class. Teachers would call on him and he still had the right answers, but otherwise he kept tight-lipped and was swift to leave class. I'd been watching him at his locker at the end of school nearly everyday, hoping that each time I'd find the courage from somewhere inside me to talk to him. I never knew it could be so hard to ask someone if they were okay.

I leaned against the wall next to the door and listened to them.

"How are you doing?" Miss K asked. "You've been awfully quiet. I know Julie is a good friend of yours."

"I'm fine," he said. "It's been hard."

"Can I help you in any way? Do you want to talk about it?"

"I don't know," he sighed. "She's going to have her second

surgery tomorrow."

I nearly dropped my books. I held them closer to my chest and held my breath.

"Oh, goodness," Miss K said. "You must be worried sick."

"I'm afraid to go to the hospital. But I'm going there later today. I was wondering if I could take her homework to her. I don't want her to fall too far behind."

"Yes, absolutely," she said.

I peered inside and saw Miss K sifting through some papers and putting them into a manila folder.

"I help her with her homework whenever I go there. During visiting hours. I'm there almost every day," Nemo said. He paused. "Me helping her with her homework—that's not cheating, is it?"

"Definitely not," she said with an emphatic shake of her head. "I think what you're doing is kind and thoughtful and I really admire you for being such a great friend to her."

"Thank you."

"I'm here for you, Nemo," Miss K said. "I'm all ears! And I've got shoulders if you ever need those, too."

"You're the best, Miss K."

She sure was.

Nemo headed for the door and I scooted back behind the wall. I held my breath again and closed my eyes as I heard him walking. He went right by me. He didn't even see me. Good, I sighed.

I peered into the room again and watched as Miss K packed away her things. I wanted to talk to her, but I got stuck. All the words that were in my head had disappeared, and my feet froze. She looked up and saw me.

"What are you doing?" she said with a chuckle.

"I don't know," I said. "I—I forgot."

"You forgot?" she asked. "You must be studying too hard, Edith. You're frying your brain." She walked up to me and when she caught a good look at my face, her whimsy turned to a frown. "Is everything okay?"

"Yes," I said, turning away from her. She glowed like an angel with the afternoon light shining behind her.

"How's practice going? For the festival?"

"I'm a little nervous, but I've been practicing every day." Well, almost every day.

"Have you told your Dad about it? I bet he's excited," she asked.

"Not yet," I said. "I want it to be a surprise."

She knelt and her warm, cocoa-colored eyes wrapped me up like a blanket in the cold. "I know I'm excited. I want to hear the rest of that song. And when I told some other teachers and the principal about it, they were excited, too. You've got a little fan club starting up. You're really talented, Edith."

Miss K stood and squeezed my shoulder. "Now hurry home and get working on your essay. I really want to hear what you have to say about the short story. I mean, assuming you're going to read it in front of the class."

"Maybe," I mumbled.

We left the classroom and said goodbye. The halls had emptied already. It was like I had the whole floor to myself. The whole world. I wallowed in it, happy to be alone for just a moment.

Yaden called out to me from downstairs, waking me up from a nap.

When he called out to me a second time, I hid under the covers. Then, he knocked on my door. I kept quiet. After a third knock, he let himself in and turned on the light. I need to learn a poem that keeps doors locked, I thought.

"It's time to eat," he said, whipping the blanket from over me.

"I'm not hungry," I said, snatching the blanket back over me.

"I already made your plate, so you're going to get up and eat." He threw the blanket to the floor. "And stop sleeping in your uniform. You always get it wrinkled and then I have to iron it."

"Fine, I'll go down. Geez."

I crawled to the edge of the bed, rubbing my face. Dinner had become the worst time of the day. I didn't feel like speaking at the table. Cannoli would ask every day when Dad was coming home, but Mom and Yaden would lie to her. I wish they'd tell her the truth.

"I want to see you stand up," Yaden said, his arms crossed.

I didn't want to. I was getting sick of watching Mom drink so much. She'd finish two or three glasses of wine before she even finished her food. When she'd ask me about school, I said very little about it. I didn't want to talk about it, but I should figure out how to say more, because Mom would always ask Yaden about his college applications and writing scholarship essays and saving up for a car so he can drive far, far away from us. I didn't want him to go.

I had to dig deep to will myself up. I pushed him aside. "Get out so I can change."

"Two minutes, Edith," Yaden said, closing the door on his way out.

"Jerk," I snarled.

I slammed my dresser drawer shut once I picked clothes and

changed. I was still groggy and tired and I wanted nothing more than to slink back to bed.

When I got to the table, Cannoli was spinning more angel hair noodles onto her fork than she could possibly fit in her mouth. Mom was pouring herself a glass of wine, of course. Yaden hadn't even set my plate, yet! All of that pretense to rush me downstairs was a lie.

"Nice to see you join us, Snowpea," Mom said.

She sat down, then Yaden gave me my plate. I looked at her and forced a smile. Did I look any different to her? Did she know that her little Snowpea had changed? Could she tell that I'd fallen in love with a boy I couldn't have? Could she tell that I had gotten into my first fight? Was there something that might have changed in my eyes or my brows or maybe even the tone of my skin that said I had hurt someone so badly with my own fists that I put them in the hospital?

"How's school?" she asked me. "Anything new?"

I shrugged my shoulders. Even if I told her how I'd changed, she wouldn't believe me. I was always going to be the little Snowpea hiding between Yaden's and Cannoli's shadows.

"Well, I found out I'm a witch." A smirk rose on my face. I glanced over at Yaden. He let out a short laugh.

"You're a witch?" Cannoli asked. She burst with excitement over the news.

"Yup," I nodded plainly.

"Edith," Mom said. I could hear disappointment hanging between the syllables of my name.

"Can you do magic?" Cannoli pressed, her voice high and squeaky.

"Yeah, but I'm still learning," I said, playing along with Cannoli's delight. "I'll show you one day once I get the hang of it."

"Don't feed your sister lies," Mom said sharply.

"It's better than feeding her the truth," I said. "Have you even told her?"

"Told me what?" Cannoli asked. "Mom's a witch, too?"

"It's none of your business if I told her," Mom said. She clasped her napkin into her fist as she narrowed her eyes at me. That was my cue to shut my mouth.

"Why isn't it?" I asked. "She's my sister."

"And I'm your mother."

I leaned over the table towards Cannoli. Softly, I asked, "Did Mom tell you about Dad?"

"No?" Cannoli said.

"Edith, I swear—" Mom said.

"She needs to know," I said before she could finish.

"No, she doesn't."

"Cannoli, Dad isn't coming home," I said in a rush. If I had said it any slower, if I had waited another second, Mom was going to cut me off.

"What?" Cannoli said, a forkful of pasta and sauce hovering over her plate. "How come?"

Mom got up from her chair and stood in front of me. When I looked up at her, she slapped me. Hard. Wind sailed from out my lungs. A sharp pang flared on the side of my face as I leaned over my chair. I took deep breaths to gather myself from the shock.

Yaden and Cannoli sat completely still. Mom's eyes and her nostrils were wide as she glared over me. Mom had never laid a hand on either of us, no matter how badly or annoyingly we behaved.

My hand at my cheek, I got up from the table, kept my head down, and walked out of the kitchen. Once I was in the living room, I ran all the way to my room. I slammed the door, scooped up the blanket, leapt into bed, and hid in my fabric fortress. A cascade of tears fell. I heaved and sniffled into my pillows. No one came to see if I was okay the rest of the night. Not Cannoli. Not Yaden. Not Mom.

Before, I had been the good kid—the one who could do no wrong. I'd never had detention at school. Mom and Dad never had to reprimand me. They never sent me to my room. But why, all of a sudden, was everything I did so awful—even when I didn't want to do anything bad? What got into me that I had to say anything to Cannoli anyway? How did it slip from my tongue so easily?

I listened from my room as everyone eventually made their way upstairs. Cannoli's tiny footsteps pitter-pattered through the halls before Mom gave her a bath. I heard Yaden playing video games for a few hours through the wall. I read "Under the Rice Moon" two more times before I started writing my essay. I played a cassette of classical music while I finished the rest of my homework. I kept the volume low, hoping no one would hear it. I didn't want to bother anyone—but I also hoped that they would wonder about me since I'd been quiet for so long.

When I was done, the halls had settled. It was nearly ten o'clock, half an hour past my bedtime. Mom still hadn't come into my room. I realized I had gotten what I wanted. All day, I had wanted to be alone. And to be alone meant that I had to push everyone away. I had to make them mad at me. And when it hit me that Mom, Yaden, and Cannoli were all mad at me, and they weren't going to say another word to me before they'd gone to bed, I didn't like the idea of being alone anymore.

I wanted to tell Mom I was sorry. I wished she could believe me about being a witch. I wished I knew how to show her what I was.

I turned out the light and flipped on my flashlight. I dug through the bottom drawer of my dresser and found my journal. I opened it to the first page and looked over the illustration again: It had since blossomed with color, my hair was a faded auburn and my dress was violet. My eyes were wide and ivory with no pupils. The swirls around me glowed cyan. I put my ear next to it hoping to hear the ocean like in seashells, or the crashing of tiny waves at the shore. Instead, I faintly heard Julie's screaming. I shut the book and shuddered.

I swallowed and reopened the book. I flipped through all the empty pages. There could be hundreds of poems for me to learn. I had a long way to go. I wished there was a poem that would let me rewind time so I could take back what I said to Cannoli. And a poem that could tell me where Dad was.

And I had to find a way to heal Julie.

I put on the fluffiest pair of slipper socks I had to keep my steps silent, then snuck out of my room and tiptoed downstairs. I picked up the phone in the kitchen. I held my breath as I listened for a dial tone first. The line was open — Mom wasn't on the phone. I called Lenore and was relieved when she picked up.

"Are you asleep?" I whispered.

"No," she said. "I'm still writing this essay. What's up?"

"Can we practice some magic tomorrow? After school?"

15

Friday was coming to an end. Only English class was left. Lenore had been dragging along all day. She dozed off in Social Studies, and said she wasn't sure she was going to hold up for the rest of the day.

"But we're still going to practice after school?" I asked.

"Don't be silly," she yawned. "I'm just tired of being here. I want to go home."

Miss K started the class first by asking who wanted to read their essay for extra credit. In a room of about twenty students, only five raised their hands—including me and Nemo. Miss K picked on him first, and he stood in front of the class.

"Miss K, is it okay if I were to read Julie's essay, too?"

Whispers rustled in the class. I shifted in my seat, and when I looked over at Lenore, her head was down. She'd fallen asleep again. I gulped.

"I think that's a fine idea," Miss K said.

"I'll read mine first," he said. He cleared his throat and

straightened his posture. He talked about birds being the luckiest animals on the planet. They could fly high in the sky or hang low on the ground. "Instead of us feeling pity for the caged bird, do you ever wonder if birds pity us? Do you think they pity us because we can't fly? I want to be a bird, someday, but only for a little while, so I can tell everyone what it's like, but they won't think I'm weird. They will see me for who I am, and they won't get jealous when I tell them what a wonderful time I had. The bird probably went on to tell his other bird friends how terrible it was to be caged, and to be sick, and he warned them to appreciate their wings and the skies and even the ground, because you never know when you, my friends, will be caged as well."

Miss K led a light applause in the class. "Nemo, that was beautiful. Truly. I didn't think of the story that way at all."

He nodded. "Thank you. I'll read Julie's now."

The students leaned over their desks in anticipation. What did Julie have to say? Was she going to reveal everything that had happened to her?

"I feel sick, like the girl in the story. I'm not really sick. I'm not sneezing or coughing. I don't have a fever. But I'm not well. I might never be the same again. And that scares me." Nemo paused.

"I've been in the hospital every day. I don't know what happened. All I know is that I woke up one day and was told I just had surgery. I've never had surgery before. And I've never been in bed for this long. If this is what it's like to be a bird in a cage, then I will never want to have a pet. Not a bird, not a cat, not a dog, not a hamster. None. Animals should be free. If not, then they will get sick like me, where they will never feel like themselves again. So fly away, birds, and be free, for sick little girls like me."

Miss K was silent, blinking rapidly as her eyes shifted from Nemo, to the class, and to her desk, and then all around again. "Th-thank you, again, Nemo. For that. And thank Julie, for us. Please tell her that we wish her well."

"I will," he said. He handed Miss K the essays and went back to his desk, his head down. The rest of the class looked at him as he hid his face in his hands.

"Everyone, what just happened was very courageous. For both of them. So let's hear it for Nemo and for Julie," she said, starting another short round of applause.

Miss K picked me next.

The students were now slouched in their seats, or had their eyes down at their own essays.

"I always wanted to know what it's like to fly—" I started.

"Wait, Edith," Miss K said. She got out of her desk and walked to Lenore. She nudged her awake. "Excuse me, Miss Close. It takes a lot to read something personal in front of the class. Show some respect, please."

Lenore nodded sleepily, rubbing her eyes before she looked at me. And when she did, my heart skipped. Her eyes had changed. They'd gone black, like the night of our slumber party. No one else in the class noticed but me. I was fixed at her. And she offered a half-smile, crooked and trembling.

"Umm..." I stammered. I had to be brave like Nemo. "I always wanted to know what it's like to fly..." I trailed, looking up from my paper and back at Lenore. She blinked, and then just like that, her eyes were normal. She raised her hand as I paused.

"Yes, Lenore?" Miss K said, annoyed.

"May I go to the bathroom, please?"

"Yes, go," she said. "But hurry."

Lenore stood, and when she was at the door, she turned her head and glanced at me. Her eyes were black and empty again.

Once she had gone, I turned back to my essay, which was rattling in my hands. "One time, in the winter, when the snow was starting to melt in the sun, a few birds bathed in the mushy snow at my window sill. They chirped and shook their feathers and they seemed happy. When I went outside, I played in what snow was left, tossing snowballs at my brother. When it was time to go home, he picked me up and carried me all the way home. He told me I was going to fly that day. We bobbed and weaved past people walking by, and we slid on a patch of ice we didn't see. We fell into a pile of snow and laughed, but my brother picked me up again and we flew. One more block. When we got home, the birds at my window were gone. I wondered where they went and if they'd ever come back. I wondered if they were bathing at another kid's window sill and inspired them to fly that day, no matter if there was snow on the ground or if they had a strong older brother to carry them for three blocks straight. I hoped so, because everyone deserves to fly."

The unenthused applause from the kids didn't need a cue from Miss K this time.

"Edith, absolutely beautiful," Miss K said.

I dropped the essay on her desk and, after asking permission to go to the bathroom, quickly made my way out of the classroom. My shoes echoed in the slumbering hallway as I made my way to the girls' bathroom. When I got there, I heard my name. I spun around, and Lenore was standing at the banister by the stairwell.

I inched over to her, taking hesitant, sliding steps. Her eyes were still dark.

"Lenore, what are you doing?" I asked

"I'm not Lenore," she said. Her voice was raspy, like she had suddenly come down with a cold.

"Then who are you?" I said, playing along.

"Eva."

She turned and leaned over the banister. "What a long jump this would be. I wonder if Lenore died, if I would die, too."

I grabbed her arms and tried to pull her away, but she was holding onto the banister. She laughed as I struggled. "Don't worry. I'm not stupid."

"Are you really another person?" I asked. I felt silly putting those words together. I was talking to Lenore, but it didn't feel like Lenore. I couldn't put my finger on it. It was like a subconscious part of my brain was reading her spirit or energy or something, and telling me this was a stranger, even though Lenore was clearly standing right in front of me.

"I am," she said. She let go of the banister and paced over to the top of the stairs. "How's your arm, by the way? I didn't mean to hurt you."

The bruise and the pain had been long gone. "It's okay."

"Can you help me?"

"With what?"

"When Lenore falls asleep, that's when I can wake up," she said. "But I want more than that. I need to get out of here."

I felt dizzy. Part of my brain knew that Lenore was still

somewhere in there, but she was far away. It was like when you know someone else is still in your house with you but you don't know where.

"You can wake me up, Edith," Eva said. "You're a witch. But I can tell from your aura that you're not just an ordinary witch. You're special."

I didn't know if I felt any different than when I wasn't a witch. What was being a special witch supposed to feel like?

"I know this must be strange." She started down the stairs, cautiously. She lost her balance, and then grabbed the banister. I tended to her.

"What am I supposed to do? I don't know any poems."

"Talk to Karen," she said. "You can let go. It just takes a while to get used to actually walking with this body. It's like when your foot falls asleep, you know?"

I backed up to the top of the stairs. She started to walk down. "Where are you going?"

"For a walk. I always wanted to know what it was like to go to school. Don't worry, I'll take good care of her. You should get back to class."

"No!" I ran down the stairs after her, but only made it halfway before she opened her palm at me.

Suddenly, I felt a strong pulse of wind that was like an invisible wall. I lost my footing and reached for the banister, my hand slipping before I found grip.

"If you don't go to class," Eva bellowed, "I'll give Lenore another seizure." She dropped her arm to her side. "We'll meet again. Soon. By then, I hope you'll have figured out a way to help me. This body can't hold on to two souls forever."

She went down to the second floor. I watched her until she disappeared around the bend. I wondered if Lenore even knew what was happening right now, if she knew about Eva at all—that she was sharing her body with another soul.

I didn't want to risk Lenore having another seizure, so I didn't follow her. I went back to class.

When class ended, Lenore's things were still on her desk. I grabbed them, left the room, and headed for my locker. I stuffed her things in there, and went all through the third floor looking for her.

No luck. I searched the second and first floors and didn't find her. She wasn't in the cafeteria or the auditorium. I went into each bathroom on each floor. The library. The nurse's office. Nothing.

Had she left the school? Was she out there alone?

I returned to the third floor, out of breath. I'd ran through the entire school. Finally, I saw her. Lenore was at her locker.

I found a little bit of strength left in my legs and ran up to her. "Eva?" I called out reluctantly. "Eva?" She didn't look up. When I got within a few feet, I called again. "Lenore?"

She turned to me with a puzzled look. "Hey, have you seen my book bag? It wasn't in Miss K's room."

I leapt at her and hugged her, still trembling. I looked into her eyes. They were chestnut and *normal*. "I have your stuff."

"Why?"

"Lenore? Do you remember anything? From English?"

"Did I fall asleep? I remember having to go to the bathroom really bad. Then I came back to class. And I've been looking for my things ever since. Did I fall asleep? I don't even remember."

She had no idea. I didn't know if that was a good thing or a bad thing.

16

As we left St. Vincent together, Lenore was bubbling over about all the poems she wanted to teach me. It was like nothing had happened in English class. How was I supposed to help Eva? How hard was it to learn and perform poems? Was I really someone special? I didn't even know what I had to do. I was nervous but I kept it all to myself.

When we were one street away from her house, Lenore took my hand and stopped me. She pulled me close next to her. "Do you see anyone around?" she asked.

"No?"

"Make sure the coast is clear. I'm going to teach you a poem."

Lenore glanced down the streets, each way then came back to me. Was I going to be able to do it right?

"I don't know, Lenore," I said. "Can't we wait until we get to your place for this?"

She took my hands in hers. "This poem isn't as fun when you're inside. Now, listen. I'm going to say a poem. And I want you to repeat it after me. You have to say the whole thing at once."

I squeezed her hands. "Lenore, I can't."

"Yes, you can. Don't be a chicken. It's easy. Now listen:

Skip and jump, over tree trunks
Whistle and run, for jolly and fun.
Wink once. Wink twice. Consider what's nice
Close your eyes, 'n be ready to glide."

She winked once. Then twice. And I felt her lift from the ground. I looked down, and her feet were an inch off the ground. My mouth fell wide open.

She smiled at me. "Say it," she said. "And be sure to wink twice and then close your eyes."

I tried to say the poem, but I forgot the second line. Lenore laughed and then corrected me. She was still floating and holding on to me. I wanted to fly, too, just like the bird in "Under the Rice Moon."

She recited the poem again for me and I let the words bounce around in my head like frolicsome butterflies. The world got quiet. No passing cars, no airplanes in the sky. The birds stopped singing, as if they were listening and waiting to see me fly.

I recited the poem, winked, and then closed my eyes.

I felt something at my toes, like my shoes had slipped off. It tickled the bottom of my feet, and my eyes sparked open.

"Try to take a step," Lenore said. She let go of my hands, but kept them close.

I did. And I would have fallen over if Lenore hadn't steadied me.

I felt light, like I was suddenly walking on the moon.

A powder-blue feather fluttered from underneath my shoe. It glistened as it made its ascent. I reached for it as it drifted past my face, but it faded once I touched it, leaving a tiny droplet that lingered on the tip of my finger.

I took another step, to turn around and look at Lenore, but I'd forgotten my weightlessness and fell back. Lenore caught me. We both laughed as she picked me up.

"It's going to take some getting used to," she said. "And I still get a little carried away with it."

"How is this possible?" I asked. I started taking more steps, hovering a few inches above the ground. Feathers trickled behind, floating up.

"You have faith in your imagination," she said. "That's all it takes. All you ever have to do is hold out your hand, and believe."

Lenore walked towards me, her feathers were as red as cinnamon. "Want to race?"

"No way," I said.

"Oh come on. When you're feather-footed, it's easier to run than walk. Trust me. That's kind of the point."

"I don't know. What if I fall?"

"You *will* fall. You have to fall. That's how you get better with poetry."

I looked down the street. If I ran, would it be hard for me to stay in a straight line? Would I topple over and crash into a telephone pole?

"Try not to think of it as flying," she said. "You're floating. Floating isn't as big of a deal. Keep your head up, one foot in front of the other." She spread her arms out, angling them down. "And hold your arms out like this."

I took a long breath and moved my feet a little, looking for balance. I tottered a little as I spread my arms.

"Ready?"

No.

"Set."

I can't believe I'm using magic.

"Go!"

I ran as fast as my legs knew how. It was like my feet had wings as a bounty of feathers burst after each step. I was moving fast but I kept stumbling. Eventually, I found some rhythm. My heart hammered in my chest. I laughed with excitement and awe.

Lenore had given me a head start. She shouted behind me. I teetered over and fell. I picked myself up, which was easy because I was so light. I floated once I stood, grit my teeth, and kept running. I nearly caught up with Lenore. I was going faster than she was.

She got to her front door and celebrated on the porch with an awkward dance as she chanted *I win! I win!*

"Shut up," I said, a little out of breath. "It was close."

She laughed and gave me a hug. Then, she gasped. "Hey, look!"

Blue and red feathers were swirling above, caught in the wind. Amazement stretched my mouth and eyes wide, pulling at my cheeks. We watched them until they all disappeared into the sunlight.

"If you had any doubts about being a witch, I hope they're all gone now," she said.

We went inside and made our way to the basement. Miss Karen was there, sitting in the tall window sill. Her legs swung back and forth in her floral trimmed dress. She put down her book, leapt from the sill, and stopped in mid-air just before she came to a gentle landing.

The basement was wide, lined with shelves and cabinets filled with an assortment of curious things. I paced slowly behind as Lenore went straight to Miss Karen.

My head was on a swivel. A tall bookshelf was stacked tight with hardcover books boasting strange titles like *The Holy Power*, *The Memoir of the Sacred Whale*, and *Alternative Poetic Theory*. Small glass jars filled with glowing liquids and glimmering powders populated a wide stand. A round centerpiece counter shone in the heart of the basement with shelves of necklaces, masks, and miniature cauldrons that could fit in my backpack. A thick, candied aroma made me think of chocolate banana bread, mixed with hints of pinewood and cool stone. A baking furnace burned in the far end of the basement. I pulled in the sweet, rustic air as much as I could.

"How was school, girls?" Miss Karen asked.

"I was tired all day," Lenore said. "I slept through my classes so I don't remember much."

I cringed. She had no idea why she couldn't remember much — at least much of English class. "It was okay." I swallowed.

Miss Karen walked over to me, moving strands of my hair behind my ears. Then, just as gently, she lifted my head up from my chin. She looked at me as if she'd found lost treasure.

"I've never noticed your eyes are blue *and* brown," she said. "Do you know what that really means?"

"Weird genes?"

"No," Miss Karen laughed. "It's a sign of your element and its strength. A witch with eyes of different colors can move oceans like the moon."

I blinked. "That sounds dangerous."

The feathers and the running had been nice, but I got the feeling the rest wasn't always going to be so pleasant. Lenore came over to us with a handful of miniature chocolate chip cookies. She handed me one.

"Eat it," she said. It was warm and soft and I wished she had given me more. She took one for herself and then gave her mom another one.

"The cookie will open up your pores," Lenore said. "But you can only have one! Two and you'll charm your imagination. You'll get hyper. And that's not good."

Lenore went off running to a closet on the other side of the basement. I looked up at Miss Karen. If she could look into my eyes and tell me that I could move oceans, then could she look into her daughter's eyes and tell that Lenore was not merely one person?

"The first thing we have to do is meter your soul," Miss Karen said.

"Say what?" I said.

"It's a way for us to know what kind of soul you have. Is it blooming in light or brooding in darkness? It's used to tell your natural element. Knowing the meter of your soul will help Lenore and I teach you."

Lenore returned with a tall chair. I climbed up on it, grateful it was comfortably cushioned.

Miss Karen told me to straighten my back and to fold my hands in my lap. "Concentrate," she went on, "and think of a memory. A place or a song, some kind of special moment that's happened recently."

I closed my eyes, and she told me to let my mind take its course.

"Whatever comes to mind, let it be. Don't force something specific. I'll be able to meter your soul after a few minutes."

My eyes shot open and I gripped the arms of the chair. "You're going to read my thoughts?"

"Relax, Edith. There's nothing to worry about."

I shut my eyes tight. How could I relax? Soon, I felt a pins-and-needles tingling in my arms and legs. It crawled through my chest and stomach and nestled right in the middle. I tried to stay in my head but it started to hurt.

I wondered if Miss Karen could see me and my thoughts the way I always saw myself in my head. I'd been curled up in a ball in the corner of my mind for weeks. All the prayers and the tears and Molly Ringwald movies helped, but only a little. Practicing for my recital was bittersweet.

The side of my face prickled when I had thought about dinner last night. Cannoli didn't speak at all this morning and Mom was silent as she drove me to school. She told me she loved me, but she didn't call me Snowpea when she did.

It'd been a month since I last saw Dad. Two weeks since I fought Julie. And a few hours since Lenore had been Eva. I didn't want Miss Karen to hear all those thoughts.

The tingling tightened like a charley horse in the middle of the night. The air became thin; I struggled to breathe. I opened my mouth, gasping like I'd been swimming underwater. I grasped the sides of the chair and squeezed with a whimper.

"I'm almost done, Edith," Miss Karen whispered. "Keep strong."

"Okay," I squeaked. *Hurry.*

Soon, my ears rang in a crescendo that got so loud that I let out a scream. Then, just like that, the pain disappeared. The ringing stopped and I could breathe through my nose once again.

I opened my eyes, dizzy like I had been spinning around and around, and I looked up at Miss Karen. Uneasiness raised her eyebrows and pulled her eyes wide.

"What's wrong?" I asked.

"Well," she started, "when someone meters a soul, they can see the person's lightness. It occurs like a scale that slides from pure white through all the grays in between to pure black. What's in your mind is a reflection of that scale. It's your *Spectrum.*"

"I bet Edith is the purest white you've ever seen," Lenore said. She offered me a glass of water but I only took a short sip.

"No one is pure white. No one is pure black, either. No one ever has been. But there have indeed been people that have come within just a sliver of one or the other."

"So I'm not the purest white?" I asked with a nervous laugh.

Miss Karen opened her mouth to speak but then took back her thought. She glanced at Lenore, then knelt to level with me, her eyes shifting. She was delving into my eyes like she was looking for a spare thought that she could borrow. "You have the darkest soul I've seen in twenty years."

My heart sank.

"Mom, are you sure?" Lenore said.

"Rest assured," Miss Karen said, "this doesn't mean you're a troubled child destined to become a super villain. But it is concerning. We'll have to be careful grooming you. The darker the soul, the more likely you are to do wrong by your poetry. But let's not worry about that too much right now."

She went to a shelf with empty jars, took two of them and filled one of them with water. "There's a lot you have to learn about being a witch. But first, I'm going to have you learn a simple trick." She put a hand towel over a small table, then set the jars on top. "Learning the simplest of poems can be exhausting for a new witch. Frustrating. Young witches tend to be loose cannons, but lucky for you, you have someone to teach you. And you have another young witch to learn with. I wouldn't wish loneliness on any young witch."

I gulped. I wasn't sure I wanted to do this. I could leave if I wanted to. I could say never mind. I could pretend that none of this was happening and I could go home and be normal again.

She kept on. "There's two types of poetry. There's *intrinsic* and there's *logical*. Logicals are poems we use to control natural elements. Fire, water, earth, electricity, air—things like that. Intrinsics are abstract poems, like healing or reading minds. Today, you're going to learn a logical.

"You're what you call a pelagic witch. A water witch. And you've got quite a strong gift. I don't normally teach new witches logicals on my first day with them. But I'm confident you can do this."

Karen squinted her eyes and lifted her open palm. The water inside the jar splashed upward, then came together into a gurgling sphere. She carried it in the air gracefully before a few droplets got away and fell to the floor. She swerved her hands and the water lost its shape, swirling in a circle like a cat after its own tail. She clasped her hands, and the water fell into the empty glass. Then, the water stirred as vigorously as she spun her finger, nearly toppling the glass with her magical whisk. She stopped, and the water relaxed.

"Whoa," I muttered.

"Have you ever danced with someone before?" Miss Karen asked me. "Do you remember what it was like when you took your partner's hand and you moved together?"

"Yeah," I said. "Last time was at the Father-Daughter dance last year." Dad and I had practiced our moves for weeks. We wanted to show the whole school that the Solstices were the best dancers in the city. If moving the water was supposed to be anything like that, I wouldn't have any problems at all.

"Think of that," Miss Karen said. "And when you do, imagine lifting the water as if you were reaching for its hand from afar, asking for a dance."

I stood from the chair and got closer to the glasses. Lenore's hands were clasped together and her eyes were wide. "You can do it, Edith," she said.

I didn't have to think hard about the dance. I'd been thinking about it a lot lately. I had worn a long, short-sleeved powder-blue dress with a ruffled skirt. I borrowed an evening clutch from Mom, and a pair of satin gloves that I wished I could wear every day. I felt elegant, and Dad told me how beautiful I was as we walked into the gymnasium-turned-dance hall. I believed it.

I felt terrible, then, for the girls who didn't have a father like mine. None of them would get to dance swing or salsa like we did, even if we were clumsy. None of them got to dance with their fathers —the first men to ever love them in their lives unconditionally. I was lucky.

The water began to lift from the glass as I thought about our first dance: The lights dimmed, the music got louder, and "1999" by Prince cued the disco ball.

The water started swishing aggressively in the glass. I breathed and tried to relax, putting my hand at my chest. I watched my breaths. Lenore inched close to me.

Then, the water lifted. I couldn't believe it! Droplets quickly started falling, so I bit my lower lip and took another deep breath. Out of instinct, I lifted my arm and opened my hand. I tilted my head as I thought to move it across to the other glass. This *was* easy. Miss Karen was right. It felt like I was dancing, so I started to rock back and forth like Dad and I did during Julie London's rendition of "Sway," one of my favorite songs.

I was using magic. I was a witch, and I was dancing with water.

"I can't believe you're my daughter," Dad had said to me. I had rested my head on his chest, his voice drumming against my ear. "It's been eleven years and I still can't believe it."

Those words stuck with me. I repeated them all the time.

After the dance, we'd gone to an Italian restaurant for dinner. I ate all of my manicotti and had three Shirley Temples. We talked about how much I loved English class and how amazing a teacher Miss K had been. Dad was happy about how fast I was learning piano. We took cannoli home for dessert for Jenna. We woke her up and shared a late night snack—we never told Mom about that part.

"This was one of the greatest nights of my life," he told me before I went to bed.

"Me too," I had said. "You're the best Dad in the world. I love you."

The water splashed to the floor, knocking one of the glasses over. It shattered to pieces when it hit the floor. My arm fell to my side. I stared, stiff as a tree in the bleakest of winters.

Karen picked up the shards. Lenore dried the floor with a poem and then swept up the smaller bits with a careful, soft wind. I didn't help. I couldn't move.

"You had it!" Lenore said with robust enthusiasm. "You freakin' had it!"

"I'm sorry about the jar," I murmured. A tear trickled down my cheek and I wiped it away with my sweater sleeve.

"You did great," Miss Karen said. "No one gets that far on their first try at a logical."

No sensation of pride or satisfaction sparked in my belly. I was suffocated by the yearning I felt after remembering the dance. I tried to swallow that feeling, but it returned like a stinging sour threat of vomit.

"Can I go home?" I asked.

"Are you sure?" Lenore asked. "That was hot water. It's a little heavier than cold water. We can try again."

I shook my head. I was done for the day. "Maybe we can try tomorrow."

Lenore came up to me and took my hands. She held them tight and pulled me close.

"What are you doing?" I asked, stumbling from her abrupt approach.

"We're going to dance," she said.

And before I could say another word, Lenore snatched me up and twirled me around and around the basement. We waltzed to a classical tune she playfully hummed.

"You're a natural, Edith," she said, still prancing me around. I choked on a fit of giggles as we awkwardly twirled about. She kept humming, and soon it became music to me, too.

When her song came to an end, she leaned her head against mine and we burst into laughter. "Think of that dance every time instead. You'll get it right tomorrow. I promise. And drink lots of water, too. It'll help you recover faster since it's your natural element."

"Thank you," I said. "And thank you, Miss Karen, for teaching me the logical."

"You're welcome. Come by anytime. We'll practice as much as you'd like. I'd love to have you as a student."

Lenore and Miss Karen walked me to the door. I gathered my things and Lenore gave me a hug. "See you tomorrow," she said.

As Miss Karen was about to close the door behind me, I stopped. I spun around, stiffed my arm against the door, and looked past her to see if Lenore was there, but she'd already gone to her room.

"Is Lenore okay?" I whispered.

Karen closed the door a little more, furrowing her brows. "She's fine."

"But what about —"

"*She's fine*, Edith," she interrupted. "Goodbye now." And she shut the door.

17

The weekend flew by. I practiced carrying water from jar to jar for hours with Lenore and Miss Karen. I wanted to nail it down until it felt easy. Lenore also taught me a simple healing poem that helped with minor aches and colds. She said I should practice this one alone next time I got sick. That should have been soon since it was October and I'd always caught a cold sometime in the early part of fall.

At the end of classes on Monday, I saw Nemo at Julie's locker. He was packing her things into a duffle bag. His back was to me as he knelt down, pulling out textbooks and shuffling through pages in marble notebooks before he stacked them neatly inside the bag.

I inched over to him, my arms crossed in front of me. We hadn't spoken in thirteen days. Yes, I'd been counting the days.

"Need help?" I asked.

He looked up at me, slightly startled or just really surprised. His eyes fixed on me for a long moment before he took them away and set his attention back in the locker. He was taking down her pictures.

The first one I saw was a polaroid photo of Nemo and Julie, side by side, his arm around her. Both of them wore their uniforms, along with big, laughing smiles.

"No," he said. "But thank you."

"Is she home yet?"

He nodded.

"Is she okay?"

"She's fine," he said without looking at me.

"It's really nice of you to be taking her all her homework to her."

"Thank you," he said.

I fell silent as he kept taking down her pictures. She had a lot of them. She even had one with Lenore from last year. It looked like it was taken in the cafeteria, too. I don't remember that picture being taken. They looked happy. Lenore and Julie were friends, but Lenore knew Julie and me didn't get along, so she didn't talk about her around me.

I noticed her science book in the duffle bag. "We don't have science homework tonight. Is she falling behind?"

"No."

"Then why are you taking her science book?"

He slammed the locker shut and stood up. I flinched.

"I thought you didn't want me talking to you?"

"I'm sorry," I said. "I didn't mean it. I was just mad. And scared. Just like you."

He took a deep breath and looked at me. "I'm sorry, too. I shouldn't have accused you like that."

"It's okay," I said. I leaned close to him and spoke softly. "Did she tell you what happened?"

"She doesn't remember," he said. "She remembers skipping rocks with you. And then she doesn't remember anything after that. Except waking up in the hospital."

I breathed, thinking *oh, thank God*. And that moment of relief was broken up quickly. I shouldn't feel relieved. I did a horrible thing and I couldn't admit the truth about it. I took the breath back in and it made my chest tense.

"I'm sorry," I said.

Nemo slipped the photos in a notebook and then zipped up the duffle bag, slinging the duffle bag over his shoulders with a grunt.

He started to walk away but I walked with him.

"What are you doing?" he said.

"Do you need help?"

"No."

"Can I walk with you?"

He said nothing.

"Are you mad at me?"

At first he said nothing, but a few steps later, he offered a soft "no" under his breath.

"Are you going to see her right now?" I asked.

"Yeah."

"Can I come with you?"

Nemo walked the entire way to Julie's house without complaint. I tried asking him questions but he was still giving me short answers. About halfway there, I decided to let him be in his little mysterious silence, taking in my surroundings.

Fall was here. It was my favorite season, and soon, my favorite holiday would come: Halloween! The relentless summer was gone for good, and the tension of starting a new grade had long faded away. I was okay with being a seventh grader. I had aced all my first tests in my seventh-grade classes.

I think being a witch had widened my eyes a little bit. If I looked close enough to a leaf, I could see tiny bits of it changing colors. The sun stung my eyes when it sparkled through the trees. I could smell rain in the air a day away.

I wished I could cast *feather-footed* so Nemo and I could hover the rest of the way to Julie's. Nemo had broken into a sweat, and he switched shoulders with the duffle bag at least once each block. I could literally take the weight off his shoulders if he let me. I wondered if he would be terrified if I did use a poem.

When we arrived at Julie's house, Nemo dropped the duffle bag on the porch. The heavy thud mixed with his deep grunt, and he leaned over for a second. I kept silent. I wasn't going to ask if he was all right. Maybe it was better if I let him feel like a big, strong hero. He probably needed to feel that way, not only for himself, but for Julie.

"I don't know if this is a good idea," he started after he caught his breath.

"Why not?" I asked. "I came all this way and now you changed your mind?"

"I don't think Julie's okay with having friends over. Especially if they're coming over surprising her."

Friends? I shook my head and chuckled. *I'm a friend?* Did I belong in the same circle as her gaggle of cheerleader buddies? Did any of them ever come to see her or did they just mourn for her at her locker?

"I want to see her. I have to," I said. I put my hands in my pockets and tightened them into nervous little fists. "I care about her, too."

I wasn't sure how true that was, but I looked at Nemo with a firm gaze.

"Fine," he said. He took a set of keys out of his pocket that was paired with a *Hello Kitty* charm. He unlocked the door and let me in first.

I entered with careful steps. The house was quiet. The living room was decorated with framed family photos. I stopped when I looked at them. Many of them were group photos, and I noticed that alongside two parents, Julie had two older boys next to her. They were both tall, lanky and pale white boys who looked like they played college basketball for the University of Pennsylvania. None of them looked anything like her. Julie was Japanese.

"Nemo?" I asked, my voice low.

"What?"

"I don't understand. Who are these people in these pictures with Julie?"

"Her family," Nemo said. "Come on, she's upstairs."

"She's adopted?"

He narrowed his eyes. "That's why she doesn't want anyone coming over," he said. "She doesn't want everybody to know."

One time in sixth grade, I asked Julie what her real name was. Julie Suzanne Cherry was not a Japanese name. I didn't mean any harm by it. I knew a girl named Michiko who went by the name Sandy. I had only been curious to know if Julie had another name. I liked knowing little things about people like that. After I asked, she left class for the restroom and didn't come back for a long time. Her eyes were puffy but I thought nothing of it. She stared at me when she came into the class, and she didn't speak to me for a week. After that, she picked on me all the time, but I'd thought all this time she was just a typical, annoying cheerleader.

He started for the stairs and I followed behind him. I grew more timid with each stair I climbed and I walked on the edge of my feet, afraid to make a sound. The hallway was dim. At the far end of it, a bedroom door was open slightly. When we got to it, Nemo turned around and put his finger over his lips, then, he pushed the door open slowly and walked in.

He took a second, looking but not saying anything. A smile briefly flickered on his face. "Hey, wake up," he said.

I peered into the room. Julie was in her bed, wrapped in a comforter. I couldn't see her face.

"Hey," she said.

I stepped inside the room, a chill sweeping down my back and my legs.

"Where's your mom?" he asked. He knelt at her bedside.

"She went to the supermarket."

"Did you do any homework today?"

"I did some of the vocab words for social studies. There's a lot of definitions. Then I got really tired after I took my medicine."

I inched closer.

Nemo glanced at me. "Umm, Julie?"

"Yeah?"

"Edith is here. She wanted to see you."

"What?"

She tossed the comforter away from her and sat up in the bed. She was wearing a mask—a gray and white wolf face that wrapped around her head with holes for her eyes, nose, ears and mouth. At the back of her head, a tail hung from the mask. The fabric looked like it was cotton, and there were stitches along the edges.

I backed away, unsure of what to say.

"What the hell are you doing here?" she growled.

"I—"

"Why did you bring her here?" she hissed at Nemo.

"She wanted to see you," he said. "Julie, it's okay."

"You could've asked me first," she said.

"I wanted to, but it was kind of random. She really wanted to see you. Today. Right now."

"Get out, Edith," she said. "Get out!"

"Julie, listen," I pleaded. "I really think we should talk."

She reached over the side of her bed and scooped a slipper from the floor. Before Nemo could react, she tossed it at me. I dodged out of the way just enough for it to fly a few inches past my face.

"Get out!" she screamed repeatedly.

Tears streamed as I stared at her. I was speechless. It was like my heart stopped beating and I got cold inside.

Nemo grabbed me at my waist and pulled me out of the room. He closed the door. I embraced him and leaned my head on his chest, sobbing. I couldn't stay on my feet. I collapsed to my knees and he held on to me.

"I'm sorry," I said. That was all I could say to him. I said it over and over. When the tears finally went away and the sobs faded to sniffles, I let go of Nemo and leaned against the wall.

"I'm going home," I said. My throat and my eyes were swollen and my mouth was dry.

Nemo climbed to his feet, offered his hands and pulled me up. He walked me to the door.

"She's not okay," I said. It was more of a statement than a question.

"She needs more surgeries," he said. "But it's not going to be enough. She'll never be normal again."

"What about school?" I said. Did school even matter anymore? I ruined this girl's whole life, all because I was jealous and I had no idea why she had really been picking on me all this time.

"I don't know. Her mom is thinking about quitting her job and homeschooling her."

I couldn't take much more of this. I told Nemo to tell Julie that I was sorry, and I walked out of the house without another word. I ran all the way home. I wanted to get away as far as I could. I didn't want any of this. I didn't want to be a witch. I didn't want to practice or get better at it or anything.

This was why I had such a dark soul, wasn't it? I was a bad witch. I was a bad person.

When I got home, I leapt into bed and looked into my journal. I wondered if I ripped out the pages if I could stop being a witch. If I purged the poems Lenore and Miss Karen had taught me out of my memory, then I wouldn't be able to cast anything anymore.

Cannoli came into my room not long before her bedtime. She crawled into my bed and got under my covers. She was coughing and sneezing the cutest little sneeze I'd ever heard. She hadn't been herself over the weekend.

I had been struggling to finish my Religion homework, reading a chapter about how Jesus healed a woman who was sick for fifteen years. I was still out of it since seeing Julie.

"I don't want to sleep in my room," Cannoli finally said.

"Why not?" I asked.

"My night light doesn't work anymore," she said.

"Did you tell Mom? She probably can just change the bulb."

"No."

"Do you want *me* to change it?"

"No."

"Then what do you want?"

"I miss Dad," she said after a long pause and a couple of sneezes.

"Me, too."

"Is he really not coming home?"

She fell into a sneeze attack, and I couldn't help but laugh. How could sneezing sound and look so adorable? I put my book aside and laid down next to Cannoli.

"Do you want to sleep here tonight?" I asked.

She nodded eagerly.

"I don't know. You're sick. I might catch your cold."

"I promise I'll stop sneezing!"

"But all your germs are going to be all over my pillows and that's just gross," I said.

"Please! I swear I won't get any germs on your pillows."

I thought about the story in my Religion book. That woman Jesus healed merely touched his cloak and she was healed. It wasn't his cloak that healed her, but because she believed. I had to believe if I wanted things to be normal again. If there was a way to help Julie, I had to believe. If I were going to do something about Lenore's two souls, I had to believe. I had to believe *in me*.

"Want to know a secret?" I asked.

"Yeah!" Cannoli said, bursting with excitement.

"Promise you won't tell *anyone*? If you tell, then the secret won't be true anymore."

"I promise!"

"Alright. Remember when I said I was a witch? Well, I wasn't kidding."

"Nuh-uh! Witches aren't real!"

"Yes they are!"

"You can't do magic!"

"Yes I can. Want to see?"

I put my hand over her forehead. She rolled her eyes as far up as she could to see. I recited the poem in my head.

> *Wounds that pulse through the skin,*
> *And illness we caught in the wind,*
> *Fade away, go astray.*
> *Everything will be okay.*

With that, an ivory aura crept from my fingertips and hovered over Cannoli's face. "Wow!" she screamed. I put my finger over her lips and shushed her. She watched as the stream found its way into her gaping mouth and her widened nostrils. There was a soothing hum coming from the aura, and Cannoli giggled. "It tickles."

I laughed. And after a few minutes, I closed my hands and the last of the aura seeped into Cannoli's ears and into her skin.

"How do you feel?" I asked.

"I can breathe!" she said, squeezing her nose. She rubbed her neck and forced a cough. She exaggerated an ah-ah-ah, but the -choo didn't come.

"You cured me!" She threw her hands up in the air and kicked her feet.

"Told you I was a witch."

She looked at me with the most curious of stares. She took my hands and opened them, touching my fingers and putting them against her face. "This is impossible."

"It is possible," I said. "But if you tell, I won't be a witch anymore. And then I can't heal you when you get sick. Which means you can't sleep in my bed when you get sick or lonely."

"I won't tell," she said.

"Good. Are you sleepy?"

She nodded.

"You want me to read to you?"

"Yes, please."

I took my favorite book, *Alice's Adventures in Wonderland* from my book shelf. Then, I grabbed my flashlight from my nightstand, turned out the light, and got back into bed. I had her read the first paragraph out loud before I read the rest to her. She fell fast asleep by the second chapter.

I kept reading on my own. I thought about how brave and how curious Alice was. She was in a different world, but that didn't stop her from trying to find her way. Even when she wasn't sure who she was going to be, from one minute to the other.

I knew then why Nemo carried all those books. I knew then why he talked to Julie so tenderly, and why he was afraid for her. I knew then, as I looked over at Cannoli in the glow of my flashlight, why I had become a witch. I was meant to heal, and I never would have known that if I hadn't hurt someone first.

I read until the flashlight started to dim and flicker. I was going to need new batteries soon. The yawns were getting hard to fight. It was past midnight, and I decided it was best to fall asleep. Tomorrow was going to be the day I woke up as a hero.

18

Lenore and I walked to her place together. On the way, she got me excited for her mom's pumpkin macarons. She said that they could help a witch's memory, something that would be useful for learning new poems. I was pumped. I tried not to show it too much to Lenore. I didn't want her to know why. Yes, I was going to be a hero, but she was one of the people I had to rescue. She didn't know that she needed rescuing.

When we got to Lenore's, there was a woman looking up at the house in admiration. She was wearing a black spaghetti-string dress dusted with what might have been chalk or flour. A green hellebore flower rested in the back of her emerald hair. White spores floated around her head and flickered like fireflies, illuminating her earth-toned skin. Her getup was strange, but she was oddly gorgeous.

Lenore, who had held my hand the entire walk from school, let go and walked a few steps closer to the woman. "May I help you?"

The woman turned with a start. "Oh dear, I'm sorry," she said.

She had a Cajun accent. "Maybe you can? Are you Lenore?"

"Yes, I am."

"Is your mother home?"

"She should be. Who are you?"

"Oh, I can't tell you my name." She glanced at me, and did a double take. The second time, she lingered at me, as if she found something else she'd been looking for. She squinted, and turned to face me. "Oh, what a powerful little witch."

I blinked. How did she know?

She paced over to me. "Are you helping Lenore?"

"No, I'm here to practice with her mom," I said.

"Oh, I mean," and then she lowered close to my ear and whispered, "are you helping Eva?"

"Eva?" Lenore asked. How did she hear that?

My mouth fell open and I shivered. She straightened up with a half-smile that twitched a little. "I hope that's a yes," she uttered.

"I don't know why you're here," Lenore said, "but you need to leave."

The woman whipped toward Lenore, white spores swirling around. "I suppose I should go," she said. She kept walking and the spores trailed after her until she got far away down the street. The spores fell gracefully to the ground and faded away.

"Stay away from her," Lenore said, once the woman was out of sight. "If you see her again, don't talk to her."

"Do you know her?" I asked.

She said nothing. She took me by the hand and we went inside.

Once we were in her house, we dropped our things and changed our clothes. I had brought the clothes Lenore let me borrow from the other day. I'd been wearing them all the time. They'd become my favorite. Lenore had even said I could keep them.

I took my journal from my backpack and we went downstairs to meet Miss Karen. I wasted no time asking about her pumpkin macarons. She gave me two of them, drizzling a warm sauce over top of them that tasted like honey, vanilla and cinnamon. She said it had a secret ingredient that she couldn't tell anyone about, not even Lenore. Whatever it was, I reveled in its deliciousness. I wanted more, but Miss Karen suggested we get to work.

Miss Karen whispered something to Lenore. It was a long thought and Lenore listened closely. Lenore nodded at first, but then, she looked at me while she listened. She didn't blink. She didn't move. She fell still and her eyes were stuck on me. I looked back at her, but I was unnerved. When Miss Karen was finished with what she was saying, Lenore left the basement.

"Where is she going?" I asked.

"She's tired, so I told her to take a nap if she wanted," Miss Karen said. "Don't worry, she'll join us later. In fact, I think it's best she not know these poems. Not yet. So let's get to it, shall we?"

I heard Lenore's footsteps continue up to the second floor of the house. Meanwhile, Miss Karen shut the blinds to the windows and switched on a dim light that filled the basement with an olive glow. I whipped my head around as she closed the basement door with a gust of wind summoned from her open palm. Then, she put her index and middle fingers together out straight and turned them ninety degrees. I heard a click from the doorknob; she'd locked the door.

I swallowed. She stood by a wall and traced her hands along the lines of cement between the bricks. Then, she put her head next to the wall, closed her eyes and smiled with a long breath.

"Come here, Edith," she said softly. "Put your head against the wall. Listen," she said.

And I did. "I don't know what I'm supposed to hear," I said. I lifted my head, but she gently put her hand at my cheek before I could step away.

"Try your other ear," she told me.

The wall felt cool. Grains of dust and cement rubbed against the side of my face. I could smell hints of bread and pumpkin in the brick, but I couldn't *hear* anything.

"Keep listening," she said. "This is the first poem you're going to learn today. But you have to open your ears and your mind. It's called *Eavesdrop*. With it, you can hear what's been said within the walls of a room. From the tiniest of whispers, to the grunts of angst and yelps of joy. So long as the sound or the words had feeling, the walls remember them."

I pushed myself closer to the wall. I closed my eyes and tried not to think too much about anything else. Was it like trying to meditate? What would the words sound like when I heard them? Did the walls have their own unique voice?

I thought of the eerie look Lenore had given me before leaving the basement, and wondered if the wall would tell me what Miss Karen had said to her.

"At first, you'll only be able to hear what's been said in the last few seconds. Maybe minutes if you concentrate hard enough," Miss Karen said. "But if you really want to learn this, you could hear all that's been said in the past hour or so."

All I heard was a swirling of air, like a seashell humming the wisp of the beach. Miss Karen urged me to keep on. A curious silence fell between us.

"Miss Karen, what's wrong with Lenore?"

She sighed. "I was afraid you'd might ask sooner than later."

I lifted my head away from the wall, but then she made a sound of discouragement through her closed mouth—*mm-nnh*—and I leaned back onto the wall.

"I had a daughter before Lenore."

She knelt, looking down for a long time before she found more words. "I was nineteen. There was a boy. And, long story short, I got pregnant. When I told him I was a witch, he got frightened and upset and then he left."

I couldn't keep my head against the wall anymore. Uncomfortable, I sat against it, beside Miss Karen. I hadn't heard anything from the walls anyway.

"I'm sorry," I said. I knew how it felt to be left behind like that. I wanted to hold her hand or hug her or something.

"It's not your fault, don't apologize. Whatever the case, I had to support myself and my daughter all alone, so I started selling magic pastries to other witches. I wasn't making enough, so I used poems to make the pastries addictive."

"Are the macarons addictive?" I asked. I still wanted more.

"No," she said with a laugh. "That's not something witches are supposed to do. Someone found out about what I was doing, and they put a curse on me and my daughter." The smile from her laugh, the one that had always made me feel safe and warm, soured as Miss Karen fell silent for a long time. "The curse was strong. My daughter died. She was two."

She took a long, quivering breath before she continued. "A friend of mine, Esmeralda, had a crazy idea. She said to me, 'we can reincarnate her.'"

Karen touched the ring on her left hand, turning it only slightly and sliding it halfway up and down her ring finger. I'd noticed it before, but it was then that I realized that was an engagement ring. Neither Lenore nor her mom had ever talked about Lenore's father.

"Reincarnation is forbidden poetry," she said. "Your soul plummets into darkness and it never comes without consequence. But with precision, the consequence can be minimized.

"Esmeralda and I practiced for months. Together, we revived flowers, fruits and vegetables at first. Some of the fruit would come back sour or rotten or sugarless. There was a banana that came back with a yellow so bright that we could only look at it with sunglasses. There was a cucumber that Esmeralda tried to eat and it made her sneeze for hours."

Miss Karen spoke with a peculiar whimsy. She hung on her words, sometimes with a smile or with an open mouth. Her eyes would strew to the corners of her eyeballs, or she would stare up at the ceiling. But she never looked at me as she talked.

"We kept going until we were able to revive fruits and vegetables to their young, nearly flawless selves. Then, we moved on to animals. We got good, but there were still consequences. Frogs couldn't leap. Fish couldn't breath underwater and drowned immediately when they were reborn. And squirrels came back without their grace.

"But when Esmeralda's pet cat Kim Chi died, something clicked. We did it right. We were in sync. We both loved that cat. When he came back, he was his normal self. Cuddly, loquacious, and loved to play with yarn more than ever before. He even learned to play fetch."

"What was the consequence?" I said, wistful.

She let out an odd, cold laugh as she shook her head. She put her hands on her face. "Twelve years later, he's still alive. Kim Chi is a twenty-seven year old cat. He was reborn with eternal life."

"That's great!" I yelped.

"No," Miss Karen said. "He'll grow old and everyone he loves will die. And he'll get lonely, like all the others I know who live eternally. Trust me, Edith, just as I would never wish death on someone, I would never wish eternal life on them, either.

"But we learned something we hadn't read in any books or heard from any other witches. With reincarnation, it's important that there is a mutually strong emotional connection within the fibers of the triangle."

I trembled. Drowning in the storied sea Miss Karen poured on me, I felt terrible for Miss Karen. I'd only ever known kindness from her. She had welcomed me into her home and taught me poetry. I was speechless. I didn't know what to do, how to move, or how to look at her.

"On my daughter's birthday, we went to her grave," she continued. "We meditated for hours together before we began. We held hands and kept our breaths as closely synced as possible. It was a cold, late November day. I was pregnant with Lenore, too, and she was due in six weeks. But we did it. I could hear my daughter's little cries and her coos she would make. But we couldn't find her. Not in her grave. Not anywhere. We looked and looked. It sounded like she was following us, like a ghost. We even had our auras appraised by a witch to see if there were any ghosts actually following us. Nothing. But soon, I realized where she was."

Miss Karen stopped for a long time. Another tear trickled down the side of her face. She sniffled, wiped it away, and put her hand on her stomach. A half-smile rose from the corner of her lips and I sat down next to her.

"Esmeralda placed her ear on my stomach," Miss Karen said.

I felt a tingling at my throat like when the first cold of the season lurks inside your neck ready to leap at the sinuses in your nose.

"I thought that was the consequence: she would have to start all over again. *I* would have to start all over. But Lenore would have a twin, and if that was the consequence, then I was happy.

"Then, Lenore's due date came. And only Lenore was born. There was no sign of my other daughter."

Miss Karen sat there, her chest rising and falling slowly. With all that, I saw something that I hadn't seen before. She was lost and didn't know what to do or how to feel. She was the kind of mom I assumed had all the answers. But she'd swept consequences under the rug for nearly thirteen years.

The basement door opened. "Mom?" Lenore called from the top of the stairs.

I was hit with a dizziness that I couldn't shake. I clenched my teeth and shut my eyes. As Lenore slowly came down the stairs, that's when I heard it. Miss Karen's voice echoed behind me, like she had repeated the words in my ear. I spun to her, but she was silent as she stood and paced over to Lenore. I put my ear against the wall. Faintly, I heard the words again: *But Lenore would have a twin...only Lenore was born. There was no sign of my other daughter.*

"Miss Karen—" I turned to tell her that it worked. But then, I saw Lenore's eyes. Her pupils were black.

Miss Karen took Lenore in an embrace. "How did you sleep?" she asked Lenore.

"It was a nice little nap," she said with a big smile. Her voice had deepened slightly. She looked at me. "Hi, Edith."

I said nothing. The two of them were facing me, standing side by side, waiting for me to return her hello. But there wasn't a sound coming out of me. Miss Karen's last words to her story swirled in my head so loudly that I wasn't sure if they were my thoughts or if I was still using *Eavesdrop*. My ears started ringing. Quickly, the ring crescendoed louder and my ears hurt.

Underneath the shattering sound, I heard Miss Karen and Lenore's voices, muffled like someone holding the receiver end of the phone at their chest instead of their mouths. I put my hands at my ears and let out a shrill cry. I swore my head was going to burst.

Miss Karen put her hands at my shoulders. "Try to listen to the words, Edith. Whatever you're hearing, listen to the words," she said softly.

"I don't want to listen!" I stumbled back, falling against the wall. I tried to gain my balance, but when my hand touched the brick, the voices only became more vivid. I glanced over at them, their mouths not moving but I heard them speaking. My vision blurred. I moved my hand off the wall—the ringing faded, and my head stopped hurting.

"How do I stop it?" I asked, shaking as tears filled my eyes. "How can I stop listening?" One voice was enough in my head. Now I had others repeating the same words over and over. I had always struggled enough to shut my own voice up. How could I possibly tell myself to shut up when it's not me talking in my head?

"You have to want to stop listening," Miss Karen said. "That can be as hard as trying to listen, sometimes."

I looked at Lenore. *Lenore would have a twin*. And I was looking right at her.

I could see another person now, one who I barely knew. I wanted to run away, but I was scared Eva would catch me and stop me. It looked like she wanted to hurt me. Her eyes narrowed as she clasped and unclasped her fists.

There was no sign of my other daughter. There was no sign of Lenore. Only a stranger that looked exactly like her.

"Please," I said, "can I go home?"

"Yes, but—" Miss Karen started.

I started for the stairs with a burst, but then the door closed and locked in front of me before I could get away. I tugged at the doorknob, "please let me go. Please let me go!"

"There's just one more thing you need to learn, Edith," Miss Karen said.

19

Eva munched on a brownie and swung her legs as she sat on the edge of her bed. Miss Karen had given her that brownie. "This is so good, Mom," Eva said. "I wished you made them more often."

"I will honor that wish," Miss Karen said.

I stood by Lenore's desk, unnerved. I couldn't stop staring at Eva's eyes. I shivered each time she spoke. How could her voice be a different pitch and oddly still sound like Lenore even though it was the same body?

Since I knew Lenore so well, I noticed other things about Eva, too. She walked at a slower pace but took wider steps. I could tell when Lenore was coming down the hallway in school or if she were walking the stairs just by listening to the way she moved her feet. But Eva could sneak up on me if she wanted to. Lenore's hair smelled like lavender. But when I got close, in a brief moment of bravery when we first came to their bedroom, Eva's hair was like mint and white chocolate.

"Is it weird that I'm already wondering if it will snow soon?" Eva asked.

"Did something make you think of snow?" Miss Karen said.

"I had a dream about it when I was napping. We were playing in the snow but then there was someone who came and melted all the snow with a poem."

"Well, it sounds like we'll have to learn how to make snow with a poem."

"Is that possible?"

"Of course it is," Miss Karen said. She turned to me. "I bet Edith could learn to easily. That's in the realm of your element."

I laughed timidly, glancing at Miss Karen before I turned away. "I'd probably screw it up."

"I believe in you," Eva said. She took the last bite of her brownie and looked at me with confidence. Lenore would do the same thing — linger at my eyes like an embrace. Eva seemed kind, and for a moment, I wasn't afraid of her anymore.

"Thank you," I said.

"I miss the sunshine," Eva said. "All the time. I can't always see it when Lenore is awake. It's like walking around with my eyes closed. But when *I'm* awake, I can see it all. I can smell it. Taste it. But then, everything's sweeter when it's not all the time. That's what Mom said."

Miss Karen nodded with a smile.

"I have to think really hard sometimes. I had to imagine what you looked like, Edith. And I got it right. You're just as pretty as I always thought you'd be."

I thanked her again as I nervously pulled at my hair.

Miss Karen sat next to Eva on the bed and rubbed her back. She whispered in her ear. I had seen Miss Karen whisper in Lenore's ear plenty of times. Something didn't feel right whenever she did. I could see Miss Karen's eyes glance at her periphery. She must have thought I'd been listening. And I was. But she was so quiet that I wasn't even sure that she was really speaking. It looked like she was only moving her mouth, whispering a wordless thought into Eva's ears. It was a secret I wasn't supposed to know.

How many more secrets did Miss Karen have to hide? What was she confiding in Eva and Lenore that made them nod with a wistfulness like they were about to float away into space with the stars?

"What are you saying?" I asked.

Miss Karen kept whispering.

"What are you *saying*?"

Miss Karen stopped after a few last words and turned to me. "You'll find out soon enough."

Eva yawned and stretched. "I feel sleepy."

"Sleepy?" Miss Karen laughed. "You just woke up from a nap."

"I know. But I can't help it. I just feel really tired all of a sudden." Eva threw herself back in bed and crawled under her blankets. "I feel weak again, too, Mom."

"It's okay," she said, pulling the blankets over her daughter.

"Will I wake up soon?" Eva asked.

"You will. I promise."

"Good," Eva said. She was nestled and comfortable. "Sometimes I really miss you, Mom. I miss when you used to read to me when I was little. I could still hear you, even when it was Lenore who was awake."

"I miss you all the time, Eva," Miss Karen said. "Even when you are around."

"Can you tell me goodnight when it's Lenore falling asleep, too?"

"Yes. I will. Now fall asleep, and dream about lots of snow."

"Okay," Eva said. "I love you."

"I love you, too, Eva."

Miss Karen kissed Eva on her forehead and stroked her hair. She took Eva's hand in hers and held it firmly until Eva drifted all the way to sleep.

I inched over to the bed. Indeed, Eva's eyes were closed. Part of me wanted to see her black pupils. I was allured by them as much as I feared them.

"When you took her to the hospital," Miss Karen said softly, "that might have been the most Eva had gotten through. Their souls are fighting with each other with nightmares and bad daydreams. A sibling rivalry in one person's body." She put Eva's hand at her side and stood straight, looking over her with longing, glassy eyes. "There's a poem that I've learned that calms them. You two are always together, so it would help if you knew how to quiet their fights, too."

Miss Karen murmured some words that rhymed as she hovered her hand over Lenore's eyes. She said it would put her into an even deeper sleep. She sustained it for a few minutes, and Lenore's breaths got longer and heavier. Shiny motes of dust danced over Lenore's head before seeping into her nose and through her parted lips. She whimpered, then sneezed, but stayed asleep.

Miss Karen stood beside me. "This isn't going to be easy. You need to memorize this chant, and you need to memorize it *now*." Her tone had sharpened.

"Why?" I asked. "What am I doing?"

"I whispered a nightmare into Eva's mind. They're going to fight. And Lenore is going to have a seizure in a few minutes. This poem is going to calm them, and you'll wake up Lenore."

"No," I said, backing away towards the door. "I can't do that!"

"You have to," Miss Karen said. "You will learn this poem. And you will help Lenore before Eva seizes Lenore's soul."

"Why are you doing this to her — to *them*?"

"If you don't do this, you may never get to speak to Lenore again."

I paced back to the bed, my brows knit. I bit my lip and tried to breath and slow my heart. "What do I say?"

Miss Karen recited:

> *Let's move together, with brio in waltz*
> *A precedence set by quintessence.*
> *When the wind currents against,*
> *Let go,*
> *And still we move with sangfroid.*

I hesitated with the words. I couldn't nail the rhythm. Each time I messed up, Miss Karen got firmer with me. "Say it again," she'd urged with a shake of her head. She repeated the poem, but the words were only escaping me faster.

"The only way for you to learn magic is to *do it*, Edith," she said. "Listen, and do it."

"I can't."

"Yes you can. You will."

"Why can't you just do it?"

"Because we're not here to *watch* me do it. Now say it again."

"Let's move together, in brio with waltz—"

"No! Say it again!"

Lenore let out a feeble sound before her lips trembled. Was she having a nightmare? What kind of nightmare did Miss Karen whisper into her?

"You don't have much time," Miss Karen said. "Say it again."

"I—Let's move together, with brio in waltz," I looked at her. She nodded. "A precedence set by…" I lingered. What were these words? They clumped in the back of my throat. "…Quintessence. When the wind…"

Lenore's fingers were stretching. She was opening and closing her hands, and then she'd reach, and pull them back close to her.

"…Currents against, let go." I stopped. I couldn't remember the last line. Lenore was shaking. Her back arched and her chestnut eyes shot wide open. She gasped for air, then her body fell limp. "And still…" She clenched the edges of her bed and started shaking again.

Miss Karen glared at me. I could see through her pursed lips all the things she would have said to me. *If you don't get this right, Lenore is going to die. Say it! Say it now!*

"We move with—"

Eva's eyes shot open again. I wondered what color Eva's eyes were when she was a baby. Were they like Lenore's eyes? Were they hazel like shrubs in the spring? Were they as blue and as big as the ocean? Why had they gone black? How had they become black like the meter of my soul?

"—Sangfroid." I said it slowly. What did that word even mean?

Lenore didn't stop seizing. "Why isn't it working?" I panicked.

Miss Karen said nothing. Her head tilted, she watched Lenore continue to have a seizure. She took Lenore's hand and squeezed it. Soon, she stopped shaking. My breaths were bated in my lungs.

"Is she okay? Did I say it right?"

"Take her other hand," Miss Karen said.

I did. She was warm and clammy. A long moment passed before Lenore's breaths returned to normal. She took her hands away, still in her slumber, and turned on her side, facing me.

"Edith?" Miss Karen said. "She cannot know."

I thought about the snow, and how last year we had a huge blizzard. We were off school for a week. We made sleds out of cardboard boxes, and Lenore and I played for hours. We built a snowman that was taller than we were.

I remembered Mom telling me that I was born during a snowing thunderstorm. That meant Lenore was, too. I started to cry. Tears fell like a flash of lightning. Minutes had gone by and I watched as Lenore slept peacefully, as if her seizure hadn't happened. As if it were all in my imagination.

In the quiet of the room, I couldn't look at Miss Karen. I feared that if she were to speak lowly enough, or lean in close to me when I wasn't aware, she might whisper a nightmare into *my* mind. The woman I once thought had such a warm and kind soul suddenly looked like a monster to me.

"Is she okay now?" I asked.

"Yes," Miss Karen said.

A hot impulse sparked at my feet and the back of my neck. I let go of Lenore's hand and headed for the door.

"Where are you going?" Miss Karen called.

"Home," I said.

I scurried downstairs and grabbed my things. I looked over my shoulder. It felt like Miss Karen had followed me. I didn't even put my backpack over my shoulders. I slammed the door behind me and ran all the way home.

20

Mom grew more and more silent with each passing day. She didn't often ask about our days and she hardly finished her dinner anymore. She spent most of her nights talking to Aunt Tegan on the phone.

A week had gone by since I'd practiced magic with Miss Karen and Lenore. I'd been crying nearly every night before I went to bed, thinking about Lenore. Thinking about Eva. I told Lenore that I needed to rest and to think about the poems I had learned on my own. It was Columbus Day, so there was no school. Still, I was awake early, and I stirred my cereal as I watched Mom go through her routine in the kitchen.

"Snowpea, can you go make sure Cannoli is awake?" she said, sifting through the refrigerator. "I don't want her to be late." She had set our lunch boxes on the counter, along with a loaf of bread, sliced turkey, and—

"Mom?" I said as she placed slices of bread onto the cutting board. "We don't have school today."

She blinked rapidly as it dawned on her that it was a holiday. "I'm sorry," she said. "I'll still make you lunch."

She prepared three sandwiches for all of us. Then, she put her own lunch together, engrossed in her own world. She had a small bag of almonds and leftover chicken salad that Yaden had made last night, and two apples from the fruit bowl.

She looked exhausted and her skin was nearly as pale as mine. "Are you going to hang out with Lenore?"

"I think so."

"Well, if you do, please page me and let me know," she said. "One of you has to stay with Cannoli."

"I know, Mom." I poured more cereal in my bowl. At least crying and praying in the mornings always worked up an appetite.

She leaned over me and kissed me on my forehead. "I love you."

"I love you, too," I said around a mouthful of Honey Nut Cheerios.

"Be good," she added as she made her way out of the kitchen.

"Mom?" I called out to her. She stopped and came back to the doorway. I looked at her for a long time. "Do you ever talk to Dad on the phone at night?"

She shifted her weight and her eyes shot in another direction. Her lips were toying with a few silent words before she spoke aloud. "Sometimes."

"Did you tell him about my recital?"

She hesitated. "Yeah," she said with a nod as she crossed her arms. "I did." She pursed her lips as she looked at me. "Did you not want me to?"

I didn't want her to, and at the same time, I was hoping she had.

"When did you tell him?"

"About two weeks ago," she said. "He was really excited."

Soggy Cheerios floated in my bowl. The milk had turned creamy gold. I clenched my spoon and took a fierce breath through my nose.

Mom took a seat at the table and held my other hand. She smiled at me. "Hey, listen. We're going through some things right now, but he still loves you, Snowpea. I promise."

"Is it my fault?"

Her eyes widened. She moved the chair closer to me. "No. God, no."

The tears were coming, again.

"Are you sure?"

"Yes! Yes, I am."

"Are you going to get a divorce?"

She said nothing. She looked away and said nothing. In my head, I pleaded with her. I pleaded with *them*. Please don't let this be, I thought. Please don't let this family fall apart.

I didn't understand why Mom was upset with him, or why he couldn't just come home. I never thought I'd see Mom be so sad, and for such a long time. If they were hiding this much from me, how could I trust anything else she was saying? I didn't know what any of us had done to make Dad go away, but I couldn't stand what he was doing to our family.

"We'll talk about this later?"

"I don't want him there," I said. "At the recital."

She paused, wiping my tears. "Are you sure?"

I nodded.

"I'll be home tonight," Mom said. "We'll have a little talk. You and me. Okay?"

"Okay."

She kissed me on my cheek despite the rolling tears, and then pecked me on my nose. "I'm going to say goodbye to Cannoli and Yaden. Then I've got to get going. But I love you. I love you so much."

I nodded. I pulled the bowl closer to me and stared at the cereal. I ate slowly, chewing and sniffling through the soggy bits. I wanted to believe that the more I ate, the faster the heartbreak would go away. Cheerios were good for the heart.

I practiced piano for the rest of the morning to make the afternoon come faster. It staggered along though, and I struggled to get any sort of rhythm with any song. I quit around eleven and had lunch with Cannoli as we watched *The Price is Right*. After, I called Lenore and asked if I could come over for a little while. I wanted to ask if her mom was going to be there, too. I didn't want to see Miss Karen. I wasn't ready. Why didn't Miss Karen ever tell Lenore about her sister? Why did she leave it a mystery to her and not to Eva?

Indeed, Lenore was alone, at least for another few hours.

I took my journal from my room. Cannoli had fallen asleep in my bed and Yaden was in his room playing video games. I lingered at his door for a while, then knocked softly, hoping both that he heard me and that he did not. He had the volume high. A few moments passed. He didn't come to the door.

I tiptoed downstairs and on my way out of the house, I gently shut the front door. At the corner, I looked over my shoulder to see if Yaden might have been creeping up to surprise me. He wasn't, but there was a surprise up ahead.

The woman who had been waiting outside of Lenore's house the other day was there. I stopped once I noticed that it was her. I wanted to hide, but I didn't know where to go. I glanced at the porch closest to me. There was an older man with gray hair and a loose-fitted button down shirt smoking a cigarette. He caught me looking at him, and waved with a smile and a hello.

"Good afternoon," I said nervously, hoping the woman wouldn't see or hear me.

"You lost?" he asked.

"Umm…"

The woman turned toward me. Too late; there was no turning back now.

"No," I said to the man. I held my chin up and walked towards her. She was wearing the same outfit as before: the string dress and the flower and an abundance of floating white spores. She smiled at me.

"Lenore said I shouldn't talk to you," I said.

"Is she home?" the woman asked. "I'd love to see her. It's been so long since we spoke. She probably didn't recognize me."

"Who are you?"

She extended her hand out to me. "Esmeralda Desjardins."

This was the same Esmeralda that helped Miss Karen with Eva and Lenore! A spark of panic took over me. I took her hand reluctantly, but my hands got shaky in hers and I pulled away. "I'm Edith. Nice to meet you."

"Edith," she nodded. "How long have you been practicing poetry?"

"A few weeks." Something about her created a warmth around me—but not the kind of warmth that makes you feel safe. I felt uncomfortable and I wanted to run away but I felt trapped. Or maybe I was entranced. One of the white spores fell on my cheek and it was soft like cotton candy. It tickled me for a moment before it disappeared.

"A few weeks?" she said, her voice striking a high pitch. "Goodness, I'm already sensing such beautiful power from you."

"Miss Karen said I had a dark soul. The darkest she'd ever seen."

"Nonsense! The light of a soul doesn't carry as much weight as you may think. You have a colossal battle going on in your spirited young mind. That's why your soul is so dark. But I see plenty of light underneath all that, my darling."

"I want to help people. I want to heal them. Like Eva. And Julie." I said. The words spilled out of me as if I had no control over it. Why was I talking to this stranger about things I hadn't even said to my best friend yet?

"Who's Julie?" was all she asked.

"A—friend. I hurt her by accident. Really bad. With magic—I mean, a poem. Before I even knew what a poem was."

Esmeralda rubbed her hand on her chin and tapped her toes. "How badly is she hurt?"

"She's not coming back to school this semester."

She knelt down at me and stroked my hair. "How badly do you want to help her?"

"I'll do anything." And I meant it. I said it so fiercely that Esmeralda flinched. Then, she put her hands on my face and stared at me with her deep auburn eyes.

"Anything?"

I nodded. "I want to be a good witch," I said. "I'll do anything to be one."

Esmeralda put my hands together, palms up, like when you scoop water into your palms. She wriggled her fingers over my hands and a cloud of smoke trickled from her fingertips. It formed a ball, and then, with a snap of her fingers, turned into a radiant, psychedelic marble about the size of a clementine.

"This is a compass pellet," she said. "Use it when you want to find me. It will take you to my home."

The sun reflected different colors against the pellet as I turned it. I saw my face reflected in the compass pellet, and at a straight angle, I was blue. When I hoisted it up higher, I was yellow, and I was as emerald as Esmeralda's hair when I held it at my sides. The pellet was smooth as glass in my hands. I was afraid that I would drop it if I didn't hold it with both hands.

"I'll be going now," Esmeralda said. "Will you send them my regards?"

"I will," I said.

"Thank you, Edith. You're truly kind. And I hope that I'll see you soon."

Esmeralda walked away and I put the compass pellet in my backpack before I rang Lenore's doorbell.

21

Lenore was ecstatic to see me. She brought me into the house and we went down into the basement to practice some of the poems I already knew. She told me one of the most important things for a witch is practice. The more you do it, the better you get and the stronger your poetry becomes.

I swished spheres of water in the air and from glass to glass without breaking anything. This time, I hardly spilled a drop. I cast a healing poem and drew a vast amount of silk fog that first embraced Lenore and then danced around the basement. The poem strung up a soft viola hum that lingered long and sweetly, and Lenore spun around in it with her arms out and her eyes closed.

We ate pumpkin macarons and chocolate chip cookies while Lenore told me what her favorite poems were. She showed me her journal, too, and told me about a bunch of poems that she couldn't wait to teach me. She spoke of logicals like blowing gusts of wind from our mouths or using a poem of fire to whisk plastic into glass.

I wanted to learn the poem that Eva had used to keep me from coming close to her when we were at school, but I wasn't sure if Lenore would know it. That poem would be great for keeping Yaden out of my room.

I hadn't heard any other walls speak to me since Miss Karen taught me *Eavesdrop*. It was probably best that I didn't. I had already heard enough out loud that I wished I hadn't. I wanted to tell Lenore that my parents might be getting divorced, but I didn't want the walls to hear me. What if Miss Karen listened to the walls after Lenore and I hung out? She must have known I would come over today. Did she trust me to keep Eva a secret? Was that a way to scare me into keeping my mouth shut?

"Can we go upstairs?" I asked. My mouth was dry from blowing wind and I had goosebumps all over my arms. "I'm getting cold. And a little tired."

Lenore made tea. After it steeped, she cooled it for me with an intrinsic poem. Tiny snowflakes fell from her fingertips and melted on the surface of the tea. She did it until the bristling steam teemed to a murmur.

I took a sip and was perked by the mix of cool and warm, and then peppermint. She had infused the tea with the petals she used for the scarlet wine, although these were a different color.

"It will help you feel less tired," she said.

"I had fun today," I said after another sip.

"You're getting really good really fast."

"Am I?"

"You'd better slow down! You're going to be better than me in no time if you keep this up."

We watched *Sailor Moon* and *Animaniacs* as we drank our tea. When Miss Karen arrived home, Lenore was happy to see her. She put down her tea and leapt from the couch, gently floating back down and falling into her mom's embrace.

"Hi, Miss Karen," I said. I curled up into the corner on the couch.

"Good afternoon, Edith," she said. "How are my girls today?"

Did she mean Lenore and me? Or Lenore and Eva?

"We're great," Lenore said. "I taught her *Zephyr* today. And she almost filled the entire basement with healing fog."

"Really?" Miss Karen said. "That's remarkable."

I watched her intently, like a wary kitten. She kissed the top of Lenore's head. I was worried that she would whisper to her, but she didn't. She walked past me and into the kitchen.

Lenore took her tea and followed her mom. She offered Miss Karen tea, pouring some into a mug and sprinkling a few snowflakes into it.

"Did you two have a nice lunch?" Miss Karen asked Lenore.

"We had sweets. That's all we need."

Miss Karen laughed. "I'll be in the basement preparing harmonies if you need me."

She ruffled Lenore's hair before leaving the kitchen for the basement. Lenore returned to the couch and sat next to me.

"Your mom makes music, too?" I asked.

"What? Oh, no," Lenore laughed. "A harmony is like a potion or a tonic. Mom sells them along with her sweets and stuff."

"Are there a lot of witches around here?"

"More than you'd think," she said.

I thought for a minute. Then, I asked, "Do you ever miss your dad?"

"I never really met him," Lenore said. She walked over to a bookshelf in the corner of the room. She leapt and grabbed a picture frame from the top. She held it for a while, dusting it off with her fingers before she brought it over to the couch. She handed it to me.

The photo was of Miss Karen and a man I assumed to be her dad. He was about the same height as Miss Karen, with a scruffy beard and an oatmeal-colored turtle-neck sweater. A two-year-old Lenore sat in his arm, with her arms around his neck. They all had big, pearly smiles.

"Mom says this is the most recent picture of him that we have."

"What happened to him?"

"He's been missing for ten years."

If we were supposed to be the cosmic twins, why did I never ask about her dad before? I felt like a terrible friend. Lenore knew everything about me, but I was starting to wonder how much I really knew about her.

I stared at the photo. What a beautiful family. How strange that there were actually four people in this photo. Lenore and Miss Karen loved each other so much. They cared for each other. They were like a team surviving together. And yet, so were Miss Karen and Eva. Somehow, they survived together, too.

I thought about that. The way she tells it, Miss Karen had done what she did because she loved both her daughters. But I still felt upset with her for what she was doing to Lenore, even if her intentions were good.

I sighed. It seemed like the closer a family was together, the sooner it fell apart.

After I left Lenore's later, I took out the compass pellet out my backpack. It felt warm in my hands as the vibrant glow drew in the sunlight. Esmeralda must've been close by. I wanted to follow its warmth and find her, but it was already late afternoon and I needed to get back home. Yaden had to have noticed that I was gone by now.

I was anxious to know how Esmeralda could help Lenore and Eva—how she could help me become a good, healing witch. I hoped she believed me when I said that I would do anything. And I hoped that I could trust her. She cared about Eva, too.

I'll go see her another day, I thought. I just had to hold on for a little bit longer.

22

I looked through my journal at all the new poems I had learned. A picture of me was forming on one of the empty pages. In it, I stood in the corner of the page, blowing swirls of wind into a tornado that spun from clouds.

I recited the poem for *Zephyr* in my head, and gently blew at my curtains and ruffled through the pages of my books to see if I could open them without blowing them away.

Mom arrived home for dinner, and as usual, Cannoli dominated conversation. That was fine with me. I didn't want to talk much. If Mom kept her promise, we would talk later tonight.

A little after eight o'clock, Mom came into Yaden's room. He, Cannoli, and I were playing *Mario Kart 64* together. Although Cannoli had been losing badly the entire time, she insisted and pleaded with Mom that she stay and play with us a little longer before bedtime. Mom stood in front of the television and Yaden paused the game. He and I both waited in silence. We didn't want to take any sides.

Eventually, Cannoli caved in, and Mom took her to bed.

We played a few more races—I won three out of four, after which Yaden called me a cheater—before Mom came back into Yaden's room.

"We need to talk," she said.

I paused the game. My body ached and I felt cold. I didn't want to talk.

She closed the door and sat between us at the edge of Yaden's bed. I gripped my controller tight as my heart punched at my chest.

She straightened her back and fiddled with her fingers as she looked at us. "If I haven't told you in a while, or even if I have," she said, "you mean the world to me. All three of you. I'll never stop loving you, no matter what."

"Even if we become bank robbers? Or serial killers?" Yaden jested.

Mom chuckled. "No matter if you're bank robbers or serial killers or just plain old you." She paused. "As you two know already, your father and I have been having some troubles over the past year. Things haven't been getting better. They've been getting worse, actually. I didn't want him talking to either of you because, well, I just didn't think he was ready to. I'm sorry for keeping him from you. He loves you, just as much as I love you. I will never deny that. But umm…he doesn't—"

She looked at each of us longly, with the warmest of loving gazes. She ran her fingers through my hair, hanging on to the curls at my ends.

"I need you both to be strong for me, okay? Be strong for Cannoli, and for each other. Can you promise me that?"

I nodded. Yaden said yes without hesitation.

"Okay," she said. "Then I think it's time that you know that your father and I have decided to get a divorce."

I had felt that word coming from a mile away, but I still sunk when I heard it.

"It's going to be a long process, and I'm sorry if I seem tired or cranky sometimes. Just tell me when you think I am, and I'll try to calm down. I'm going to need you as much as you're going to need me."

I lowered my head. I was sick of this already. I didn't want to hear anymore. The walls were listening, and I was afraid they'd repeat these words to me over and over.

"Right now, there's a ton of paperwork to do," she continued. "I don't know how long it'll take, and what the terms are going to be. But something you'll have to think about is that you may have to spend time with him. It might be half with me and then half—"

"No," I interrupted.

Mom put her hand at my shoulder, but I pulled away from her and stood up.

"I'm not staying with him," I said.

"Edith," Yaden said, "let Mom talk."

"Shut up!" I yelled. "It doesn't matter to you anyway—you're leaving."

Mom reached out to me. "Hey, sit down," she said softly. I slipped out of her reach, stumbling over the Nintendo 64.

"You're just like him," I told Yaden. It was like a revelation, the kind that takes your breath away and leaves you speechless.

"I'm going to *college*," he said back. "That's not the same at all."

"Why can't you go to college here?"

"Because I don't have to!" he yelled.

"Hey," Mom called out.

"That's what boys do," I growled. "They leave."

Mom shot a glare at me. "Yaden is not leaving you."

"He's not *staying*, either."

Mom knelt in front of me. She took the controller out of my hands. "Yaden loves you," she said. "He's going to miss you, too. And he's going to come visit sometimes on weekends. All we have to do is call him when we miss him. Right, Yaden?" She turned to him.

"Yeah."

"And there's always summer and winter breaks. You'll be tired of him then," Mom said. "And he'll be here on holidays, too."

"What about Dad? Is he going to be here on holidays?"

Mom looked down and shook her head before she returned her eyes to me. She squeezed me tight, rubbing her thumbs on the backs of my hands. "I don't know, yet."

"Are you going to tell Cannoli?" I asked.

"I will."

"I don't want to talk about this anymore," I said. "Can we just keep playing *Mario Kart* now?"

Mom turned to Yaden as she stood. "Okay. Go ahead." She kissed me and Yaden on the cheek and headed for the door. She told us she loved us, and Yaden said it back. I didn't. I hopped back onto Yaden's bed. I hadn't thought about not having Dad around for the holidays. He was the one who brought home pumpkins. He cut the turkey every year. He brought home the Christmas tree. Now Mom or Yaden had to do it. Didn't they have enough to worry about already?

The game wouldn't unpause. I pounded my thumb on the Start button over and over but nothing happened.

"You froze it when you tripped over it," Yaden said. He went to reset the game.

Mom's voice echoed in my head from the walls. I couldn't stop it. My ears rung as the walls swathed her words into my mind. I almost screamed *shut up!* but Yaden would have thought I was yelling at him. I threw myself onto my back and pulled the covers over me. I needed to hide.

23

Ten days had passed since Mom had announced that Dad wasn't coming home. I carried the compass pellet with me each day, safely tucked in a tiny pouch cushioned with cloth that I kept inside a lonely compartment of my backpack.

The only time I could have gone to see Esmeralda was after school, but I couldn't shake Lenore. I loved spending time with her, and I enjoyed practicing magic with her—as we'd done every day since last week—but I was itching to know what Esmeralda had for me.

Once classes had ended, I scurried to get to my locker. I had places to be. Things to fix. People to heal. I quickly sorted through what books I needed—I had homework in all my classes so I was in for a long night. I had the compass pellet in my hands when Lenore snuck up on me. Startled, I nearly dropped it. I shifted away from her and shoved it in my sweater pocket.

Lenore held books to her chest. Her backpack was as stuffed as mine. She'd been mellow and quiet today. She hadn't even sat with me at lunch. She leaned against the locker next to mine and she gazed at me for a long moment.

"What's up?" I said. "You're being creepy."

"Can I ask you something?" she said.

"Since when do you need to ask if you can ask me something?"

I closed my locker and kept my hands in my sweater pockets.

"I don't know."

"What's up with you today?"

"Nothing." She squeezed her books closer to her and looked around her. "I just—umm, so, okay. I'm just going to say it. My friend Jesse, from the baseball team, is having a Halloween party next week, on Halloween, and I was wondering if you wanted to be my date."

"A Halloween party?" I asked. "I've never even been to a party."

"Neither have I," she said.

"And I don't know your baseball friends."

"That's okay," she said. "They're really funny. And they're not as jockey as, like, the basketball team. You'll like them."

"You sure?"

"Yeah. I always tell them all about you and how cool you are."

"The baseball team thinks I'm cool?" I asked her twice. It sounded silly to me. I barely knew any of their names. Jesse was the only one I knew. We said hi to each other in the hallways, and we had Miss Martini's Science class together. And there was one time he sat with Lenore and me at lunch but that was it.

Lenore pulled at her hair. "Well? Do you want to go with me?"

I was nervous with the idea. I was flattered by being famous amongst her baseball buddies, but I didn't fit in anywhere. I didn't have many friends at St. Vincent, and I wasn't looking for any, either. But Lenore was fixed at me, biting her lip and rocking her leg, left and right.

"Okay. I'll go."

"Yeah?"

"Yeah."

"Yes! It'll be fun," she said. "Let's go shopping for costumes this weekend."

"Only if I get to be Alice."

"Alice?"

"In Wonderland?"

"Oh," she laughed. "Of course you can. I want to be Dorothy Gale. We'll look cute together."

I wanted to ask if she knew whether or not Nemo was coming, but I imagined he wasn't in much of a party mood. He was quiet in class, and he never sat at our table at lunch anymore. He was still turning in Julie's homework. Part of me wanted to try and find him before Lenore and I left. But what if I asked him and he said no? That would be twice as embarrassing if Lenore was with me.

Lenore relaxed her shoulders. "Umm, well, I have to go see…my Spanish teacher for a little while. You should probably head home without me."

"No practice today?" I asked.

"We should take a break," she said. "Just, umm…call me, tonight. And we can go over Social Studies for the test tomorrow."

"Alright," I said.

Lenore backpedaled with a wave. She spun around and she was

back to her normal, skipping self. I took the compass from my sweater and slid it back into my pouch and into my backpack.

I went to Nemo's locker but he wasn't there, so I hurried down the stairs to the cafeteria. Sometimes kids would hang out there on cold days. But he wasn't there. I left the school through the courtyard and he wasn't there, either. There was just a bunch of girls playing double dutch. *Apples, peaches, pears, and plums...jump out when your birthday comes! January, February, March...*

I waited at one of the benches hoping he'd walk by. Nemo and I hadn't spoken more than a few words to each other since he'd taken me to see Julie. I missed him. I missed my friend. I worried about how he was. Maybe a party would help take his mind off things. He could be the Mad Hatter!

I debated whether or not to tell him that I might have found a way to help Julie. No way would he believe I was a witch, though — and the only thing that could convince him was if I used poetry in front of him. That might shatter his whole world. But if I were going to help her, I might have to reveal my secret, anyway.

If I stayed any longer, Lenore might have run into me. I had to find Esmeralda.

Using the compass was like trying to find Esmeralda through a game of Hot or Cold. After dropping my backpack off at home, I walked two streets past Lenore's house to Alford Street. The compass warmed.

I turned and walked down Cullen Avenue. I'd never walked too far on my own — this was as about as far as I'd ever gone. It was a busy street with outdoor vendors selling random wares on their foldout tables and tall shelves. The vendors' faces were hidden by the hoods of their heavy coats. Most of them didn't notice me, but I was getting nervous. Should I turn back and go home even though the farther north I walked, the warmer the compass grew?

I kept my head down and didn't look at anyone. I turned onto Robin Street, which was a bit more peaceful and quiet. I passed numerous stores like Hogan's Hoagies and Armour Guitar & More. The compass was getting hotter. I was going in the right direction! It made me walk faster, running across the streets when the street lights turned yellow.

I was a ways away from home now. I didn't think anyone would think to find me out here if I went missing. I hoped that I could remember the way back. Things looked different when you were going back.

I arrived at a house that was shaded by a tall, orange-leafed tree. Colorful plants and flowers decorated the porch: lillies, cedar bonsai, aloe and ficus shrubs. Wind chimes sang in the breeze. Chinese lanterns hung from the porch awning.

The compass burned in my hands. I fought the impulse to drop it, but a second later, the compass lifted and floated over to the front door. It hovered for a moment, flickering an assortment of colors before it thrust itself to the floor and shattered. I flinched.

I hurried up the stairs and tried to gather the pieces of glass, but the shards turned to water at my touch. I looked at the chestnut-colored door. I didn't see a doorbell. I peered into the mail slot, but it was so dark inside, I couldn't make out what I was seeing. Growing more nervous with every second, I finally summoned the courage to knock. *Knock...knock...knock...*

I turned to look at the other houses while I waited. Not even one of them had a hint of decor—nothing but long chains of row homes. No one was walking by, at least as far as I could see. This street felt lonely and empty.

The door opened, creaky and rickety. I spun back around and found Esmeralda standing before me.

"You decided to visit."

I nodded. "I guess so."

"Come in," she said, stepping aside.

She closed the door behind me. Inside, the living room was dim. The curtains were closed. Mountains of books were piled around the room, and mason jars were filled with herbs and powders. African masks and paintings hung from her walls. A cat scurried up to me, his bell jangling as he pranced.

"May I get you something? Water? Tea? I have some fresh banana bread that's still warm."

"Water, please?" I asked.

I followed her into the kitchen, the cat following close behind. Esmeralda walked with an accelerated step but she had a slight limp, like her foot had fallen asleep.

She poured a glass of water, and added a few drops of another clear liquid. "Drink this. I included a little harmony made with enchanted aloe—it will help open your pores and relax your mind. I can tell you're nervous."

"Thank you," I said as I took the glass from her. Our hands touched, and I felt a chill run through my fingers like a cold, electric shock. I nearly dropped the glass.

"I'm so glad you came," she said. She sat down at her kitchen table. "It's been weeks since we've had any visitors. We get lonely."

"We?" I asked.

The cat leapt onto the table, his purr vibrant enough to hear even a few feet away.

"Kim Chi and I. I think he likes you."

This was Kim Chi, the immortal cat! Kim Chi walked across the table and stood at the edge. He meowed at me, his eyes intent and unrelenting. I sat down in the chair and gave him the attention he wouldn't stop meowing for. There was something about him that felt old, but not in that walk-with-a-cane, rickety bones kind of way. I could see wisdom in his eyes when he looked at me. If only I could speak to him.

"He's such a flirt," she said with a laugh.

I smiled. He was friendly and I didn't think he was going to let me stop. His fur was golden and he purred like a tiny lion.

"So," Esmeralda said. She leaned in. "How does it feel being a new witch?"

"Scary," I said.

"Indeed," she said. "I felt the same way when I was a young witch. It takes a long time before that feeling goes away. But it's good to be scared at first. Otherwise, you get cocky and cross boundaries too soon."

Kim Chi crawled into my lap and laid down, pawing at my skirt as he got comfortable. Esmeralda smiled. "How is Eva?" she asked.

"I don't know," I said. I drank the last of my water. "She keeps asking for my help."

"She knows you can help her. She's a smart girl. I could tell that when she was little."

I explained that I knew the story about the reincarnation. But there was something else I needed to know.

"Why are you here?" I asked. "Miss Karen thinks you're far away."

"I'm here for Eva," she said. "There is a way to help her."

I swallowed my excited curiosity.

"But it's complicated. Have you heard of *The Collateral Art of Poetry*?"

I shook my head.

"It's a series of doctrines for all who practice poetry," she continued. "Within the doctrine, we learn about collateral in many aspects of poetry. The one that's important for you to know about right now is *The Collateral Art of Favor & Apology*. Edith, I can help Eva. I'm directly tied to her. The fibers of her existence have become intertwined with mine. But I have also wronged her, according to the rules of reincarnation. Thus, if I have to heal her, I must express my remorse by performing a favor."

"A favor?"

"I have a poem that I can recite to separate Eva's soul from Lenore's body. But in order to cast it efficiently, I have to do a favor for someone close to Lenore—a favor that involves poetry. I must do *you* a favor, but it must be asked by you. It has to come from your heart."

I shuddered. Kim Chi leapt from my lap as I leaned back into my chair. What did I want? What did I *truly* want? There was more than one thing that I wanted to ask for. Do I ask her to help me with Julie, or do I ask her to bring Mom and Dad back together happily?

"I know you have a troubled heart," Esmeralda said. "I can tell by the way you breathe and the way your eyes shift. But deep down, you know what to ask. That is, if you think it's in the fairness of rescuing Eva."

"I do," I said. "I want to help her. What would you do with Eva once her soul has left Lenore's body?"

"I have a body waiting for her," Esmeralda said.

I was learning something new each day, but there were still so many aspects to this world of being a witch that I didn't understand. I couldn't imagine what else was out there. How did Esmeralda have a *body* waiting for a soul?

Here I was, sitting in the dreary afternoon light that seeped through thick, cream colored curtains in a kitchen dank with unfamiliar aromas, with a woman I had known for but all of fifteen minutes combined. I felt light-headed, knowing that there were doctrines I hadn't heard of and practices and beliefs that had yet to be shared with me. I was only a few weeks old at this witch thing, and I was already being asked to help with something that a month ago would have sounded like science fiction to me.

Esmeralda was right, though. The first person I thought of was not my Dad. It was Julie. I wanted to return her life to normal. I hadn't meant to hurt her. I felt remorse for that. Esmeralda and I both had remorse for things we'd done wrong, and maybe that is why I felt like I'd known her for so long. Our hearts thumped with grief and pinged with contrition. She had carried sorrow for a dozen years, while I hadn't even gotten through a dozen weeks.

"You said you wanted to help someone else the other day," she said. "Julie, right? Is she a friend?"

"Yes," I said.

Esmeralda stood from her chair and came over to me. She knelt and extended her pinky finger to me. "If you pinky swear with another witch when you tell a secret, the other witch can't tell the secret to anyone else. They won't be able to speak it or write it. Ever, unless you were to pinky swear with me again."

I wrapped my pinky around hers.

"Now, tell me what happened to Julie."

"I burned her face by accident," I said. The tears started falling down. "We got into a fight and I burned her face with poetry. I didn't even know I was a witch, and I couldn't stop it, and now she has to stay home and she wears a mask and no one thinks she'll be normal ever again."

"And you want to heal her?"

"Yes," I said.

"Are you sure?"

I nodded affirmatively.

"I can help you, if you help me," she said.

"I'll do it, I'll help you."

"And I promise to keep your secret, okay?" she said.

"Okay," I said.

"And with a kiss, I seal this secret under my tongue and before my wrists," she said. She kissed her hand. "And kiss your hand now."

I wiped my tears with my other arm, sniffled, then kissed my hand.

"Good, then it is a secret," she said, letting go of my finger. "And it is a promise, a contract between the two of us, in the name of *The Collateral Art of Favor and Apology*, that you and I shall extract Eva's soul, and restore Julie's countenance."

"Thank you, Miss Esmeralda," I said.

"Just call me Esmeralda," she said. "We're poetic partners now. Equals. It is important to feel equal when you enter a contract with a witch."

"Alright," I said. "So how are you going to get Eva's soul from Lenore?"

"I can't."

My heart sank. "I thought you said we were going to? I thought you knew?"

"I do."

"I don't understand."

"Karen placed a blocking poem between Lenore, Eva and I. My talents are stifled when I'm near them. There's no way I could perform such high witch poetry while in their presence. It's quite a powerful intrinsic that she cast on me."

"Then who is going to do it?" I asked. "Do we have to find someone else? A *high witch* or someone?"

"We've already found who's going to recite the poem," she said with a smirk. She squeezed her hand on my shoulder.

No.

No way.

24

On Saturday morning, Mom gave me cash and an old wallet of hers. It was a violet, leather-bound wallet that she had used back when she first started working at the hospital. She set it on the table as I forked away at my french toast, eggs, and bacon.

"Are you sure about this?" I asked her.

"You're practically a teenager, Snowpea," she said, "I think you're ready to learn."

I'd been expecting Mom to take Lenore and me to the mall, but that morning, she decided that we should go on our own. She told me she'd gotten permission from Miss Karen, too. It was time for Lenore and me to learn to be without adults.

I opened the wallet and counted the cash. I'd never seen so much money in my hands before. "Fifty dollars?"

I was nervous. Leaving a twelve-year-old with all this money to take the bus to the mall and go shopping might have been a bad idea.

After breakfast, I called Lenore. She was excited *and* nervous that we were going to the mall on our own. We promised to meet outside her house at around noon, then we'd walk to the bus stop together. It was only a block away. Mom gave me a bus schedule, telling me with that it was only about a half-hour ride.

"That's a long time," I said. "Can't you drive us there and pick us up?"

"I was twelve when I first went to the mall with my friends," she said. "My mom didn't have a car, so we had to walk or take the bus or the train everywhere. You and Lenore will be fine."

There was no use trying to change her mind. I got dressed and looked through my journal to pass the last bit of the morning. I had quite a few illustrations now. *Feather-footed, Eavesdrop, Healing Fog, Zephyr...*and then there was the first page. The fight with Julie still haunted me.

Hardly anyone was on the bus. We sat together near the back door. Lenore let me have the window seat, which also meant I had to keep a closer eye out for our stop. A few minutes into the ride, an older woman boarded. She said good afternoon to us and sat in the seat in front of us. Lenore said good afternoon in return. I stared blankly at her. I couldn't muster a smile or a nod, let alone words, to talk to a stranger on the bus.

I pulled the string when we got close to our stop. We got off and were immediately immersed in busy street traffic, tall buildings, and strangers passing by. As we crossed the street to the mall, not one person noticed me. Strangely, it was comforting to be invisible, even if only for that afternoon.

Lenore found a plush cairn terrier at Toys 'R' Us, perfect for a

Toto. She bought a basket to go along with it. We spent most of our time exploring a vintage store called Alandrea. They had so much cool stuff that I couldn't afford. I found a gold pocket watch with embroidered cogs and wings that made me think steampunk. I loved the way it fit in my palm. I opened and closed it over and over again. I wore it as we sifted through dresses and fabrics and shoes in the young women's section. We tried a few things on, and eventually, we found what we were looking for. I put the pocket watch away before we went to the register, deciding it was too expensive. I told myself to keep it in mind, hoping that maybe it would still be here come Christmas time.

I was nervous when the lady at the register rung us up. I carefully pulled out enough cash from my wallet and handed it to her. When she gave me change, I didn't want to put it all back into my wallet, so I shoved it into my pocket. I felt strange about having a wallet and my cash out there in the open. What if someone were to snatch it from me?

We still had some cash to spend, so Lenore wanted to go to the record store. She made a big deal about Dr Pepper lip gloss, and raved about a band called Princess. She bought one of their cassettes, and insisted that I take it as a gift. I refused, but she said it was her favorite band and swore that I was going to love them, too. I bought my first CD ever: *Left of the Middle* by Natalie Imbruglia. I also got a purple beanie hat that I wore out of the store.

Lenore and I made our way to the mall food court after our shopping spree. Our destination was Samurai Pizza Kitchen—they had the best burgers in the world and it had been months since we'd gone. There was always a long line, but it was worth the wait. We grew excited as we got near the register. We didn't have to deliberate over the menu. We knew what we'd come for. By the time only one person was left in front of us, we were dancing. We were carrying shopping bags and about to order our own food. Lenore and I were proud of ourselves, and we were ready to celebrate our young adulthood with a coma-inducing lunch.

We gained some composure and placed our orders together. Both of us got double cheeseburgers and ninja fries—which should be considered world famous—and we even added two strawberry milkshakes.

The cashier looked annoyed at us. He probably wasn't much older than we were, perhaps a sophomore or junior in high school. His hair was shaggy and his uniform polo was about two sizes too big. It draped, just like his posture. When we put the last few of our dollars together, we realized we had enough, but we'd be short two dollars on getting back on the bus.

Lenore and I scrambled to find what might have gotten lost in our back pockets or wrapped up with the receipts in our bags. I offered to skip my milkshake, or that we could share one order of ninja fries, but Lenore called me insane. There was no way she was going to share an order of food at Samurai Pizza Kitchen. And she swore that she had more money somewhere.

"I can help you ladies."

I looked over my shoulder. The woman standing in line behind us smiled brightly. She had a sprinkling of freckles, a southern accent, and the most perfect teeth I'd ever seen. She was tall with long, curly cardinal-red hair. She rubbed her round, baby-bearing belly with her hand.

"Umm…" I responded, not-so-gracefully. Lenore and I looked at each other, flushed and blank.

The woman laughed. "I'll take that as a yes." She added two orders to ours and then handed the cashier her credit card.

"Thank you," Lenore and I said together, blushing.

"I've been where you are," the woman said. "I used to go to the mall all the time when I was a teen. I'd spend all my money and forget to save something for food. And I would have to beg my friends to spare me a few dollars. Every time."

I laughed nervously.

"What are your names? I'm Fiona," she said, extending her hand for a shake.

"I'm — Madeline," I said.

Lenore shot me a glare. "And I'm — Roslyn."

"Those are such pretty names," Fiona gushed. She went on to ask about our day as we waited for our food. She lit up when I told her that I was going to be Alice for Halloween. "I was Alice when I was sixteen. I remember that Halloween like it was yesterday. But here I am, an Alabama girl turned receptionist living in a big city eating for two. Times flies, girls. Be careful not to grow up too quick."

Whoever she was or wherever she came from, Fiona was beautiful and her happiness was contagious. Something about her seemed awfully familiar.

"Is it a girl or a boy?" I asked.

"Girl," Fiona said. "And I've been thinking of the name Coral. But Madeline would have been nice. I can't steal your name, though."

"I wouldn't mind." I beamed.

The person behind the counter called Fiona's name. Our food was set on three food trays. Fiona asked for a fourth one. We waited with her, and offered to help her carry hers.

She giggled. "I had to convince my boyfriend to let me buy lunch. Sure as the rain, I can carry the food that I pay for, too."

"You're not married?" Lenore asked, her voice low.

"I'm sorry?" Fiona said.

I nudged Lenore. "Thanks again!" I said.

Fiona started on her way with a wave. "You're welcome. Have fun, ladies! It was nice meeting you."

Lenore and I found a table in the food court not far from where Fiona now sat. I watched as she set two trays down and separated the food. There was an aura about her, warm and serene and jolly. She was like the southern version of Molly Ringwald. Lenore, on the other hand, was already unwrapping her burger and had taken an obnoxiously loud sip of the milkshake.

"So you're going by your middle name now?" Lenore asked after her first bite of her burger.

"Strangers don't need to know my first name," I replied.

"She has the right. She paid for our lunch."

"Well, Madeline is still my name. So I didn't lie or anything."

"Fine, fine." Lenore waved her arm up in defeat and took another bite. "This is so good! Why aren't you eating? You were complaining about how you were starving like ten minutes ago."

I said nothing but ate a pair of fries before unraveling my burger.

A few more bites were mixed with hyping up for the party, slurping on milkshakes, and ruffling napkins on our hands. The food court was crowded. Entire families, complete with baby carriages, sat in the highly sought out food court booths. Other teenagers were gathered at tables, some of them standing, talking and laughing loudly. I spotted a table with four men in business suits munching away on ninja fries and pizza slices talking about stock shares or something. I tried listening to all the conversations and sounds. A booth crowded tight with high schoolers gossiped about homecoming dance rumors and bickered about whose sneakers were "phatter." I tuned in on a kid talking breathlessly about some Playstation game I had just heard Yaden raving about the other day.

"Oh, hey," Lenore interrupted. "I meant to ask you if you wanted to practice with Mom soon. She's been asking about you."

It had been almost two weeks since I'd practiced poetry with Miss Karen. That was also the last time I'd seen Eva. I looked at Lenore, wondering if Eva was listening to me now. How much of Lenore was Eva aware of?

"I guess I've just been practicing alone," I said.

"You shouldn't. At least, not a lot. You're still new. You need someone to practice with."

"I know."

"Are you still scared?"

"A little." *A lot, actually.*

"Come over tonight! Mom has some great poems to teach you, and they're easy to learn."

"Okay." I said, unsure what else to say. I took a handful of ninja fries, the cheddar cheese strung along stubbornly.

"So have I ever told you my theory? On the circle of life?" she asked.

"You have a theory?" I joked.

"I have a bunch of them." She playfully poked my foot with hers under the table. "You're not the only smart kid in the seventh grade."

"If you think I'm smart, you haven't seen my math grades lately." I sucked at Pre-Algebra—I'd been getting B's and C's all semester.

"You know what I think?" Lenore said. "I think people die. They all die. And then they decompose."

I held my burger at arm's length. "Perfect mealtime conversation," I said.

She ignored me and pressed on. "When they decompose, that gets into the dirt, you know? And then! It gets into our plants and vegetables, like our potatoes." She held up a ninja fry, wagging it like it was part of a presentation. "And then it gets in our blood and it becomes us. *And then!* We get older, and we have babies—and those parts of the people that died are, like, *infused* with all the babies, right? So what if someone died and were cremated and their ashes found their way into a garden or a farm where your Mom ate something from and then she had you? We're all just recycled dirt, you know?"

"Are you sure this is an original, umm—*theory*?" I asked.

Lenore's wide eyes collapsed to a dull flutter of blinks. "Well, no, but still."

I laughed. "What made you think to tell me this?"

"I've always thought about it," she said. "But that pregnant lady? Part of you could be in that little munchkin in her tummy. Which, by the way, I never want to be a mom. Or a wife. I don't like dealing with boys, let alone babies. Yuck. So glad I don't have a little sister."

I cringed and took another bite of my food.

I looked over at Fiona. And that was when I saw *him*. I dropped my burger, and what was left fell into a sloppy mess of a pile.

"Edith?" Lenore said. "What's wrong?"

There he was. My Dad. And he had just kissed Fiona. Right on her lips.

Lenore shook me out of my stare, calling my name. I took her with a tight grip and swung her in front of me. "Shut up," I said through my teeth. "You'll make a scene."

"You're the one making a scene right now," Lenore said. "And you're getting grease all over my hoodie."

I let go, and then pulled my beanie as far down my face as possible. I whispered to Lenore to look over to Fiona.

She glanced over her shoulder. Then, she spun her head back to me, squealing out the F word.

"What do I do?" I said, tears welling in my eyes and a hot fury swelling at the back of my neck.

"Calm down first," Lenore said. She put her hands firm at my face and tilted my head to look up at her. "We don't want him to see you. Right?"

"I don't know," I said. I leaned over to try and see them. Was it really him, or had I accidentally cast an intrinsic poem that put illusions in my mind?

But then, I heard his laugh. His distinctly peppy, rumbling chuckle boomed from across the food court. I hadn't heard that laugh in a long time.

"Let's go," Lenore said.

"No, I have to stay!"

"And do what? Say hi?"

"No," I said. "I have to know where they're going."

"I thought you didn't care about him anymore?"

I looked up at Lenore. I didn't care about him. But I wanted to know if he still cared about me, and Mom and Cannoli and Yaden.

I stood and took a step past Lenore before she grabbed me by my arm and swung me back to the table. "You want to know where they're going?"

I nodded, looking past her.

Lenore went into her pocket and pulled out a charm. It was shaped almost like an arrowhead, bronze with a tail of blue feathers threaded at the ring.

"What is that?" I asked.

"I'll explain later," Lenore said. "Take our bags and sit by the bench at the record store over there. I'm going to give this to them."

"What? No!" I said, gripping her by her sleeves.

"Yes," she said, pulling away from me. Then, she grabbed my beanie, put it on her head and pulled it down to her eyebrows. "Now grab our stuff and go. And keep your head down."

I gave in and did as she said. I looked over my shoulder as I was walking to the record store, and bumped into a man and nearly fell. "Watch where you're walking, little girl!" I apologized, then walked faster to the bench and sat down, watching Lenore from afar.

She walked over to their table and tossed the charm in one of their shopping bags. Dad looked up when she did, and he called out to her. She walked away with brisk steps. Dad called again. He stood up, the chair sliding against the floor. The sound launched Lenore into a dash.

I shot up from the bench and grabbed our bags. Dad was walking towards her, calling out. "Hey! Hey! You dropped something!"

Dad was right there. And I was frozen as Lenore came near me. I hadn't seen his face in so long. I hadn't heard his voice. I was suddenly miserable with yearning that ached in my chest and my stomach.

"Let's go!" Lenore called. She grabbed at my arm and tugged as I fought to be still. "Come on, Edith!"

"Wait."

"No, we have to go."

He was coming through the food court.

Suddenly, I felt light, and before I could turn to look at Lenore, she pulled at me. Had she recited *Feather-footed* on me?

"Come on!"

"No!"

But her pull was too much. For a moment, I was floating. I wished I was invisible again because it would cause a stir if people saw that I was floating an inch off the ground. I stomped my feet down and stumbled into a run as Lenore kept pulling at me. We were heading straight for the escalators, right towards the exit. I turned to look one last time.

Our eyes met. I was certain the way he looked at me that he knew it was me. I felt cold all over. He was still and we didn't take our eyes off each other until we were out of sight. He didn't chase after me. I didn't try to snatch myself away from Lenore's mighty grip.

Up the escalators we ran, bumping into an older woman halfway up. Lenore apologized. We went through the exit doors, and Lenore didn't let go of me until we got to the bus stop. The bus had arrived just as we did.

I fought to hold it together. Lenore and I didn't say a word for the entire ride home. I wasn't sure that I could speak. Was that baby his? My half-sister? My stomach lurched at the thought. How could he have done that to Mom? To us?

By the time we got to Lenore's house, I couldn't hold it in anymore. I collapsed into a vicious cry right on her porch. I heaved and sobbed like I'd never done before. Lenore lay beside me. The floorboards were cold against my arms and legs. She pulled away the strands of hair that clung to my face.

"Why doesn't anybody love me?" I cried.

"Stop," Lenore said.

"No," I shouted. "No one loves me. Not my Dad. Not Nemo. Everybody hates me."

"I don't hate you," she said.

"You should. Julie does. She's your friend, right? You should be on her side, not mine."

"Edith."

"Yaden hates me."

"Your brother does not hate you."

"Yes he does. That's why he's going away for college. He doesn't want to have to deal with me." I got into a coughing fit between my sobs. "Dad didn't even come after me."

"He saw you?" Lenore asked.

I nodded.

"Damn it. I'm sorry. If it makes you feel better, I don't hate you. I love you with every piece of my heart. And I promise I always will.

No matter what."

We sat on the stairs together and she put her arm around me and kissed me on my cheek. "You should stay over tonight. It's my turn to host a slumber party."

"Okay," I said, the last of my crying quivering out.

Lenore reached into her pocket and pulled out another one of the charms. "So this is a Locus Charm," she said. "I gave the other one to your Dad. When these charms get made, they are broken in half and then enchanted with a poem that attracts the two together. Using another poem, you could find the other half of the charm. We can find your Dad. But only when you're ready. When you are, I'll teach you the poem."

I was far from ready. I wanted to scream. I wanted to kick and break things. I wanted to shatter lamps and bang skillets until I dented the iron. I'd rip every music sheet and break every key on that God-forsaken piano if I went home.

He wasn't coming home anymore because he had Coral—the little girl he'd *never* leave.

25

Monday came and went quickly. I daydreamed the whole day away with thoughts about Dad and his new family. My memory had gotten stronger since I'd begun practicing poetry, because I kept seeing him kiss Fiona over and over again.

I asked Miss K if she would meet with me in the auditorium after school. I sat at the piano, playing chords to warm up while I waited. A few minutes after three, Miss K's shoes clicked and echoed in the quietness of the auditorium. She smiled at me as she came down the aisle, the curls of her sienna hair bouncing and her dress swaying back and forth. She was the youngest of the teachers at St. Vincent, and while she commanded respect among both faculty and students alike, she did so with the same kind of grace and elegance that she walked with. She felt more to me like an aunt or an older sister than a teacher.

She was everything I wanted to be when I grew up.

She sat down next to me at the bench. The song I had been

writing was open in front of us.

"Is this it?" she asked.

I nodded.

She narrowed her eyes as she read it. Then, she rested her hands on the first chord and proceeded to play through it fluidly. She hummed along with the keys.

"This is very good, Edith," she said after she'd gotten through the half the score.

"Thank you," I said. "I finished it last night." I had spent all of my Sunday writing it. It was the only thing that was going to make me feel any better.

"Can *you* play it for me?" she asked.

I played the song, flowing through it naturally. I'd been relentless in learning the song after I'd finished writing it. I hadn't gotten up from the piano except for breakfast and dinner. Playing it felt like moving water from one glass to another. I was swimming in my own music.

"Do you think it needs something?" I asked.

She took a long breath and closed her eyes. "I don't know," she said. "It's beautiful. It's complex. I don't think I would add anything. You may find something on your own, but this is fantastic. You're going to make a great musician one day."

"I don't think I want to be a musician," I said. I'd only ever played because of Dad. Playing piano only seemed to fill a void with another lately. I played to get through sadness.

"Well, whatever you do, you have a gift. And I support you no matter what you do."

"Can I ask you something, Miss K?"

She nodded.

I leaned over, my head close to the keys as I whispered. "Do you believe in magic?"

Miss K chuckled, tilting her head back as if she were shifting all her thoughts and memories to the top of her head. "What if I told you that, once upon a time, I was a witch?"

I sat still, cold from shock. Her face was straight, absolved from sarcasm or wit. She looked at me with conviction.

"Are you kidding?" I asked.

"Do *you* believe in magic?"

"I do, but…"

"I'll believe in anything," she said. "I've never seen any sorcery in my life. And I've never cast a spell. But if you tell me you believe in something, I'm going to believe it, too."

"So you're not a witch?"

"No," she laughed. "But let me tell you something. We grow up and we forget how to believe in what we don't see. We can't imagine it anymore. Just think what it would be like if we could all imagine the way we did when we were little kids."

"I believe in a lot of things," she continued. "If you told me why you believe in something, and you can convince me that you feel something from that belief, then to me, and to you, it's true! What if I told you that I'm actually only eight years old?"

"That's not possible," I called out.

"Yes it is," she said. She danced her fingers along, tapping on eight keys. "I've only had eight birthdays."

"How?"

"I was born on February twenty-ninth. And I don't turn nine for another three years."

"Oh," I said. "Then what do you do when it's not a leap year?"

"I used to celebrate on the twenty-eighth, because my dad didn't want to have me wait an extra day for on March first."

"So technically you're younger than me?" I asked.

"Yes, we can say that," she said.

I felt safe with Miss K. I took one long breath and let it rise from the center of my chest. The sun from the windows warmed my back.

"I've been practicing piano by myself," I confessed.

"I thought your dad was helping you?"

"No," I said. "My parents are getting a divorce."

She covered her mouth with her hands. "Oh, goodness," she said, "Edith, I'm so sorry."

"It's okay," I said. I didn't want to talk about the details. "But I still need to practice with someone before the recital. I was hoping you could help me."

She pulled me close, squeezing my shoulder. "I'd love to be your piano teacher. We can practice after school whenever you want."

Miss K walked me out of the auditorium. She told me how proud she was of me and promised that she would be there for me whenever I needed her.

"I know divorce is hard," she said. "Just don't blame yourself for it, Edith. Being in love is complicated, and it only gets tougher the older you get."

As if on cue, I saw Nemo walked by and headed out the front doors. I wanted to catch up to him. We hadn't spoken in such a long time and I wanted to know how he was. I wanted to know how Julie was, too.

I thanked Miss K and left in a hurry. I flung through the doors, across the courtyard, past the parking lot. When I saw Nemo, I froze. If he turned right, he was going home. If he went left, he was heading to Julie's.

He went left. And so did I.

I let him gain enough distance from me so if he turned to look over his shoulders, he might not notice me. Or I'd at least be able to hide behind a tree or a car. But part of me wanted him to catch me. I'd be stuck with nowhere to run, and I'd have to confront him.

Deep down, I knew I still liked him. With us not spending time together, I missed him more and more. He was the only boy in St. Vincent that accepted me for who I was—smart, quirky, sometimes blunt. He was the first person I'd ever been attracted to.

When we arrived at Julie's house, I wanted to call out to him, but I knew he didn't have a clue that I was there the whole time.

Instead of going through the front door, Nemo went between the small alley next to the brownstone house and banged at the aluminum gate.

"Hey! Open up!" he called.

I watched from the alley entrance, peering out from behind the trash can by the neighboring house.

Julie came to the gate and unlocked it. I leaned over a bit more to see her better. When I did, a cat leapt from above and startled me. I yelped.

Gasping, I covered my mouth and hoped that the sound of my voice hadn't drawn Nemo and Julie's attention. I curled up close to the trash can and the cold brick wall of the house next door. The cat, cute and tiny with white spots on its mostly black fur, purred and meowed at me.

"What was that?" Julie whispered.

"Just that cat," Nemo said.

"No," Julie said. "The cat is sniffing at something. Someone is there."

"But—"

"Go check!" Julie said. I heard her lock the gate back.

As Nemo's footsteps approached, I tried to shoo the kitty away with my hands, but he was too curious. The cat walked closer to me, its cool, wet nose tipping my knees.

"Edith?" Nemo said.

The cat scurried away as I jumped to my feet. "Hey, Nemo." I glanced over at the gate. "Hi, Julie."

Nemo crossed his arms and knit his brows. "What are you doing here?" he asked.

"Nemo," Julie said through her teeth and mask. "Get her out of here. Tell her to go away."

I couldn't tell if she was looking at me or at Nemo through her mask.

"You know she doesn't like being around other people," Nemo whispered. "You have to go."

I swallowed. "I'm not leaving." I said it loud enough for Julie to hear.

"Yes, you are," he said.

"No, I'm not." I stepped past Nemo, bumping my shoulder into his and started for the gate. When I was a few paces away, Julie clasped the gate door tightly. She was about to swing it shut when Nemo pulled me back from my sweater. I fell, nearly onto my back, but Nemo caught me. His eyes widened when I looked up at him while in his arms. He helped me back to my feet.

I faced Julie. "Do you want to be friends or not?"

"I never wanted to be your friend," Julie said.

"No? Not even when we skipped rocks at the creek? The day you got hurt?"

"Only because..." she trailed off, looking past me at Nemo. I filled in the blank in my head: *only because Nemo told you to?*

This was no time for pride. I didn't want to fuel hatred anymore. I walked up to her. She backed away. She went to slam the gate door shut, but I dove and shoved it back open before she could lock it. She stumbled back and fell on her butt. Nemo came into the backyard right behind me, grabbing my arm.

"She doesn't want to see anyone!" he said to me.

"I don't care!" I shouted at him. My voice bounced between the houses and down the alley. I turned to Julie and lent my hand. She was reluctant to take it. She grunted, clutched her hand in mine, and I pulled her up.

"I'm here to help," I said to her. "I have a way."

"Help how?" Julie asked. "You know a doctor or something?"

"No, not really," I said.

"Then, what? You know, I've had four surgeries the past month and none of them have *helped*."

"I'm sorry," I said.

"Why do you care?" she asked. "Only reason why you give a shit is because you're still mad that Nemo's my boyfriend and—"

"Julie, shut up," I yelled. "I'm being serious. You want your face back to normal?"

She was silent. I could see her narrow her eyes through the mask.

"I have a way, and I need you to believe in me," I said. "Otherwise, it's not going to work."

I glanced at Nemo over my shoulder. I hoped he wasn't piecing things together to fill in the blanks. I hoped he didn't find it strange that I was trying to come to Julie's rescue, as if I had something to do with it.

"Don't fucking joke like that, Solstice," she snarled as she got in my face. Last time she was that close, I punched her.

"This isn't funny," Nemo said.

"Close the gate," I told him.

"You have to go."

I stomped my feet. "Close the fucking gate!"

I'm going to need a few Hail Mary's for that one. And once it left my mouth, I felt like a fool. *If you're going to cuss, at least try to sound cool and drop the g at the end.* I sucked at cussing. I didn't even like to say the word *cussing.* It's *cursing.*

Nemo closed and locked the gate. Then, I told them we should go inside. We went through the backdoor and into the kitchen. Julie said her Mom and Dad wouldn't be home for about another hour.

I took two bowls from the cabinet and filled one of them with warm water. I placed them on her dining room table.

Nemo and Julie stood on either side of me.

"What the hell, are you trying to baptize me?" Julie asked. "You think just because you're all Catholic and learning about Confirmation that you've got the hands of God?"

I tried to be as calm as I could. I shut my eyes and held out my hands like I was stretching forward. Should I be doing this? I bet there were rules about a witch showing poetry to normal people—or whatever the proper word was for non-witches. Maybe the rules were in one of the *Collateral Art* books. But right then, I didn't care about the rules. Anxiety pulled at my insides and I felt nauseous. My face blushed bright cherry.

"What I'm about to do," I said, first looking at Nemo, and then Julie, "you can't tell anyone, okay? If you do, then—well, it can go badly for you." I imagined I could make up all sorts of things if I showed them I was a witch. I could make false threats about losing their voices if they told someone my secret, or that I'd cast a curse on them so that they'd have nightmares every night for the next seven years.

Julie shrugged her shoulders. She was not into this at all.

For a moment, I wanted to know what her face looked like underneath the mask. Was it still fleshy in some parts? Was her skin scarred? Did she have stitches on her cheeks and her chin and under her eyes? Did it still hurt?

I thought of a song in my head. The first thing that came to mind was *Masquerade Waltz* by Aram Khachaturian. I closed my eyes and wiggled my fingers and toes. My heart throbbed like a dancing metronome. Between the instruments playing in my head, I heard the swishing and swirling of water. It was as pronounced as the sea. I could feel the water and its warmth even though I wasn't touching it. I lifted it with my hands, and I opened my eyes. The water hovered above the bowl in a perfect sphere.

"Edith?" Julie said.

"It's okay," I said softly. I smiled at the sphere. Somehow, I sensed kindness from the water. I moved the sphere above our heads, first over mine, and then at Julie, and finally at Nemo. His mouth gaped open, and I let a few droplets fall down. He recoiled as the water hit his tongue, as if he had swallowed a bug.

Julie laughed. My head swiveled to her when she did. I couldn't believe it. I made Julie laugh.

"Do you want to touch the water?" I asked her.

"Can I?" she said. "How are you…"

"Don't ask," I said. "Just believe." I moved the sphere in front of her. She eased her hands closer and closer to the water. She poked the sphere with her index fingers. She flinched as the structure of it broke for a moment, and drops trickled down the back of her hands. I moved it away from her and gently placed it into the other bowl. Then, I shifted them back and forth from one bowl to the other, before I split the water into both bowls.

Nemo and Julie were speechless.

"I can help you, Julie," I said. "Do you believe me now?"

"Am I dreaming or something?" Julie put her hands into the water in the bowls. She splashed it a little. Then, she lifted one of the bowls and looked under it. She knelt and glanced under the table. Then, she looked at Nemo.

"Are you in on this?" she asked him.

He threw his hands up in the air. "No," he said.

"I had a hard time believing it, too," I said. "But it's true. I'm a witch. And you can't tell anyone, or else."

"Or else what?" Julie asked.

"Trust me," I said. "You don't want to find out."

Julie laughed mockingly until the stern look I gave her seemed to settle her. Her laugh turned into a nervous fit of giggles, and eventually, hiccups. She sat down in the chair. Those giggles and hiccups turned into a quiet sob as she buried her head in her arms on the table.

I was afraid of what I'd done— frightened by the idea that rumors would spread about me. What if everyone in St. Vincent found out I was a witch? Could there be some kind of witch hunt? I wanted to believe that no one else would believe in it. I hoped Miss K was right about how people lose their imagination, and that all the kids could never believe in such a thing like me being a witch.

As much as I wanted to help Julie, I was unnerved. I could fail. I could make this worse. I might hurt Lenore, too.

I put my hand on Julie's shoulder. I decided none of that mattered anymore.

"Do you want my help?" I asked her.

"Yes."

26

Two days later, I was on my way back to visit Esmeralda. I walked to her place through a nasty storm. The wind snapped my umbrella inside out and it broke when I tried to fix it. I *Feather-footed* when no one was looking; I didn't want to get completely soaked on the way, and the thunder clapped so loud and close that I had to hurry inside.

Esmeralda rushed me in through the front door and dried my clothes with a pair of logicals. She lit a small blue ember that hovered above me. Then, she stirred the air around me, like a warm whirlwind. I had trouble staying on my feet as the wind grew vigorous, but within a minute or two, my clothes were dry—all the way down to my socks. I thanked her.

"You know," she said, her voice low and raspy, "I didn't expect to see you back so soon."

I had thought many times about turning back around when I was caught in the rain. But each time I did, I remembered that I had made promises. I was going to help Eva and Julie, and I had a contract with Esmeralda. Mom always told me that when you made promises with someone, you have to keep them.

"I'm ready for this," I said.

"Great," Esmeralda said. "Shall we go to my shrine?"

I followed her upstairs. In the hallway, she pulled the attic stairs down and we made our way up. I was shaky as I climbed.

The attic was dusty and muggy. The ceiling was low and the space was bare, except for a large blanket on the floor and a small set of shelves far back in the corner. Esmeralda took a large jar from one of those shelves and made a moat of sand around the blanket. The grains shimmered silver.

I stepped over the circle and sat on the blanket while Esmeralda went deeper into the attic. She'd fallen so deeply into the shadows that I couldn't see her.

Was there something I should be doing? Should I be meditating or preparing with a mental chant? I closed my eyes and pretended to be doing all of the above. After a while though, I peeked one eye open slowly.

Esmeralda made her way back toward me. She was holding her cat Kim Chi in one hand and an empty jar in the other. She sat the jar down and held Kim Chi, stroking his hair and rubbing his head.

"You are brave, Edith," she said. "I've never known such a young child willing to learn such an advanced poem to help her friends."

Kim Chi's eyes blinked long and wearily as he dug his paws into her arm.

"Thank you," I said.

"Kim Chi has all nine lives, so it'll be okay to practice with him," she continued. "You're going to extract one of his lives. You won't *kill* him, you'll just take one of his lives out as pure energy and trap it into this jar. I hope you don't have homework tonight, because this is an exhausting recital of poems. Not even a healing poem will help you. You'll be tired for a few days."

"Is it hard to do?" I asked.

"Yes," she said. "And it's dangerous."

"What happens if I get it wrong?"

"Kim Chi might lose one of his lives."

"What happens if I get it wrong with Lenore?" She didn't have nine lives.

"If you fail, you may end up losing one of the girls' souls. Or worse, you might kill one of them."

I put my hand over my mouth. I'd gotten queasy fast.

"And I'm sorry," Esmeralda said, "but if you don't come back with the soul of Eva, then the contract is voided. And that won't go well for you."

"What do you mean?" I said, my lips quivering and my hands trembling.

"Just don't fail, Edith. Do as I say, and you'll have nothing to worry about."

I was twisted in knots like a shoelace strapped too tight for my tiny feet. My eyes fixed on Kim Chi. It gave me an ounce of comfort looking at this canny sage of a cat. Most of his life had been an accident. He wasn't supposed to be alive. How long would he live on for? Would he feel any different when I took one of his lives away? Was I going to get it right? If not, Julie would end up stuck the way she was forever. And I'd have killed Lenore.

Killed.

There was no other way to make things normal again. I couldn't fail.

Kim Chi paced about the circle as Esmeralda talked about extracting a soul. The first poem would be *Silence Echo*. It would trap energy in the space and it had to be cast with enough thought and feeling for it to last for a while. Then, there was a second poem called *Awake*. It was a poem that forced another person to fall into a state of lull—kind of like sleep-walking. Originally, it was a poem that balanced energy within a person's body, but Esmeralda said she had modified the poem to make it balance Lenore and Eva's souls. The third poem, *Vigor*, would strengthen the soul that was to be extracted. The fourth and final poem, *Extraction*, would pull the most pronounced soul from the body. That's when I'd have to capture Eva.

This was going to take a while. I should have called home and told Yaden that I was staying over at Lenore's until the rain calmed down. The thunder and lightning boomed and flashed and I could feel the rumble in the floor.

Kim Chi came close to me and rubbed the side of his face against my knees. I pet him to hold his attention as Esmeralda finished explaining the poems I had to recite. I was having second thoughts again.

"Do as I say," she said, "and feel as I do."

Esmeralda held her arms out straight and her palms open. I did the same. Her eyes were closed and her head tilted back. I repeated the words after her:

> *My heart's blood flows like the sea*
> *With all the things that have tided me*

Troubles and whim and vigorous winds,
Seal into a case, these rambunctious vims.

A faint aura of light circled around her hands. When I said the last line, the same thing happened to me. The light was warm and it tickled my palms as it swirled.

"Think of the fear of running out of air," she said, "and imagine that all the energy you're trapping is the air you need to breathe. Create claustrophobia. And then fix it."

I felt the air go thin and I began to take longer breaths. My panic grew and I felt energy seeping out of my body like a cold sweat.

"The room feels tighter," she said. "You did it."

I choked a little when I tried to speak. "But Lenore's going to notice this."

"Don't worry, she won't know that it was you," Esmeralda said. "Now, try to relax. Let's go right into the next poem while you still have the energy. You'll have to recite these poems within a small amount of time. You're a young witch. This is going to burn you out very quickly."

She took in a long breath, like it was nothing for her to be caught in this thin air. Maybe that came with age—and practice. She recited another poem:

To be awake and to be asleep
To be between
To be everything
To be nothing
All at once

To be awake and to be asleep.

I repeated it, and once I finally got it right, she told me to repeat it in reverse. I had to say this poem twice.

"These are the words we witches use to describe the moment between being awake and falling asleep. Think of that moment when you recite the poem, and be sure to be looking at your subject when you do. You're going to lull them into that state, and they'll be suspended there for a time. This is an excellent poem to learn when you want to swoon an enemy."

An enemy? I hoped I never had enemies.

Kim Chi's eyes grew heavy with blinks and long stares. His pace slowed and he stumbled as he fought to stay upright.

I looked at Esmeralda. "Did I do it right?"

She nodded. "Now let's wait a minute or two. Tell me, Edith. Are you an artist?"

"I like to play piano," I said. "And I like to read and write. Does that make me an artist?"

"Yes, of course," she said with a smile. "Can you hear the music of his souls? The great thing about cats is that if you are good with sound, you can hear a symphony."

I listened. Soon, I heard a viola, a flute, and a xylophone. A bass cello hummed distantly. I closed my eyes to listen closer. An accordion grew louder and louder until it was the loudest of all the instruments.

"I hear it," I said.

"The one that's the loudest is his strongest soul," she said. "We're going to make it stronger."

She taught me the next poem:

> *The spirit of the body*
> *Sleeps in the dark*
> *And in its dim,*
> *I give it sunlight.*

I performed the chant and the accordion grew even louder. I stumbled over the words. If I messed this up, Kim Chi would be a little less immortal. If I messed up with Lenore, then she would be a lot less alive.

"Close your eyes," she said, "and get ready to extract."

> *Now rise, rise*
> *Above the chains*
> *Be free, free*
> *Away from pains.*

I felt something like silk at my fingertips. I opened my eyes and saw a long, glimmering white cloth hovering above my hands.

I held my breath. My heart thumped against my chest.

"Hold on to it," Esmeralda said.

"Is this…?" I asked.

Esmeralda smiled. I clasped it gently, running my fingers along its smoothness. I was holding pure life.

I admired its shimmering ivory glow. It was so bright that I had to squint my eyes to look at it. I still heard the accordion faintly in my head. I wondered if what I was hearing had come from a memory

Kim Chi had.

Then, as I was about to lift the life closer to my face, a screech burst as it shot from my grasp. Esmeralda grabbed the empty jar and opened the lid. The life flew into the air, but it bounced off an invisible wall. It soared over my head to another corner of the room, its sound a mixture of a shrill scream and an out-of-tune accordion on a skipping record. The cloth—the life—flung from corner to corner, fighting to get away.

Kim Chi had fallen asleep.

The life plummeted down to the floor towards Kim Chi. It hit my leg and I cried out from a stinging pain, growing cold all over.

"You need to carry it into the jar," Esmeralda said, "much like you would carry water. You are a pelagic witch, right?"

"I guess."

"And Karen taught you how to move water?"

I watched the life gliding above like it was a seagull waiting to dive and poke at my head. "Yes."

"Then move it, just like you would water, into the jar and seal it tight."

"It's too big to put into that jar!" I protested.

"No it isn't," Esmeralda said. "Trust me."

I waved my hands in the air until the life followed my movements. It was like moving water, but it was heavy and it resisted. I fought back, taking strength all the way from my gut. I felt it in my toes.

I jumped to my feet as I found control over its momentum. I governed it into a ball and carried it down to the jar, my arms burning against its weight. I stuffed it into the jar, leapt at it, and put the lid on as tightly as I could. The soul's screams became muffled.

I held on to my breath, staring at the soul in the jar. It was bright and it swirled like a dense white fog.

I laughed, rolling on the floor as I held the jar. I wasn't laughing because it was funny or that I was victorious in learning an advanced poem recital in one try. I was in disbelief. I was terrified. I was holding one of Kim Chi's lives.

I had gotten it right, but I felt like a thief. This life didn't belong to me.

27

Halloween was finally here. At last, a chance to take my mind off trying to save the whole freaking world.

When I put on my costume, I felt like a different person. I was Alice. I looked in the mirror squeezing my plush Cheshire Cat and twirling around. The dress whirled and bloomed wide with grace. Tonight was going to be my first party ever, and I couldn't wait.

Yaden knocked on my door and I let him in. He told me I looked adorable, and then pinched my cheeks. My face got hot and I pushed him away.

"But seriously, you do," he said after a laugh.

I looked at him with a broken smile. I hadn't told him about seeing Dad in the mall last Saturday. I had been dying to say something to him all week, but I was afraid of how he'd react. Sometimes not knowing the truth is better.

There was part of me that didn't want to hate Dad anymore. Hate had been sitting on my heart for months. It had come to me in aches and seeped through my hands with water hot enough to burn someone's face. It had made me a terrible person and forced me to keep secrets.

On the other hand, Yaden was a good man and our family was going to need him. I hugged him as tight as my arms could. "You're the best big brother ever," I whispered, resting my head on his chest.

"I know," he said through his laughter.

"Are you doing anything tonight?" I asked him.

"I'm playing *Nightmare Creatures*. That's how I'm celebrating Halloween. Bring me back some candy, and I'll let you play when you get back."

"I'm not going trick-or-treating."

"You're not?"

"Nope! I'm going to a party."

"Does Mom know this?"

"Duh."

"You're lying," he said. "Mom!" Yaden went to the top of the stairs and shouted down to her. "You know Edith is going to a party?"

"Yes, Yaden," she called.

He lingered there for a moment, saying nothing, then came back to my room, giving me a look. "I bet you think you're cool."

"Cooler than you," I said, hitting him on his arm with my Cheshire Cat. "I'm not the one staying at home playing video games like a nerd."

"You're dressed up as Alice in Wonderland. You're a nerd, too."

"Shut up!"

"Just don't kiss any boys tonight. Or any night. Not until you're eighteen. And no drinking! Not even any soda or punch. You can't trust kids these days."

"I don't drink soda," I said, turning away to hide my face. I was flushed red and fighting a shy smile. I wondered if Nemo was going to be at the party. It would be nice to see him. He'd like my costume. I thought about how nice it would be to have had my first kiss on Halloween.

I went downstairs with Yaden. Mom insisted on taking pictures with her disposable camera. She took one of me at the bottom of the stairs. Then, she paired me with Yaden, and then with Cannoli, who had dressed up as a witch. It was Cannoli's idea, and she said I was her inspiration. She was excited about going trick-or-treating with Mom, who wore all green and a pair of wings and called herself Tinkerbell.

Lenore arrived with Miss Karen a few minutes later. She looked pretty as Dorothy Gale. Her hair was tied in pigtails with blue bows and she carried a willow basket that was filled with candy and her plush Toto. Yaden took two pieces of candy from her, while Cannoli grabbed two handfuls. Halloween was her favorite holiday, too.

Mom and Miss Karen took more pictures of us all together. Both Mom and Miss Karen got teary eyed when it was time for us to go.

"Look at our daughters, Anita," Miss Karen said. "Aren't they something?"

"They look like twins," Yaden said.

"That's because we are," I said.

Miss Karen dropped us off at Jesse's house. She gave us the *be on your best behavior* speech before we left the car, but only half-heartedly.

She laughed at the end of her bit and told us to have as much fun as we could. Miss Karen worried about us much less than Mom did. She must have been confident that we were smart, young witches who could use poetry to keep ourselves safe.

Out on the lawn, we were greeted by a scarecrow and a murder of fake crows that flapped their wings and cawed at the front steps. Rows of illuminated pumpkins dotted the porch.

Jesse answered the door. "Lenore! I didn't think you'd come!" He was dressed like Superman.

"Of course," she said. "And I brought Edith with me."

"Whassup, yo?" he said, offering his hand for a shake. I wasn't sure if I was supposed to give him a normal handshake or one of the ones that all the cool kids did that ended in a hug.

"Hi," I said. I decided to give him a classic handshake.

"Come on in," he said, stepping aside.

Inside, music blared from a stereo with large, booming speakers. A few kids were gathered there, clamoring about which CD they should put on next. A furry lion walked by me, saying "'sup Edith?" but I couldn't tell who it was. I said hello with an awkward wave and a crooked smile. Someone was dressed as the Pink Power Ranger, complete with the helmet. She was in a circle that included a boy in a suit with a green mask and a girl pirate. I didn't know any of these people.

"Lenore?" I said, tugging at her shoulder and pulling her close. I whispered, "are these all eighth graders?"

"No," she said. "Some of them are ninth graders. Jesse has a lot of friends at Ave Maria."

The excitement I had slumped into nervousness. I followed her and Jesse into the kitchen. She let out a shriek and jumped into the embrace of a boy dressed as Super Mario. Then, she hugged the boy dressed as Luigi right next to him. I recognized Luigi—that was Emanuel from the baseball team. I watched the three of them chat from the other side of the kitchen until Lenore turned and realized I wasn't beside her. She pulled me over and introduced me to her friends.

"Good to see you again," Emanuel said. He had a slight accent that was African but I couldn't place exactly where.

"Where are you from?" I asked bluntly.

"Philadelphia," he laughed.

"No, where are you from?"

"Eritrea. You know where that is?" he said.

"No."

"I'll get a map one day, and I'll show you."

"Okay," I said. I hoped he didn't think I was an ignorant little white girl who had no idea other kinds of people who didn't look like me walked the earth. He smiled at me, though. And as if on cue, the music stopped and a new song played. The kids around the stereo shouted, "seriously? Celine Dion?"

Lenore and her friends were talking baseball. I didn't understand much. I just wanted to find a wall to lean against, but there were kids everywhere.

I drifted into the backyard. A group of kids turned their heads toward me when they heard the backdoor shut loudly behind me. They stared at me with their brows knit and their eyes narrowed. I froze.

I recognized one of the boys: Fred King, a boy in my social

studies class who didn't speak much and always wore black on dress down days. He wasn't dressed much differently today: he wore loose-fitting black goth trousers with silver chains hanging from them, a red headscarf in his back pocket, and a bandana with an engraved silver plate. He normally wore glasses and had freckles and looked unassuming and unthreatening in class. But there, he looked like a punk rock hoodlum.

"What's up?" he asked, his nostrils flared.

"I—nothing," I said.

"You should peace out," he said with a nod. The other four boys stared at me in stoic agreement.

"What are you doing?" I took a few steps over to them.

"Go back inside, Edith," he said firmly.

I looked past him and saw plastic bags filled with something that was greenish-brown that resembled oregano or basil leaves. Fred shifted in front of my face and extended his arms.

"Fine," I said. I backed away but when I turned around, Lenore and her baseball buddies were coming outside.

"Hey," Jesse said, walking past me towards the group of boys. "What have we here? Enough for everybody I hope."

"We might," said a boy dressed as a ninja. He wore a curly ginger afro wig.

"It's my party, Jew-jitsu," Jesse said. "Which means you're sharing, right?"

Fred stood aside. The ginger afro ninja held what looked like a handmade cigarette. Another boy, dressed like Duffman from *The Simpsons*, took a can from his belt and tossed it at Jesse.

"You were going to hide all the beer and weed from me?" Jesse laughed. "Jerks."

The group of boys and Lenore and her friends got into a circle. I didn't want any part of this. I tapped Lenore on her shoulder.

"Can we go inside?" I asked.

"Yeah," she said. "In a second."

"No," I whispered. "Now. We aren't supposed to be doing this."

"I'm only going to have a little," she said. "You don't have to."

"I can't believe you!" I said.

"It's a party, Edith," she said. "What did you expect?"

Something a little more wholesome. Maybe some candy and some scary stories over a fire. But not that. I couldn't believe Lenore, of all people, was in line for drugs and alcohol. I stared at Lenore as the kids passed around a joint. I was so upset at her that I was shaking. I wanted to pull her away. When the joint came to her, she took a long drag and blew smoke into the sky. I thought she'd leave the circle after that. Nope.

I went back inside and walked through the kitchen and to the living room, past more kids I didn't know all dressed up. I wished I could've left and gone back home. But I was on another side of the city. And it was dark out. Halloween suddenly got a little frightening. I sat at the stairs, my head against the banister. I hoped no one spotted me as I turned into a wallflower cuddling with her plush Cheshire Cat.

I watched the kids in the living room. There were about a dozen of them dancing and chatting and laughing. These kids couldn't dance. I chuckled when one of them fell, stumbling on the robe of his vampire costume. Watching the party was more fun than being in it.

A few songs later, Lenore and her friends came into the room.

They all jumped into the dance party, except Emanuel, who started up the stairs in a burst but stopped abruptly when he noticed me.

He smiled at me. "Hey."

"Hi," I said. I was nervous. I knew it was going to be hard for me to talk. I didn't have anything to say to anyone here, let alone the boy who I'd accidentally insulted. I clutched onto the Cheshire Cat, silently wishing him away.

He sat next to me. "You okay?"

"Yeah, just having a good time."

"Doesn't look like it," he said. "You've been hiding up here all this time?"

"They were smoking outside," I said. "I don't do that."

"Oh, right on. You're a smart girl. Don't ever start," he said.

"But you did it?"

"Only a little. It makes things more fun. That's all. I only ever do it at parties."

"You go to a lot of parties?" I asked.

"Not really," he said. He gazed into me. "I like your costume."

"Thank you."

"So how do you like St. Vincent?" he asked.

"It's okay," I said.

He asked a million more questions, like what my favorite food was, where *I* was from, and if I really liked the music they were playing. I didn't even know who it was, and when I guessed Wu-Tang, he laughed at me. I blushed.

"Not even close," he said. "It's A Tribe Called Quest."

"I don't really listen to rap."

"What do you listen to?"

I blushed more. "Jazz. Classical." I was such a nerd.

"That's great," he said. "You play anything?"

I lit up a little. "Piano."

"That's dope," he said. "Was it hard to learn?"

"Not really." I fixed my posture. "It's just a lot of practice. I have my first recital soon. On Christmas Eve." Why was I telling him all this?

"That's really cool," he said. "A cute girl who plays piano."

I laughed. "Umm, no, I'm not cute."

"I'll have to go to your recital."

"That'd be cool, I guess. I mean, you don't have to…So how do *you* like St. Vincent?"

"Oh, I don't go to St. Vincent," he said. "I'm at Ave Maria."

My heart skipped. "That's a high school." I didn't mean to say it out loud.

"Yeah, it is," he said with a chuckle.

"Oh, well, I should catch up with Lenore," I said as I stood up. I tucked a strand of hair behind my ear. "It was nice talking to you."

"You're leaving because I'm a high schooler?"

"No," I said.

"Okay, well if you find yourself at the stereo picking out a song, come find me." He put his hand on my shoulder, smiled and winked at me. "I'll help you pick a good one."

I nodded and tried to smile back at him, but what I made on my face instead was broken, anxious and awkward. He was charming, but I didn't know how to act being hit on by a ninth grader.

He went up the stairs and I made my way back to the living room. I scurried to Lenore.

"You're not high, are you?" I asked.

"What? No way," Lenore said with a laugh. "I had like one toke. I felt bad."

"Why?"

"Because I shouldn't have done it, not if you weren't going to."

One of the kids switched on some uptempo house music. Lenore took my hands and started dancing. I cringed as I tried to move along with her. I was afraid I'd step on someone's toes. I couldn't follow the beat.

She laughed at me. "You're a horrible dancer," she said.

The party had died down. I'd lost track of time. A few kids were left playing video games. A pair of kids were sitting on the couch, holding hands and their faces close to one another. The boy was laying on the sweet nothings thick—I could tell by the way the girl giggled and blushed and playfully shoved him away. For a long moment, I was mesmerized by them, looking at them from afar. I felt a weird mixture of disgust and envy.

Lenore came up next to me and gave me a nudge. "Come on," she said, taking my hand.

We went through the kitchen, where Jesse mingled with his older friends. They were drinking out of red cups. Emanuel was there. He looked at me, beaming.

"Hey, you two," he said, "come here. Have a drink."

"No, thank you," Lenore said. "We're going outside for a bit. We'll catch you in a second."

He looked at me while Lenore spoke. "Alright. We're playing Truth or Dare soon. Don't be too long."

Truth or Dare? I panicked.

"We'll be there," Lenore said. She pulled me along and we went out the backdoor. No one else was back there.

"You want to practice?" Lenore asked. "It's really humid. We can probably make rain."

Lenore made sure the backdoor from the kitchen was shut tight. She pulled up her sleeves, closed her eyes, and took a long deep breath. She told me to do the same.

"Then, try to feel the vapor in the air," she said. "Breathe it in, and then imagine the vapor trickling down your arm, underneath your skin, all the way to your fingertips. You'll feel a tinge at you elbows if you're doing it right."

I did what she said.

"Now, think of a cloud. A rain cloud. If you want a lot of rain, think of the scariest storm cloud you've ever seen."

That was easy. The storm I saw on the way to Esmeralda's made it look like the world was ending. As I thought of the clouds, I could faintly hear the party still happening inside.

Lenore shot her arm up sharply. A white bolt flashed from her hands. It exploded a few feet above, and with a rumble, a cloud that looked as soft and white as a feather pillow formed about ten feet above the ground.

I watched as it floated there above the garden. Then, a single droplet fell onto a flower petal. Another fell, then more, and soon, the cloud was pouring like a watering can. A smile blossomed on my face.

"I do this to water our flowers at home. Sometimes. Only really good witches can make rain when it's not humid."

I watched every drop with awe. Soon, the cloud separated and faded.

"Now you try," Lenore said.

Excited, I held my arm up, just like Lenore. Nothing happened. Lenore corrected me, telling me that I had to put my arm out with force, like I was trying to throw a ball as far as I could. I tried again, this time a little worried that I was going to mess up and throw a rain cloud into someone else's yard. I was terrible at throwing things.

The tinge at my elbows gathered into my hands as I threw my arms up. A bolt shot up a few feet above us, a little higher than where Lenore's had been. My arm fell numb and cold for as long as it took the cloud to take form. It was grey and thick and long. No raindrops fell, but something else did.

Lenore covered her mouth and muffled a shriek. My eyes widened as my mouth fell open. Snowflakes fell from the cloud. When they hit the ground, they flickered in various colors like a flashing rainbow, then melted.

"What did you do?" Lenore jumped. "How? How did you do that?"

"I don't..." I realized that I hadn't been thinking about rain. Instead, I was thinking about winter and the Christmas Eve Festival. About January and my thirteenth birthday, and how Lenore and I were born during a snow thunderstorm. I thought about how she was my best friend and how important she was to me.

Lenore and I touched the snow. Flakes fell into our open palms, and the colors were vibrant on our skin. I stuck my tongue out and tasted a snowflake. "It tastes like raspberries."

"Really?" Lenore said. She stuck out her tongue. "Mine tastes like butter pecan ice cream."

"Maybe all the snowflakes taste different. Like the different colors?"

"Edith, you just fused snow and ice cream together. Think about that!"

We tried to taste more of the snow as it fell. We sampled vanilla, maple, strawberry, and cinnamon before the cloud floated up and faded.

"I've been practicing a poem where I can shoot stars," Lenore said once the last snowflake fell. "I suck at it though. I was hoping to have it down before tonight so I could show you."

"You can still try," I said.

She shook her hands and then took another deep breath. She looked up, scanning the sky, then waved her arms and pulled down like she was dragging something invisible to the ground. After a long pause, she forced her arms up, and a streak of light trailed out of her hands and burst like a firework above the house.

"That's not it," she said.

But I was impressed. "Try again," I urged.

"Maybe another time," she said. "It's hard making your own poetry."

"So those baseball friends of yours," I started, "do you like any of them?"

"They're cool."

"No. I mean, do you *like* any of them?"

She went through the motions of the shooting star poem again like she was only practicing. When she threw her arms up, nothing happened. "I—no, not really. Jesse tried to kiss me before the first game of the World Series. But I didn't let him."

"Why not?"

"Because," she said definitely.

"How come you don't talk about boys? I talk about Nemo all the time. And Emanuel said I was cute. I think he was hitting on me."

"It was kind of obvious," she said, turning away. "Are you going to go out with him or something?"

"Well, no," I said. "He's in high school."

"Good."

"Jesse seems nice. Maybe you should give him a chance."

"Edith," Lenore said. She'd given up on her poem. She turned and stared me, her eyes glossy.

"What's wrong?" I asked. She moved close to me and put her hand on the side of my face. She glanced over at the backdoor. It was still shut.

She swallowed before leaning her face up to mine, our noses touching. Her hands were firm and warm against my cheeks. She looked into me, her eyes crossed because she was so close. She breathed, and stared down towards my chin. Then, she firmly pressed her lips against mine.

It took a moment before I realized what was happening. The taste of her Dr Pepper lip gloss was in my mouth. I squealed and then pulled away.

"What are you doing?" I said sharply.

She stared at me. Her face flushed cherry-red. She wiped her lips with her hand. "I'm sorry, Edith. I—"

The door swung open, crashing loud as it banged against the outside wall of the house.

"Yo, are y'all crazy?" Jesse shouted. "It's cold out here. Come back in, we're going to play Truth or Dare now."

Lenore glanced at me before she abruptly scampered off. I tried to reach over and grab her arm, but she slipped away and bumped past Jesse.

"Lenore?" Jesse said. Then, he looked over at me. "The hell did you do?"

I ran after her.

Lenore hid in the bathroom for the rest of the party. I kept calling out and knocking at the door, begging her to unlock it and let me in. She wasn't responding, and when I put my ear against the door, I could hear her crying softly. Jesse arrived and tried to do the same thing, but Lenore remained silent. It was almost midnight, and I knew Miss Karen was going to be here soon. She was going to have to open the door eventually.

Other kids came up to see what all the noise was about.

"It's none of your business," I told all the kids whose names and faces I didn't recognize. They were reluctant, so I stomped my foot and raised my voice at them. "Get out of here!"

"What happened?" Jesse whispered to me.

"Nothing," I said. "Can you keep guard at the stairs or something? She's not going to come out if there's a bunch of people here gawking."

He nodded. I heard him announce that the party was over, and that everyone needed to call their parents and get on home. "Halloween is over. It's All Saints' Day now. You jerks need to go home and pray away your sins from tonight."

Groans and hisses erupted in a harmony of disappointment. I sat against the bathroom door.

"Lenore, your mom is going to be here any minute," I said. "Can you come out?"

Nothing.

"I'm going to wait here, whether you like it or not," I continued. "You can't stay in there forever."

Still, nothing. Other kids came up the stairs to use the bathroom. I told them that it was out of order and that I was guarding the door to make sure no one used it. One of them didn't buy it.

"Go pee in a bush somewhere, dork," I barked.

A few minutes after that kid left, I heard the door unlock. I leapt to my feet and waited to greet Lenore. When Lenore opened the door, her face was puffy with tears and her nose was snotty. She walked by me without a word. I followed her close, down the stairs and through the living room. She went outside, passing Jesse as she kept her head down.

Her willow basket was on the counter in the kitchen. I grabbed it and went to meet her outside. She was sitting on bottom of the front steps with her back to me. As I got nearer, she mumbled, "leave me alone, Edith."

I sat at the top of the steps and we waited until Miss Karen arrived. She drove up a few minutes later. Lenore wiped her face with her sleeve while Miss Karen parked.

"Did you ladies have fun?" she said as we got into the car.

"Yeah," Lenore said, masking her trembling voice with a high pitch and a smile.

I said nothing.

Neither of us said a word to each other on the ride home. Lenore talked about the party to Miss Karen like nothing had happened. She didn't mention the ninth graders, the beer or the marijuana. She said she had danced, but didn't say she had danced with me. She didn't tell Miss Karen that she had her first kiss.

Miss Karen dropped me off and she bid me good night. I thanked her, and then I told Lenore good night.

"Good night," she said glumly.

I got out of the car and immediately went to my room. I leapt into bed, not bothering to get out of my costume. I played the kiss over and over in my head until I fell asleep.

28

For three weeks, I was lost. November had come rushing in, the days going by too quick for me to get my footing. I prayed every night, asking God to slow time down. I was still acing all my tests and turning my homework in time. I was practicing piano nearly every day, either on my own or with Miss K, who met up with me after school on Tuesdays and Thursdays. But everything else was slipping away.

Yaden and Mom were working more. It was now my job to pick up Cannoli from day care after school. Often, I skipped lunch to save money so that Cannoli and I could get snacks at Manuel's Candy Shop. I skipped lunch, too, because it was hard being around Lenore. She hadn't spoken to me since the party.

Mom wondered where Lenore had been. I only told her that Lenore and I had a fight. I wanted to tell her everything that happened at the Halloween party but I curbed my tongue.

Some days I'd lingered at the phone, unsure if I should pick up and call Lenore. When I took the receiver, I would start to dial her number, but stop at the fifth or sixth digit and hang up.

On Mondays, Esmeralda and I practiced the extraction recital. I was getting good at the poems. By our second visit, I had them memorized by heart. I was more confident. If I could make snow and extract souls from kittens, then I was surely making progress.

The Monday before Thanksgiving, Esmeralda told me that there was no need for me to come practice the recital anymore.

"Why not?" I asked.

"There isn't any time left for you to practice. The new moon is this Saturday."

"So?"

"Your strength is at its peak during the new moon. You have to do it then. You're going to need that advantage."

Practicing on cats was easy. But it was when she told me about the new moon that I got nervous again. If I failed, Lenore could die by my hand.

"Can't I wait until the next new moon?" I asked.

"Eva is getting strong, and fast," she said. "I could tell when I saw Lenore. Eva's going to take over Lenore's body soon if you don't help."

So I had five days. Great.

The last day of school before Thanksgiving break, I went to Lenore's locker to say hello and she slammed her locker door shut, shot me a glare, and briskly walked away. Part of me was getting annoyed. Why was she doing this? "You can't keep this up forever," I shouted at her down the hall for everyone to hear.

She kept walking. I had three days.

That night, I waited by the phone again. Mom, Yaden and Cannoli were in the living room getting ready to watch *Planes, Trains, and Automobiles*, something we always did on Thanksgiving Eve. Yaden called out to me, "the movie is starting!" while I sat in the kitchen by the wall phone.

I dialed Lenore's number. The whole thing. And I let it ring. Once. Twice. Three times. Four.

Voice mail. My heart sank. I listened to half of the greeting before I reluctantly hung up.

Then, the phone rang again. I picked it up before it even rang one full time.

"Hello?" I said.

"Hi." It was a boy's voice. "Is Edith home?"

"Yeah—yes, she is. Who's calling?"

"It's Emanuel."

"What? How did you get my number?"

"A friend gave it to me. I hope that's cool."

I thought for a moment. I peered into the living room. They'd started the movie without me. "Yeah, it's cool. How—how are you?"

"I'm good," he said. "What's up with you?"

"Nothing," I said. "Just, umm, watching a movie with my family."

"Oh, I'm sorry, I called at a bad time," he said.

"No! Not at all," I blurted out. "It's fine. I've seen this movie a million times."

We spoke for another fifteen minutes or so. He asked me what my favorite movie was. *Sixteen Candles*, of course. Then, he asked what I liked about Thanksgiving and if I preferred turkey or Christmas ham. I asked him if Eritreans in America celebrated Thanksgiving. They did, but it wasn't a big deal. He said he gets more excited for football than he does for an enormous meal. His mom and dad always overcooked even though the rest of his family never came over on Thanksgiving. It was always just him, his brother and sister and his mom and dad. They preferred it that way.

"You sound like you're feeling down," he said.

"I'm sorry," I said.

"So you are?"

"A little." If only he knew the weight I was carrying on my shoulders.

"Can I tell you a joke?"

"Sure."

"Knock knock," he said.

I rolled my eyes. "Who's there?"

"Adore."

"Adore who?"

"A door is between me and you!"

I chuckled. "That was so bad."

"Isn't that the point?" he asked.

"I guess so."

"Can I tell you another?"

"Okay," I said. "One more and then I have to go."

"Alright. Knock knock."

"Who's there?"

"Needle."

"Needle who?"

"I'm going to need a little money when I take you out to the movies this Saturday."

"What?" It was like a punch to the gut.

"The movies. This Saturday. Would you like to go with me?"

"Emanuel, no," I stuttered. "I'm only in seventh grade. I can't go out on a date."

"You sure? Did you ask your parents yet?"

"You *just* asked me."

"Oh. No one has asked you on a date before?"

"Duh, I'm only thirteen," I lied.

"Then you should ask your parents."

"I'll think about it."

"I'll call you on Friday and see what you think," he said.

"Alright," I sighed.

"Cool. Well, Happy Thanksgiving."

"You, too."

And then I hung up. I was shaking all over. I leaned against the counter and took in what had just happened. A boy just asked me out. He came out from nowhere, and he asked me out. The more I thought about it, the dizzier I felt. Soon, I caught a short fit of laughter. I just got asked out. Someone *liked* me.

I went into the living room and sat next to Mom and Cannoli on the couch. Yaden was on the club chair playing his Game Boy Color, occasionally grabbing a handful of popcorn or laughing at John Candy. Cannoli would laugh when Yaden did, twice as hard. I looked at Mom and she smiled. We didn't have to say a word to each other, but I felt like I knew what she was thinking with that smile. She was happy because she had us with her, keeping a tradition that we had done since I was Cannoli's age.

Dad wasn't here, and for a moment, no matter how brief it might have been for her or me, that was okay. Maybe when the movie ended and all the snacks were gone and the yawns came, then we'd feel a hum or whisper in our guts that reminded us that we were without him.

When the movie ended and Mom started to put away the snacks, I noticed that she wasn't wearing her wedding ring. That's when that whisper rose in my belly, mingling with the brownies and spinach dip and cheese curls. Yeah, I missed Dad, but was it already time to start moving on? Missing someone doesn't bring them back home.

"Mom," I said when it was just her and me in the kitchen. "I saw Dad the other day. With a lady. She was pregnant and they kissed."

She let out a long sigh as she washed dishes. She asked me where and when and I told her the whole story.

"Did you know already?" I asked.

She shut off the water, dried her hands, and turned to me. "Yeah, Snowpea. I knew."

I hugged Mom. I didn't want to let go.

29

I couldn't bring myself to leave my house right away. I sat on the couch staring at the door in silence. It was a little bit past noon. My hands were folded over my lap as I tucked myself into the corner. I grew more and more afraid of what I was going to do. I was riding on an impulse, one that crashed into a wall as soon as it had started. But I knew I had to pick myself up.

Today was the day of the new moon.

Mom and Yaden were both at work and Cannoli was upstairs napping. I knew I shouldn't be leaving her alone, but I had to go see Lenore. I had to get her to come over. A phone call wasn't going to be enough. I had to *see* her.

I made sure the windows and the back door were all shut and locked before I walked to Lenore's house. I rang their doorbell and Miss Karen answered the door. She greeted me with a bright smile and hurried me in from the cold.

I had to make this quick.

"Where have you been?" she asked. "You haven't come over in a while now."

"I know," I said. "I've just been practicing—my recital—lately."

She clapped her hands together. "I'm excited about it. Are you nervous?"

"Yes," I said. "A little." I was more nervous about the recital I was about to perform on Lenore and Eva. I couldn't look at Miss Karen in the eyes. She was a mystery to me. I didn't know what she was ever thinking.

"Have you come to practice poetry?" she asked. "I have more pumpkin macarons, if you'd like."

"I just wanted to see Lenore," I said.

"She's out in the yard," she said.

I walked with Miss Karen through the kitchen to the backdoor. She opened the door and called out to Lenore.

"Someone's here to see you."

I peeked from behind Miss Karen. Lenore didn't see me at first, but when she noticed me, she narrowed her eyes and furrowed her brow. I moved past Miss Karen and said hello.

"I'll make some tea for you girls," Miss Karen said as she went back into the kitchen.

Lenore pulled her beanie down to her eyebrows. She stared at me for a long time without saying a word. I walked up to her with tiptoes crunching fallen leaves.

She took a step back when I got close. "What do you want?"

"To see you," I said. "I mean, we're still friends, right?"

Lenore had a baseball and a mitt, and a target drawn over a thick piece of wood that hung from the fence. She turned away from me, got into her pitcher's stance, and threw a pitch with a hefty grunt. The metal fence rattled and the ball popped up and bounced with a dull thud close to the rainbow assortment of flowers. When it came to a complete stop, Lenore held out her hand and the ball rolled to her feet. She picked it up and got into her stance and threw another pitch.

"Lenore," I said. "We're still friends, *right?*"

She rolled the ball back to herself. As she went to pick it up, I nudged past her and grabbed it.

Lenore shoved me a little. "Quit it," she snapped.

"We're still friends, right?" I said, as firmly as I held the baseball in my hand.

"You're so annoying right now," she said.

"I don't care," I said.

She lifted her open palm. The baseball moved in my hand, pulling towards Lenore like a magnet. I fought to hold on, squeezing it with both hands. I dove to the ground and curled up, holding the ball close to my stomach. She kept pulling and pulling, and it was spinning in my hands and burning my palms. I cringed and grit my teeth with a relentless grunt.

"Let go, Edith!" The ball stopped spinning as she knelt over me and pulled at my arms and my wrists. I squeezed it tighter, but Lenore was much stronger than me. She was winning. I lost my grip, and she snatched the ball away from me.

"That hurt," I said. I climbed to my feet and grasped my left wrist.

"You shouldn't have taken it from me."

"Why are you being such a bitch?" I spat.

Her mouth fell open, my hand rose halfway to my mouth. "I'm sorry," I said.

The way she looked at me was like she didn't recognize me. I turned away. My thoughts were beating me up, and it was cold and I wished I'd brought a bigger jacket. I wanted to run back home. Forget the extraction. Forget getting my best friend back. Forget trying to help Julie and Eva.

"I hate that you don't talk to me anymore," I said after a dreadfully long silence. "I don't know what I did."

"You didn't do anything," she said. She kicked through the leaves and stood beside me. "I was, I don't know — I was scared to talk to you."

"Why?" I asked.

She put her hands on her hips and tilted her head. "Really?"

I didn't say anything. I moved a strand of hair behind my ear and then winced when my wrist cramped with a shock of pain.

"You okay?" Lenore said as she took my wrist in her hand. "I'm sorry."

She closed her eyes and wrapped her hand around my wrist. I felt warmth coming from her, and that gentle healing viola hum whistled. The pain in my wrist faded.

"Thank you."

She let go of my wrist. When she did, I took her hand in mine. "Let's have a slumber party. Tonight. My house."

"You know we can't do that," she said. "Not anymore."

"Why not?"

Lenore let out a frustrated sigh. "Are you stupid? Did you forget what happened on Halloween?"

I said nothing, but I pleaded with the saddest eyes I could make. I fluttered my eyelids and frowned and everything. Lenore's eyes shifted as she thought to herself. "Fine."

At first I smiled, but then it faded like the sun behind a thick grey cloud. I broke out into a sweat and I pulled my hand away. It seemed the whole world had gone surreal. The flowers in that backyard were ingredients in healing a fever I had in my hands. Magic could burst out from my pores when I recited poems. I had hurt someone badly and I had kept it a secret. I had a best friend with two different souls in her body. And there was a chance I might make things worse.

I knew I could do this. I had to make things right.

"I'll see you tonight, then," I said. "I have to go."

"Bye, Edith," she said.

A smile flashed onto my face, then I turned and quickly went through the backdoor. Miss Karen was in the kitchen, pouring tea into three mugs.

"I'm sorry, I have to go now," I said as I stormed through the kitchen. I waved at her in passing.

I got home in a dash, and collapsed at the door once I was inside. The feelings in my stomach were tearing me in two. I wrapped my arms around my knees, closed my eyes and prayed. "I don't know how you feel about me being a witch. I know I don't like it. I don't know if this is a curse or if what I'm doing is a sin, but please, help me do this right. Help me keep Lenore alive, and punish me later if you have to."

"Edith?" Cannoli called from the top of the stairs. "I'm hungry. Can we have lunch now?"

30

Everything was going to be okay. This was going to be painless. Lenore would never have to have another seizure again. I would bring Julie back to normal, and then I could stop having nightmares about the fight night after night.

Time passed slowly. I watched as clouds passed by and the blue sky reddened into late afternoon. All of my earlier confidence unraveled. My threads—my heartstrings—were getting thin.

The doorbell rang.

I swallowed. The rigid silence I'd been hiding in was going to do me in. I realized I was more afraid of my own thoughts than I was reciting these poems. This was my chance for redemption, forgiveness, and contrition.

I leaped from my bed and peeped into Cannoli's room. She was sound asleep again, this time because I cast a strong sleeping poem on her. I didn't want her to be awake during the extraction.

I scurried downstairs. When I opened the door, there she was.

Lenore, her eyes chestnut and wide and wrinkled by the smile I'd come to miss.

"Were you sleeping?" she asked.

"I just didn't hear the doorbell at first. Did you ring it more than once?"

"Yeah, but it's cool," Lenore let herself in, taking off her shoes and coat before she made her way to the kitchen.

"Do you have a radio?" she asked as she peered into the refrigerator.

"Not in the fridge," I answered.

"I didn't think so," Lenore said. She pulled out milk and chocolate syrup and cookie dough ice cream. She seemed casual, as if nothing had happened between us at all the past month. It made me feel uneasy.

"What do you need a radio for?"

She poured milk and chocolate syrup into the blender. Then she added ambitious scoops of ice cream and then some ice. The blender screamed, and I flinched.

"I hoped you had a radio, but no problem. I brought my walkman. I wanted you to listen to Princess. They sound better with headphones anyway, so I guess that works out."

She took two tall glasses from the cupboard and poured the smooth, dense, swarthy milkshakes. She handed me one of the glasses.

"We can listen to them now, if you want," I said after a sip of the shake.

Lenore nodded. I looked at my glass as she left the kitchen ahead of me. I wasn't going to be able to stomach it, even though it was delicious.

She burst into my room and tossed her backpack onto my bed. She sat down, unzipped the bag, and dug through it.

I glanced over at my desk. My journal was out. I didn't want her to see the illustrations that had drawn on the pages for the extraction. While she searched her bag, I snagged the book. I looked around my room. My closet door was partly open. I threw the book in there and then slung a handful of clothes that were on the floor on top of it.

"No point in cleaning up," Lenore said as she untangled the earbud cord. "I've seen your room dirty before. I don't care."

I shut the closet door and let out a nervous chuckle. "True."

Lenore rejoiced when she straightened the cord. Something about her little triumphant hop made me smile. For weeks, Lenore had become a walking pile of gloom. At least, when she walked in my line of sight. Now, she was as radiant and warm as the sun. She had spun completely around, and that got me worried. Maybe she had spun too hard. Maybe she was only pretending to be cheerful. I couldn't help but wonder if she felt as anxious as I did.

"I'm just rewinding it now," she said. "I can't wait for you to hear this."

I sat next to her and she blushed and smiled at me. She handed an earbud to me.

"Ready for this?" she asked.

Yeah, I am. I think I am.

She pressed play and thumbed at the volume dial. A little static filled my ears before wind chimes crept in. A bell followed, bold and haunting but soothing all at once. Crisp hi hats sparked the metronome, and the rest of the percussion kicked in shortly after. A woman's silky voice started singing, like she was made for lullabies. Synth sounds backed her, rounding a full harmony.

Lenore was nodding her head with her eyes closed. She mouthed the words. I liked the song, too, but then the words to *Silence Echo*, the first poem, came to mind. If there was any time to get started, it was then. She was wrapped up in a sonic daydream.

I thought about the words to the poem in my head. I closed my eyes and repeated them a few times. When I opened my mouth to whisper them as softly and as quietly as I possibly could, a coldness spread through my body. Lenore had inched closer to me and her arm rubbed against mine.

My eyes shot open. She kept nodding her head and breathing the lyrics. The coldness turned warm. I didn't want to move. I might not have been able to move. I was scared. I was scared to recite the poem. And I was scared that I might have been leading Lenore on by letting her sit so close to me.

Not only did I have nightmares in my sleep about Julie, but when I was awake, I thought about the kiss. Every day. I had my first kiss on Halloween, just like I wanted, but not from who I expected. I admitted to myself that I actually liked it, even if I didn't react the right way towards Lenore when it happened. It was kind of romantic, I guess—kissing your best friend.

I shook my head. No more daydreams. If I delayed the extraction any longer, Cannoli might wake up from the sleeping poem, Yaden would get home, Mom would get home *early*, and then I'd be out of luck. I would have been all worked up only to chicken out. No more chickening out. I had to do this.

My heart's blood flows like the sea
With all the things that have tided me
Troubles and whim and vigorous winds,
Seal into a case, these rambunctious vims.

The air was tightening up. I'd said it all the right way. Step one was done.

"You like?" she asked after the first song came to an end. She hadn't heard me utter a word.

I nodded. "Mm-hmm. Yeah."

The next song faded in. "Do you remember what I told you when we went to the mall? My little theory?" Lenore asked.

"I remember," I said, winded.

"Well, sometimes I can see other people in people. Does that make sense? Like, I can see dead people or whatever in alive people."

I would believe anything by now. I gave her a gaze and another nod.

She took a deep breath. "And sometimes..." she said, then paused for a long, *long* moment. She stared forward. "Never mind."

"Sometimes, what?" I nudged her gently. "You can't leave me hanging like that."

"You'll think I'm weird," she said.

"Of course I think you're weird," I laughed. "I'm weird, too. We're witches."

She stopped. Her gaze was still fixed forward—she was looking at the mirror across from the bed. There we were, sitting close together in the reflection.

"Sometimes," she said, "when I look in the mirror, I look

different."

"You mean, like, you see yourself as a dead person? Like a zombie? Or something?" *Or like Eva?* I broke into a sweat and clutched the edge of the bed.

"No, a totally different person. I don't look like me. My nose is smaller and my chin is wider. My eyes are almost black. But when I touch my face, it feels like *my* face. It used to only happen sometimes, but it's been happening a lot the past few weeks. I don't know..."

"It's just your imagination," I said.

"I know, but what if my theory is right? What if I can see all the people that are part of me?"

"Now you're starting to sound like Sister Maggie."

"This isn't funny," she said. "I hate the way I look in the mirror. It's not me. I don't know what I *really* look like anymore."

The song played in between our silence. I looked at her. What was Lenore really going through? How had she really felt all this time? She was always spunky and upbeat. Now, her lips trembled as she sniffled. A single tear fell down her cheek.

"I'm scared, Edith," she said. "I've been having seizures almost every day since Halloween. It hurts, so much. I don't know what's wrong, but I just want them to stop. Whatever they are, whatever it is, I want it to stop. My body aches and I get so tired, and it's no point in going to the hospital because they're just going to tell me it's some stupid sleep epilepsy. I can't sleep because I'm afraid to go to sleep. I..."

I put my arm around her shoulder and leaned my head against hers.

"What about now?" I asked. "Do you see yourself in the mirror as you?"

"No." She paused. "Edith? Do you think I'm pretty?"

"Of course you're pretty."

"Don't say it if you don't mean it."

I felt something go pit-a-pat in my stomach. "I mean it, okay? You're beautiful."

Butterflies.

She smiled. "Thank you."

"Can I tell you something?" I asked.

Big butterflies with electric purple and violet and ivory patterns on their wings.

"Yeah?" She faced me.

"I promise that you'll never have to see someone else in the mirror ever again."

Plucky, fearless, bold butterflies fluttering at the back of my throat.

"What are you talking about?" she breathed.

I'm only feeling this way because I'm trying to distract you. I thought of the words for *Awake.* They were brimming and stirring in my head, ready to burst from my mouth. But I kept my lips shut. I knew if I concentrated hard enough, if I recited them loud enough in my head, it would be the same as whispering them. I screamed the words and drowned every other thought. All except for one. One tiny little thought hung in there.

Our eyes were locked. The tip of our noses touched. I shut my eyes and let my face drift forward the rest of the way until I landed on her lips. I kissed her, for as long as it took me to recite the poem.

To be awake and to be asleep

To be between
To be everything
To be nothing
All at once
To be awake and to be asleep.

I pulled away. I felt everything: I was awake. I was in a dream. All at once. And all in between. I had said the poem, and the butterflies burst from my nose and my ears and from the tiniest sliver of my smiling mouth. I breathed a long sigh, and when I opened my eyes, Lenore was looking back at me. But her pupils were widening between drowsy, dreary blinks. They were swelling, blackness rooting out from her iris.

Eva was awakening.

Here we go.

I took the earbud from my ear and stood from the bed. It was time to recite the final poem. I thought nothing of any *what ifs*. I wasn't going to fail and Lenore wasn't going to die. No one was going to catch us. I was going to capture Eva's soul. I was going to bring Julie a remedy. There was no way I was going to mess this up.

I was invigorated. I was invincible.

The spirit of the body
Sleeps in the dark
And in its dim,
I give it sunlight.

"What are you doing?" Lenore asked sleepily, falling into a daze.

I'd said the words aloud. A song played in my ears. The voice of the singer from Princess had become pronounced and the instruments ebbed back and forth in volume. But the song wasn't playing from the cassette. I was hearing it from Lenore's spirit. The chimes, synths, percussion, and the keys and the bass guitar all spiraled around me as I healed her. I could sense Eva getting stronger. Lenore's eyes were fully black now.

Now rise, rise
Above the chains
Be free, free
Away from pains.

Lenore let out a scream that started out shrill and deepened into a bellow. She collapsed to her knees on the floor and then onto her back. Controlling the soul of a kitten had to have been much easier than extracting a human soul. What if Eva was too strong?

No, no more what ifs! I bit my lip and held a deep breath. A stream of ivory light glimmered from Lenore's mouth, her bellow turning into a ghostly hollow hum. I still heard the music, but the bell pealed in my ears, startling me with each thunderous, metallic hit.

The light gathered into a dress-like figure. It hovered over Lenore.

Eva. This was the girl who had begged me to help her. Who had died years ago and come back. This was the girl with the smaller nose and wider chin that made Lenore afraid to look in the mirror.

Eva wasn't bouncing off the walls or trying to get away. She seemed to want Lenore's body. She was scared, just like me.

Eva had only impressions of limbs and a contorted body. She had no eyes, yet I felt like I was being glared at in a duel and Eva was waiting for my move.

My gaze shot across my room. I needed the mason jar. It was on my dresser and I hadn't opened it. *Idiot*, I thought. *I should have done that first.*

I sidled along, not taking my eyes away from Eva. Her figure turned as I moved. It was getting hard to breathe. My heart beat twice as fast as the kick and snares. I was only a few inches out of reach of the jar when Eva lunged at me.

I stumbled backwards, banging my head against the dresser and knocking some knickknacks to the floor. The mason jar fell, too, the carpet kept it from breaking. I snatched it up and opened it. I cursed. The lid was on there tight.

Eva waved her arms. Behind her, another stream of energy was rising from Lenore.

"No!" I screamed. She was taking out Lenore's soul.

I squeezed as hard as I could to open the lid, and finally it gave. I tried to lasso Eva's spirit, but she was heavy, much heavier than any of the souls of Esmeralda's cats. I fought through it until I got her to budge. Lenore's soul stream stalled.

Eva spun around and flew at me again, thrusting her hand toward my mouth. A cold pain like a migraine shivered from my head and shot through my body. My knees buckled. She shoved me against the closet door. I blacked out for a moment. I couldn't hear the music. I couldn't see. But I felt pain all over.

When the cold left my body, I opened my eyes. Eva was lifting Lenore's soul from her body again. The stream rose like thick steam from a tea kettle.

My head and my throat ached. I staggered to my feet and tried to lasso her away, but I didn't have much strength. The room was warm. Sweating, I wiped the side of my face. I wasn't just sweating, I was bleeding.

I grit my teeth and lifted Eva's soul. I pulled her away a little, but it wasn't enough to stop her from withdrawing Lenore's soul.

My arms fell to my side. I couldn't hold them up anymore. Esmeralda hadn't prepared me enough for this. I wasn't ready. I'd only been a witch for three months. How was I supposed to do this? Why had she chosen me?

Now Lenore was going to die. And it was my fault. I was watching my best friend die.

"No!" I said. "Eva, I'm trying to help you. Please, stop."

Lenore's soul kept rising. It was starting to take form.

"Please! Stop," I screamed.

The music was deafening in my head. The rising of Lenore's soul whistled like a sharp gale.

"Please," I said. "I know you're scared. So am I. But please, let me help you." My voice rose again. "That is not your body. Not anymore. I have another one for you. I promise."

I wasn't going to quit. I'd gotten this far. I was performing poetry that was so far beyond my age.

Lenore's soul stopped streaming and Eva turned to me. With the last bit of energy I had, I moved Eva with a hefty, courageous heave. I shoved her against the door. The mason jar was on the floor by the dresser. I dove for it, rolling on the carpet. I nearly lost the lid out of my grasp.

Eva lunged with a chilling scream but she missed. She recoiled, spinning and stirring inches away from me.

I lifted her one more time. I twirled her around until her form melted into a cloth. She was feeling lighter to me now.

"Trust me, Eva," I said. I pulled her into the jar and spun the top on as tightly as I possibly could. Heat burned from the jar like a hot saucepan. I grit my teeth as I tightened the lid more and more, then dropped jar to my side. The music in my head stopped, but then I heard the music playing faintly from the walkman. I fell to my back, breathing rapidly.

I turned my head. Lenore's soul still hovered over her. I crawled to her and ushered her soul back into her body. Panting, I grasped my hands.

It's over. It's all over.

Lenore breathed slowly. Asleep. Eva was in the jar and when I reached out to touch it, I noticed it had cooled. Faintly, I could hear Eva's cries from within. I nestled the jar close to my chest and shut my eyes. Visceral sobs erupted from deep in my stomach.

When I finally stopped crying, my eyes and my throat dry and swollen, I climbed to my feet. I wrapped the jar in a throw blanket and tucked it under my bed. I went to the bathroom to clean my face and my hands of the blood. I had a cut on the side of my face near the top of my ear that I healed. It left a small scar, and I hid it with my hair.

Before I returned to my room, I checked in on Cannoli. She was still sound asleep. I smiled. What a sleepyhead. When I walked down the hall, I heard the front door open downstairs. I craned over the steps to see who it was.

"Edith?" Mom called out.

"I'm here," I said. "And so is Lenore. We're in my room."

"Are you okay?" she said, looking at me from the bottom of the stairs.

"Mm-hmm," I nodded.

She gave me that look that she always gives me when she's not sure that she completely believes me. "Well, are you hungry?"

"Can we have pizza?" I asked. "I don't really want leftovers."

"Neither do I. Sounds like a plan."

I hurried back to my room. Lenore was still on her back sleeping. The walls in my room were faintly replaying what had just happened. My ears rung as I let them say what they had to say before I took a blanket from my bed. I lay down next to Lenore, and spread the blanket over both of us.

I fought to stay awake as I watched Lenore sleep. Esmeralda didn't warn me about any side effects or anything. And whenever we practiced, the cats behaved as they normally did once the recitals were finished. But I wanted to be sure that she would wake up okay.

About half an hour later, the play button on the walkman popped. The tape stopped. Lenore's eyes blinked slowly, right on cue.

"Hey," I said. Her eyes were normal. "How was your nap? Did you have any bad dreams?"

"No," she said, stretching. "I had a weird dream though. You and me were having a tea party with a ghost."

"That's weird," I said.

"I don't remember falling asleep," she said. "I definitely don't remember falling asleep on the floor."

"You drank your milkshake too fast," I said. "Got a brain freeze and passed out."

"Well, that's embarrassing,"

We laughed. Goodness, we laughed together. It'd been so long. We talked sleepily about her odd dream, and then about Thanksgiving and all the poems she'd been learning the last few weeks. She told me that she missed walking home with me, and every day, she'd looked over her shoulders on her way home, hoping that she'd see me walking not too far behind. She never saw me.

I told her I was sorry. I was sorry about Halloween. I was sorry for not being there for her when she was having all those seizures. I wished I'd known.

Lenore was going to be okay. And so was Julie. And so was I. I could see the light from the mason jar seeping a bit through the blanket, illuminating the carpet underneath the bed. I hoped Eva didn't feel scared anymore.

"Hey, look in the mirror," I said.

Lenore crutched herself up on her arm, looking past me to see herself in the mirror. She gasped, tossing the blanket aside and climbing to her feet. She touched her face and laughed. "It's me. Edith, it's me! How? What did you do?"

"A little poem I learned," I said. "No big deal."

"No big deal? This is a big deal! Where did you learn it?"

"One of the books your mom gave me," I said.

She squealed in excitement and locked her arms around me, rocking me side to side in a tight embrace. "You're the best," she said.

When she let go, she looked at herself in the mirror again. "I can't believe it," she repeated over and over again. "I was starting to forget what I looked like."

Mom called out from downstairs. "Pizza's here!"

"Coming!" I shouted back.

Lenore turned to me. Her lips curved in a crooked smile. She twiddled at her hands, looking away from me. "That part before the brain freeze," she said. "That happened for real, right?"

"Yeah," I nodded. "It did."

31

I couldn't help but admire myself in the mirror. My long, ivory dress swayed with me as I spun. It looked like I was floating. A delicate crystal embellishment was sewn into the bodice and it dazzled under the lights. I wore strappy white flats and long white gloves to go with it. Mom had braided my hair into pigtails. I glowed a pure aura, the aura I hoped reflected the meter of my spirit by now. Christmas Eve had finally arrived.

Three weeks had passed since Eva was extracted. Lenore hadn't had any seizures. She didn't complain about being sleepy. She was back to being Lenore. It was difficult for me to not tell her about Eva.

I gave Eva's soul to Esmeralda. She wouldn't tell me where she had to go or to whom the new body belonged, but she said she would let me know when her end of the contract was done. She would introduce me to Eva then. It could be days, weeks, or even months before the procedure was completed. I didn't want to know how it all worked. I was afraid of the worst, and my imagination made me queasy thinking of all the possibilities.

Esmeralda gave me a harmony that would heal Julie completely. It was a rare and powerful harmony. When Julie drank it, she took off her mask and tiny sparkles of light seeped through her skin and glimmered on her face. Within minutes, she was normal again. She cried and cried with happiness, and she hugged me tight and thanked me. I was happy for her as I tried to swallow the last of the guilt.

I accepted that I made a mistake. I tried to fix it with more mistakes. But my intentions were always good. Esmeralda told me that making mistakes was part of growing up. Doing my best was what was important.

On the last day of school before Christmas break, Nemo had asked me if *I* was okay. I insisted that I was — I was happy to have him back as my friend. I did tell him that being a witch meant keeping secrets and telling white lies. I wasn't perfect.

I wondered if I had a pure spirit before Dad left for his "business trip." He had told me with the straightest of faces — not a trace of a lying muscle flinched at his cheeks or underneath his eyes. It was like he had convinced himself he was telling the truth. Was that how I'd become such a good liar? Had I been born with it?

This recital wasn't a gift for him anymore. It was for Mom and Yaden and Cannoli. It was for Lenore and Nemo and Julie. It was for me.

I was excited to see Aunt Tegan and Uncle Neil in the auditorium — they had made it into town earlier that day. When it was time to go backstage, I walked out of the row and down the aisle. I looked over my shoulder. Cannoli and Yaden were bright with smiles, but Mom was even brighter. She beamed and her eyes were glossy with tears. She mouthed "I love you," and blew me a kiss.

Nemo and Julie sat near the front of the stage with Nemo's dad. They called out to me and waved. All three of them gave me thumbs up.

I didn't see Lenore in the audience. Lenore had been strangely quiet since the day before. She hadn't called me last night, and when I tried calling her this afternoon, she didn't pick up. I trusted that she'd be at the recital, but I was worried. She had mentioned the other day that her mom had been acting strange. Lenore said she even heard her mom crying a few times, cursing at herself in French. She'd stopped baking, and she would often lean her head on the walls in the basement.

I worried about Miss Karen realizing that Eva was gone. Would she have known that it was me? Each day, I got closer and closer to telling Miss Karen and Lenore about what I'd done. I wanted them to see Eva as another person. I wanted that to be a gift.

Miss K greeted me backstage.

"You look wonderful," she said. "Are you excited?"

"Yes, I am," I said.

I watched a group of eighth graders performing a dance routine. They were good, but I didn't care for their music choices. Britney Spears, Backstreet Boys and Mariah Carey were too pop for me. When they were done, the audience erupted in cheers. So did Miss K.

After that, Miss K squeezed her hand on my shoulder. "Hey, time to loosen up. This is it. This is your moment. It's all yours. Show them what you've got, Edith."

I nodded. Miss K went out on stage and gave me a warm and thoughtful introduction: "This year, I've had the honor of teaching our next performer, practicing piano with her, and watching her grow into a beautiful young woman. Ladies and gentlemen of the St. Vincent community, please give a cheerful round of applause for Edith Madeline Solstice and her piano recital."

While I had heard every word, I had my eyes shut and folded my hands in prayer.

The audience applauded and the curtains re-opened. The spotlight beamed from the top of the stage and followed me as I walked to the piano. I bowed, then took a deep breath once I sat down on the bench. I traced along the piano's ebony finish as it glimmered underneath the stage lights. The claps and cheers faded, and the light in the auditorium dimmed.

There was a microphone near me. "Thank you," I said to the ocean of Santa hats and ugly sweaters. "This song is called *Apology*. I wrote it with…Miss K. I hope you like it."

I rested my fingers on the keys. A faint and short applause sparked from somewhere in the audience. And then, I started to play.

I bit my lip as I went through the progression. The first prayer I'd said on my own a few months ago suddenly came to me. I could remember each word, as clumsy as they were. It rose from a corner shadowed deep in my mind. The song sounded like the words were moving with the music. I was playing piano for all these people. I could feel them all looking at me, pleasant with their holiday joy.

I could feel Aunt Tegan gathering up for a roaring ovation, even though it was only the first song. Then, as I kept playing, I found myself smiling. I felt Lenore's energy boring onto me. She had just arrived.

What I didn't feel was Dad's energy. Either that, or after four months, I'd forgotten what it was like.

The song came to a close. I rested my hands on the keys, and applause erupted. That was much more than I'd expected. As the applause faded, I fixed my hands at the keys again. I flinched. Something wasn't right. I sat my hands on my lap and stared at the keys. They looked like they were vibrating, shifting.

Dizzy, I shut my eyes. A commotion rose from the audience. I closed the lid, pushed back on the bench—the sound of wood grinding on the stage gave a heavy echo.

I felt it again. The siren fever. I thought Lenore said it was never going to come back?

I glanced at Miss K. She nodded with encouragement. "You can do it," she whispered.

I shook my head vigorously and walked off the stage. I went down the stairs into the aisle, and my walk turned into a dash as I got near the row my family was sitting in. I didn't look at them. I buried my face in my hands. Miss K asked the audience to give me another round of applause.

I hadn't even finished my recital. I had three other songs I was going to play. How could they give me a round of applause?

"Snowpea!" I heard Mom call out to me.

I felt her running behind me, but I sprinted out of the auditorium and into the main lobby. She caught up to me, nearly diving at my shoulders. She stopped me and pulled me into her arms. She held me tight, tighter than anyone had ever held me. She rocked me and nuzzled in my hair.

Tears streamed down my face. I wiped them with my hands — my silk gloves. "Why isn't he here?" I repeated it over and over.

"I'm sorry," Mom said. "I'm so sorry."

My heart fluttered with ache. My hands burned. There was no way I was going to get back on stage. I had suddenly become overwhelmed with emptiness. I didn't know what his energy was like because he wasn't here. He hadn't been around since I realized I was a witch. He wasn't there for me as I went through all this. He might have believed me, too, just like Cannoli did. He might have stuck around.

It finally hit me. Dad was gone.

"I'm so proud of you," Mom said. "I love you so much. I really do."

We hugged in silence for a long time, alone, until I decided I wanted to go home.

The siren fever had gone away by the time we'd gotten home. Mom offered everyone hot chocolate to go along with the chocolate chip, gingerbread, and snickerdoodle cookies she'd baked. I was still in my recital dress. Mom and Aunt Tegan were talking about Uncle Neil and giggling about the way he'd fallen asleep and snored during the dance act.

Cannoli wanted to hurry to bed; she was anxious to unwrap her presents the next morning. She begged me not to eat all the cookies and to leave some for Santa. I promised her that I would leave him plenty of chocolate chip, since according to Cannoli, that was his favorite kind. I took her to bed for Mom, and sung her another lullaby — a sleeping poem — to make sure she didn't have any trouble sleeping.

I went back to the kitchen. I wanted more hot chocolate and cookies. I wanted to call Lenore, too. I didn't want to talk to her about my recital, but it would have been nice to hear her voice.

Since the extraction—the last time she'd stayed over—we'd been holding hands a lot. She would tell me how pretty my eyes were and she'd play with my hair when we walked home from school. We hugged each other when we said goodbye, but that was it. We called each other every night, sometimes talking for hours until we fell asleep with the phones in our hands.

When I dialed her number, she didn't pick up. Maybe she wasn't home. I left her a message.

Once I finished my hot chocolate and had my fill on cookies, I went into the living room. Aunt Tegan and Mom were drinking wine and still wearing their Santa hats, loudly reminiscing about grown-up-sister things. Christmas music played softly from the stereo. I watched them for a bit before either of them noticed me. I loved it whenever they were together. Mom would always end up laughing until she broke into tears. Aunt Tegan was robust with an energy that filled the room and never flatlined. I bet her spirit was close to pure.

"Hey there," Aunt Tegan said when she saw me. "What are you up to?"

I smiled. "Oh, nothing. I was just on my way to my room."

"What are you going to do, go to bed? It's Christmas Eve! No one goes to sleep this early on Christmas Eve."

"I was going to read," I said.

"Nope," Aunt Tegan said. She patted a spot on the sofa between her and Mom. "You're going to sit right here and hang out with your

Auntie."

I didn't fight it.

"You're still wearing your dress," Aunt Tegan said. "You're going to get it stained."

"I don't care."

"But it's beautiful."

"That's okay. I don't think I'll wear it again. By the time I get the chance to, I'll have outgrown it." Or at least, I hoped would.

"Well then," Aunt Tegan laughed, shooting a look over at Mom.

"Really, I will. I didn't grow at all this year. So I know I'm going to have a growth spurt soon."

"You sure? 'Cause your Mom is kind of short. This might be it for you."

"Tegan!" Mom shouted.

"Dad's tall," I said. Immediately, I wished I hadn't said it.

"Well, you don't want his genes. Trust me. You'd grow up to be a tall, lying, cheating bastard."

"*Tegan!*"

"Come on, Anita. You think Edith doesn't know these words? She probably calls that man even worse."

I said nothing. Mom sighed and Aunt Tegan went on. "So any boys at school? Tell me their names."

"I don't like any boys. Not right now." And that was the truth. It had been a long time since I thought of Nemo the same way. The time I tried to kiss him seemed so long ago, even though it was just the first day of the semester. Emanuel hadn't called. I hoped he'd moved on. There were plenty of other pretty ninth grade girls for him to choose from. He didn't need me.

"What?" Aunt Tegan gasped. "Such a pretty girl, and no boys? You know what, that's good. Keep your nose in the books. Trust me. You don't need a boy. Especially the older you get. All you ever need is books and masturbation."

"Okay," Mom said, taking Aunt Tegan's glass of wine. "You've had too much." She poured Aunt Tegan's wine into her glass and then handed her the empty one. The two of them laughed heartily.

In my head, there was a tiny voice begging them to ask me about the *girl* at school. But when I really thought about it, I wasn't even sure about how I felt about her—how I'd answer, even if they did ask. I just knew that Lenore was giving me the same butterflies I used to get around Nemo.

Aunt Tegan went into the kitchen. From there, she said loudly, "but seriously, Edith. You were wonderful up there. That song was fantastic." Then, she returned to the room with a full glass and three cookies. "And I listen to classical all the time. That was one of the best songs I've heard in a long time."

"Really?" I blushed.

"I mean it." She handed each of us a cookie.

I looked at Mom. She nodded, and that made me smile. She was proud of me, and had been there for me when I wanted to run away from that stage—from that piano and from the feelings that had bundled in my chest.

I spent the rest of the night with Mom and Aunt Tegan. I didn't know what time I fell asleep but I fought the drowsiness for a long time before I gave into it. The Christmas tree and its flickering lights and zealous decor blurred. The giant loop of holiday melodies and stories of Mom and Aunt Tegan when they were younger cradled me to sleep.

When I awoke, I was in my bed in my pajamas. Cannoli pounced onto the bed and jumped up and down.

"It's morning!" she repeated each time her jumps reached their zeniths.

I was happy that she was excited about Christmas. For me, it was bittersweet. Our stockings were stuffed. There were plenty of gifts under the Christmas tree. But none of them had come from Dad —they were all from Mom, Aunt Tegan, Uncle Neil, and even Yaden. He'd bought me a leather-bound music composition book and a copy of *Through the Looking Glass*. He said he was tired of seeing me read *Alice's Adventures in Wonderland* all the time.

After we finished a smorgasbord of a breakfast—which I called a *breakfeast*—the phone rang. It was Lenore.

"Hi," I said. "Merry Christmas!"

"Merry Christmas to you, too," she said.

"I miss you," I said quietly.

"I miss you, too."

"Why haven't you called?"

"I—there's something I need to tell you. And I can't wait to tell you anymore."

My heart thumped. "What is it?"

I don't know why she thought it was a good idea to tell me what she said on Christmas. The first Christmas without my Dad. The first Christmas I was a witch. My last Christmas before I became a teenager. When the words left her mouth, my whole world shattered into tiny little shards of broken dreams, broken hope, and undeserved contrition, and there in the center of the mess was my consequence.

"We're moving."

32

The morning of my birthday, I awoke feeling older. January fourth had arrived. I was turning thirteen years old, but it wasn't official until I blew out the candles and made a wish.

I knew what my wish was going to be, too.

Cannoli dragged me out of bed. It was close to noon and I was awake, listening to Princess. Lenore had given me her cassette and insisted that I keep it, and I had gotten a new walkman for Christmas. I loved the album. I played it twice over that morning.

I thought about the extraction every time I heard the first song. At first, it was hard to listen to.

Lenore was turning thirteen, too. And this was going to be her last day here. No longer would she live down the street from me, but she'd be across the border in a town called Whitby. I think she said it was in Ontario.

Every year since we'd been friends, Lenore and I had a tradition where we'd share a slice of our own cakes with one another and choose who had the best cake of the year.

Aunt Tegan and Uncle Neil had come down again for the weekend. Even though they'd just been here for Christmas, I missed them dearly. I wanted them to move closer instead of living all the way up in New York. I considered that to be my wish when I blew out the candles on my cake.

Mom made a stack of double chocolate chip pancakes for breakfast. It was my personal request. I'd asked for the same thing last year. Before we all dug into our food, Aunt Tegan poured herself a glass of champagne mixed with orange juice—gross—and insisted on proposing a toast.

"Edith, you beautiful little rascal," she said after she stood from the table. "We love you so damn much. I remember the first time I got to take care of you all on my own for a day. You were five and we went to the circus—just me and you. We had corn dogs and cotton candy and we played in the park the rest of the day 'til you got tired out. I told your Mom when we got home, 'Anita, I want a little girl just like her someday.' Your Mom is lucky to have a girl like you. Trust me.

"Remember to love your Mom. Every day. Even when she acts like an ass sometimes. She'll lighten up. Just give her a hug. That's all it takes. And when you're twenty-one and she *still* acts like an ass? Buy her a bottle of wine, and then give her a hug. She'll shut right the hell up.

"Being a teenager is going to be the best and worst years of your life, all at the same time.

"To Edith, my little teenage niece."

Everyone cheered, *To Edith!* and raised their glasses of orange juice or coffee (or chocolate milk for Cannoli) and dug in.

Once breakfast was over, we all gathered into the living room for presents. There were two things that sucked about my birthday every year: one, it was usually either the last day of Christmas vacation or the first day of school. Two, when your birthday is that close to Christmas, you don't get nearly as many presents. I swore Yaden and Cannoli always got way more presents than I did. They were summer babies.

But this year I'd specifically asked that I not get a lot gifts. Eavesdropping the walls, I'd heard Mom say that she was likely going to get laid off from the hospital. She'd told Aunt Tegan that she'd find out this week. That was why I was torn about my wish. Aunt Tegan said she'd be happy to help Mom out, but what if me wishing her and Uncle Neil here was like a jinx or something? I didn't want Mom to lose her job. I wanted that to be my wish, too.

Yaden was reconsidering going to college. He'd gotten accepted to the University of Pittsburgh, but they hadn't offered him enough scholarship money, and he didn't want Mom to have to pay for the rest. That, too, I learned from eavesdropping the walls.

All I wanted this year was a few books, butterfly clips, and maybe an inexpensive pet that I could keep in my room, like a fish. And to be a normal kid again.

I got most of those things. Aunt Tegan and Uncle Neil bought me the first four books of the *The Baby-Sitters Club*. Yaden bought me a Tamagotchi—which was technically a pet, too—and Mom got me an assortment of things, including slap bracelets, hair clips, and my first pair of Chuck Taylors. She also gave me a packet of pictures, all of them from the night of the Halloween party, and frames to put them in.

Cake came after that. Thirteen candles were lit on the cannoli cake. I think Cannoli was more excited about the cake than I was. I'd asked for it since it had been a long time since we had any cannoli. It was more of a nod to her than it was a cake for me.

While Mom brought it to the kitchen table, Aunt Tegan slapped a birthday crown on my head.

Happy Birthday Snowpea was written on the icing. Everyone started to sing.

…Happy birthday dear snow peaaaaa. Happy birthday to youuuuuuu.

My heart was as warm as my face was red. I felt pure joy right then.

"Make a wish," Mom said.

I watched as the candles danced. The joy flickered away. I was seconds away from being a teenager. Being thirteen wasn't going to be so bad, right? Thirteen meant that I only had one year left before high school. I was officially a young woman, and I could go see PG-13 movies on my own. Soon, I'd be making new friends and thinking about high school dances, homecoming games and college applications. I had so much to look forward to.

But I wanted to do all that as a normal girl. And so, I took in a deep breath, and blew out all the candles. The smoke rose from the wicks and the whole family applauded. I smiled.

Uncle Neil handed me the knife. "You're old enough to cut your own slice now."

I cut two slices. One for me, and another for Lenore. Uncle Neil cut the rest and we all enjoyed the cake together.

The furniture in Lenore's house was gone. There was no couch or dining table. The bookshelves were gone. There were boxes stashed in the living room. I couldn't believe it; she was really leaving.

"She still hasn't told me why," Lenore whispered. From the living room, I could see Miss Karen wrapping plates and mugs with newspaper and carefully placing them in a box.

I didn't want to say hello to Miss Karen. I was afraid that it would hurt too much and I would unravel and tell too much of the truth.

Lenore and I went upstairs to her room with our slices of cake. All of her furniture and posters were gone. There was a blanket and a pillow on the floor. She unfolded it and we sat down and exchanged cakes.

Lenore had a red velvet cake. I thought hers was the better slice, although I was reluctant to admit it. She agreed triumphantly. I ate too quickly. I lay on my back. There was too much cake and too many pancakes sitting in my belly.

"What did you wish for?" I asked.

"I didn't wish for anything," she said. "I do wish mom wasn't being all weird, though. I don't know why we're moving."

"Why didn't you wish to stay?"

"Because last year I wished for a puppy and I never got one," she said. "Birthday wishes obviously don't come true."

"Maybe there's still going to be a puppy in your future."

"I hope so. But I don't know."

"I think wishes still come true," I said.

"Oh yeah?" Lenore lay down next to me. "What did you wish for?"

"I wished..." I trailed off. I wasn't sure I wanted to tell her. "Aren't we not supposed to tell?"

"Then why'd you ask me?" she said, laughing. "What if I'd told you?"

I looked at Lenore. My wishes hadn't come true once yet, but I kept making them anyway. Every year. I wished for world peace when I turned ten. Then I wished that Lenore would win a championship with the baseball team when I was eleven. Last year, I wished that Nemo would be my first kiss. And I'm glad *that* didn't come true. This year, I'd wished that when I woke up tomorrow, my journal would be nothing but empty pages and I wouldn't be able to cast a poem ever again.

"Hey, I want to give you something," Lenore said.

She climbed to her feet and opened a box that was tucked in a corner in the room. She pulled out two locus charms. They were different colors, but their shape was similar. These were like the charm she dropped in Dad and Fiona's bag at the mall. She handed them to me.

"I think you're ready to decide on your own if you want to find your Dad or not," she said. "The blue one is linked to his. The red one is attached to one that I have. If you ever find yourself in Canada, you can come find me."

"How does it work?" I asked.

"Just hold it close to your heart and think about that person as hard as you can. It'll send a little light into the sky, like a north star, and you can find your way to that person."

"Is there a poem for it?"

"Nope. Just don't lose them. Keep them somewhere safe."

I put the red charm around my neck. "I'll wear this one. Every day."

Lenore laughed. "You're so cheesy."

"I have something for you," I said.

I gave her a framed picture of us in our Halloween costumes that Mom had taken. Thankfully, Mom got duplicates of all the pictures. Lenore was thrilled, laughing at us and how big our smiles were. "We look like a couple of dorks. Thank you, Edith. This is the best picture ever."

We lay on the blanket for a long time. She told me how amazing my song was at the recital. I thanked her for being there, and for being my best friend. She told me about the harbor by Lake Ontario and the Whitby Brass Band and how she thought that I'd really like them. She told me that she thought I was brave and that I was going to be a powerful witch someday.

The afternoon sun was turning crimson. Dust motes hovered in the empty room. We held hands and fell silent. Finally, we kissed, like Samantha kissed Jake with the cake and sixteen candles lit between them. I'd been waiting for that all day.

I never wanted to leave. This was the most perfect afternoon in my thirteen years. I was never going to have another one like it.

But it was all going to end soon and Lenore would be gone. I couldn't help but feel like everything that was happening now was my consequence. Like it was happening because I'd wanted to take a boy back from someone I once hated. Because of the fight with Julie. Because I'd taken a soul from my best friend's body as if it were my responsibility to save her and her sister.

I meddled where I shouldn't have meddled, and now it was time to repent.

"I have to go," I said finally. It was getting dark outside. "Aunt Tegan and Uncle Neil are taking me to the movies."

"I wish I could come," she said. "I have to help mom finish packing. And we're leaving before dawn tomorrow."

"I'll wake up early, and I'll look for you with the charm."

She smiled. "So will I."

We walked to the front door. Miss Karen was sitting at the kitchen table, drinking tea. She wasn't reading or packing or eating or anything. She was sitting there, alone and quiet and looking forward.

"Hey, Miss Karen," I said, pulling at my fingers as I stood at the entrance to the kitchen. "Thank you. For everything."

"You're welcome," she said. She didn't turn her head to me.

"And I'm sorry," I said.

"For what?" She looked at me.

I turned. Lenore was sitting at the bottom of the stairs in the living room. I whispered, "about Lenore. And Eva."

"It's not your fault."

"I—"

"Happy Birthday, Edith," she said.

"Thank you."

I lingered. She took a sip of her tea and kept looking forward. She wasn't looking at anything. Her eyes weren't shifting. She was hardly blinking. It was like she saw something else beyond the walls or something that was invisible to me was visible to her. She had a tight clasp on her mug handle. The smoke from the tea rose high. I wanted to hug her. I wanted to cry for her.

Stay just a little while longer, I wanted to shout. *Don't go before you get to see your daughter. I did this for you. I fixed it. Everything's going to be okay. Everything's going to be* better!

Please don't go.

I left Miss Karen and returned to the living room. I embraced Lenore. I didn't want to let her go. "I'm going to miss you so much."

"I'll write to you," she said. "I'll write you poems that I'm learning and take lots of pictures."

"Me, too."

That was it. We said nothing else. We held hands for a long time and gazed. We hugged one last time. If I said another word, I'd burst into tears and I'd be late getting home. Who knew when I was going to see her again. All I knew was that we had two matching locus charms, and one day, we would find each other.

I hoped my wish didn't come true.

I set my alarm for four-thirty in the morning. I awoke with a jolt. I had my locus charm at my nightstand. I put it on, climbed out of bed, and quietly made my way downstairs. Aunt Tegan was sleeping on the couch, Uncle Neil was on the floor. I crept past them and opened the front door. I stood on the porch, with only a T-shirt and my pajamas. I didn't care that it was cold and that it had started to snow.

I pressed the locus charm close to my chest. *My best friend, Lenore Roslyn Close. I don't know what I'm going to do without you,* I thought. *I don't know if I'll ever be able to watch another baseball game or have another slumber party. I won't exchange birthday cake with anyone unless I'm sharing it with you.*

Nothing happened. The charm was nothing but a cold, grainy,

rose-colored rock in my hand. Maybe they'd left earlier and had gotten so far away that the charm wouldn't work.

Or worse. Had my birthday wish come true?

"I wish you'd stay," I said aloud. "I wish we could go to the same high school and be best friends forever. I'm sorry, Lenore. It really is all my fault."

Still nothing. I took a step to the edge of the porch and looked down the street. I couldn't see far through the snow. Was their car still there?

Please tell me where you are.

The charm warmed and the grains glimmered like crystals against the moonlight. The grains trickled off the charm like sand, blowing in a wind and flying into the sky, just below the clouds. The grains were bright and bountiful, streaming into a flickering white wave. They took the shape of a shimmering, chalky dove bird. It flapped its wings, soaring higher and farther away, heading north.

They had gone. Lenore and Miss Karen on their way to Ontario.

I smiled. "I'm still a witch."

33

The first day of the spring semester was unlike any other. I walked into school feeling like a brand new person. I was part heartbroken, part hopeful, but one hundred percent certain that everything was going to be okay. I wasn't afraid of seventh grade anymore. I wasn't worried about getting a B or a C in Math class. I didn't stress myself out about Sister Maggie's farfetched morality lessons. And a few people stopped me in the hallway to tell me they really liked my song at the recital. I didn't even know their names.

I put the picture of Lenore and me in our Halloween costumes in my locker. On my way to homeroom, I noticed there was a new girl at Lenore's locker. She didn't look familiar—probably a sixth grader or a transfer student. Seeing her there instead of Lenore didn't make me feel as sad as I thought it might.

Julie had come back to school. A lot of the students congratulated her and told her that they'd missed her. Her skin was like it was before the fight. The only blemish she had was a scar near her left eye.

I walked up to her. "You look great," I said.

"Thank you," she said. "I'm really grateful for what you did." Her eyes shifted, like she was nervous. "I still can't believe that you're a—"

"Me neither," I said.

She extended her hand out to me. "Can we be friends? For real?"

I looked down at her hand. I was hesitant. Although she had given me plenty of thanks since I healed her, the last time she asked me that question, we wound up fighting. But I took her hand, not afraid that history would repeat itself.

"Yeah," I said. "I'm so sorry. What I said about your name, I wasn't trying to be mean. And I had no idea about your family." I was the bully to Julie before she was the bully back at me.

"It's okay," she said. "There's a way you can make it up to me."

"Sure."

"We have a few minutes," she said. "Can I measure you? At the Sacred Wall?"

I looked at Julie at the top of her head. "Umm...that's a waste of time. I know I haven't grown."

"You sure? Come on!" She took my arm in hers and took me down the hall.

When we arrived at the Wall, she gave me a marker and a ruler. I measured her first. She stood next to her initials from last year.

"Julie," I said, "you're still the same height."

"Really?" she huffed. "I could've sworn I was taller."

Nemo came walking down the hall. He and Julie hugged. Nemo

said hello to me, and I hugged him, but I didn't leap into his arms like I had always done. I wasn't desperate for him anymore. We were friends and only friends.

"Want me to measure you?" he asked me.

I looked at Julie. "Julie's going to do it."

He put up his arms and backed a few steps away. "Oh?"

I stood against the wall by my initials from last summer.

Julie traced the marker across my head and wrote my initials and the date. I turned and looked at the wall as she took the ruler and compared the dashes.

I smiled.

"Edith Madeline Solstice," Julie said. "Congratulations. You've grown two inches since last June."

I was five foot *something*.

The End

Acknowledgements

I spent my summers in elementary school at my grandmom's—Nanny's—house out in Darby, Pennsylvania. When I was a kid, I would spend sometimes my entire days writing stories, some of which I illustrated, and Nanny was always the first reader to all these books I'd write. She loved my work. She saw the potential in me, and she believed in my talent, and her encouragement was the reason why I kept at it. I could never thank her enough for being my first fan.

I want to thank my Mom and my sister for being the strong women that they are. They are the reason I see the beauty in all women. They are the OG reason I have the capacity to fill the responsibility to write strong female characters in my work. They formed the unique ideas of richness and wealth that helped me see light and promise regardless of how low we rung on the fiscal ladder.

My 7th grade teacher Evanthia Filiou was the first person outside of my family that filled me with faith and encouragement. We would talk about writing, and that meant a lot to me to have someone else be enthusiastic about it. It's rare to have people like that in your life where I come from.

I'd like to thank my cousin Jesse for being a huge supporter of me. If you knew how incredibly talented this man is, you'd know how lucky

I am to have such a brilliant person at my side.

Thank you Yvonne, Nashely, Tony, and Lindsay B. for reading The Recital when it was in its rawest form. Sharing those first 50 pages took a lot of courage for me. Your honest and critical feedback pushed me forward. Thank you for taking the time out of your days to read the book.

I can't sing praises loud enough for my editor, Kate Angelella. You helped guide me in the rightest directions, helped sculpt Edith's voice, and gave me the confidence in this book that I couldn't have gotten anywhere else. And your TV show recommendations are impeccable. I hope we work together again.

Shout out to the cast and crew of Candles, the TV pilot we filmed in 2013 that sparked the idea for The Recital: Airen, Chris, Danielle, Lucia, Katie, Suzann, Dave, Michelle, Carolyn, Heather, Robin, Joenell, Terrell, Meg, Kat, Lacy, Thang, Baron, Luba, Epic, Quill, Angela P., Derrick, Mr. Ron, and everyone else who had a hand in the production (the list goes on quite a bit). You all believed in my foolishly ambitious vision. Although the pilot never went anywhere, seeing what we created with what little we had made me feel like I could do anything I freaking wanted to. All I needed was support and love, like you all gave me.

A round of applause for Jessica Bastidas. You did an amazing job with the promotional art and the book cover. I'm so grateful that I got to work with you and I hope I get to put something together with you again in the future.

Holly, my paramour, was a pillar for me during a long, long year of writing and revising. She kept me going through a series of nervous breakdowns, disappointments, transitions, empty pockets, and so much more. I was exposed and vulnerable and she treated me with patience, love, enthusiasm, hospitality, and faith. I don't know if I would have survived the gauntlet without you.

Thank you to everyone who contributed to The Recital's Crowdfunding Campaign:
John, Amanda, Freddy Fingers, Marcus, Fred, Jellybean, Kris aka Scully, Jayna, Leah, Jan & John, Jane, Kathy, Denise, Christina, Sam & Aaron, Carina, Noah & Ashley, PJ, Theresa, Dave & Katie, Alexis, Sonali & Peter, Luke & Jess, Aunt Lynn, those who I've mentioned above, and my BFF Tori.

Shout out to Isabella Capelli and Morgan Perry for doing a wonderful job acting in the book trailer. Shout out to their awesome Moms, Amanda Capelli and Angie Perry, too.

Thanks to Chris a.k.a. Blocade, who produced the music for the Crowdfunding Campaign and the book trailer.

And to you, the reader, thank you for picking up a copy, and I hope this story resonated with you in some way.

Kyle is a West Philadelphia native, with no relation to The Fresh Prince. He attended Temple University's Tyler School of Art, with discipline in English and Filmmaking. He spends his free time running to 80s & 90s pop and hip-hop, outpacing rude hipsters in the bike lane, and cooking up culinary masterpieces. His aspirations include fluency in French and Japanese, moving to Canada, and finally beating Contra III on Super Nintendo.

You can follow his hustle by subscribing to the Seven in the Afternoon newsletter at www.sevenintheafternoon.com.